AS LONG AS
I LIVE

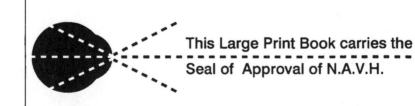

AS LONG AS I LIVE

I LIVE

EMILIE LORING

Thorndike Press • **Thorndike, Maine**

Published in 2000 by arrangement with
Little, Brown & Co., Inc.

Thorndike Large Print® Candlelight Series.

The tree indicium is a trademark of Thorndike Press.

The text of this Large Print edition is unabridged.
Other aspects of the book may vary from the original edition.

Set in 16 pt. Plantin by Al Chase.

Printed in the United States on permanent paper.

Library of Congress Cataloging-in-Publication Data
Loring, Emilie Baker.
    As long as I live / Emilie Loring.
        p.   cm.
    ISBN 0-7862-2459-2 (lg. print : hc : alk. paper)
    1. Women in advertising — New York (State) — New York
— Fiction.   2. New York (N.Y.) — Fiction.   3. Large type
books.   I. Title.
PS3523.O645 A7 2000
813'.52—dc21   99-086472

TO
ROBERT MELVILLE LORING

1

The elevator shot to the fourteenth floor.

"Far's we go," announced the grim-faced operator. The crow's feet deepened at the corners of his fretful eyes as he glowered at the girl who was the only other occupant of the car.

"Down," she answered.

She colored as he looked at her curiously. Doubtless and with reason, he thought her a little mad. She had entered the car on the ground floor and custom warranted the expectation that she would leave it at one floor or another, but on the way up her courage had oozed through her fingertips.

"Quitter!" she berated herself as she was dropped earthward with breath-snatching speed. "One would think this was the first time you had approached an advertising agency, Joan Crofton. Your work was accepted by several firms in New York. Will you let Boston frighten you?"

She strengthened her morale by repeating to herself a bit from a Thomas Burke novel she had memorized to use as a prod on just such an occasion as the present.

7

"Life is a one-way road and once you've got on a particular road the law says, keep straight on. And you've got to, whether you want to go that way or not."

The present was undoubtedly one of those one-way thoroughfares. She must keep straight on if she intended to reach her goal of financial independence. Did she intend to? She did. She loved her work, it was stimulating, exciting, besides, the income from the trust fund her father had inherited should be used to keep up a dignified and beautiful home, with a bit of travel on the side for her parents. It was up to their daughters to provide the luxuries and smart clothing which they loved, for themselves.

She tightened her grip on the portfolio under her arm. The feel of it stiffened her determination and incidentally her spinal cord. Hadn't every proof between those black covers been accepted, published and paid for?

The operator clanged open the elevator door.

"Street."

"Out eight!" Joan said.

She regarded the man coolly as he stared at her.

"Ridin' for yer health?" he inquired caustically. He winked at the starter in his gold-

8

braided uniform and tapped his forehead.

"Round and round," he muttered before he clanged shut the door.

The car shot up and stopped with a tooth-loosening jerk.

"Eight," the man growled.

"Thanks, thanks very much. It's almost like having a private car, isn't it? Don't you ever have passengers? With your sunny nature I would think they'd flock here."

"That's a come-back for intimating that my brain goes round and round," Joan told herself as she stepped to the corridor. She heard the operator mutter as the car ascended.

Before her courage had a chance to ooze she turned the knob on a door marked Craig Lamont, Inc. It was the firm on the list of Boston advertising agencies given her in New York which Mrs. Shaw, her next door neighbor — if one could call a six-acre estate next door — had advised her to try first.

She entered an unpartitioned space. There were a dozen desks at which sat men and girls. On her left were three doors which doubtless opened into private offices. The room was spacious, airy, flooded with light, a-click with typewriters, a-stir with salesmen going out with brief cases, giving place to others who sat down to confer with men at desks. The activity stimulated her, filled her with a tingling zest to make good.

In her immediate vicinity a girl presided at a switchboard. Joan had time only to think that she was the plainest person she ever had seen, to appreciate the smartness of her hair-cut and ensemble before the operator inquired crisply;

"Appointment?"

"No. I would like to see the art director. May I?" Joan inquired with the smile her father had told her made him want to pull down the moon and hand it to her.

"Okay, I'll try for the A.D."

"The A.D.?"

"Art director, Tony Crane. Lucky it's him instead of the boss, in case you care. Say, did Mr. Lamont come in with a grouch after lunch? I'm telling you. Must have lost an account." She plugged in a switch. "Long distance calling, Mr. Parks."

Joan drew off her gloves and surreptitiously kicked off the shiny black rubbers she had bought near the motor mart where she had left her sedan when she had observed that the city streets were rivers of slush in spite of the fact that overhead it was a turquoise and gold day. She couldn't keep her mind on an interview when aware of those glittering pedal extremities. Besides, the art director might have a galoshes inhibition. Trivial events ofttimes had decided the fate of nations, how much more likely that they would affect the fate of drawings.

With her eyes on the gleaming gilded dome of the State House flanked on one side by the Stars and Stripes and on the other by the fluttering white of the State flag against a clear blue sky, she mentally rehearsed her approach to the object of her visit to the accompaniment of the telephone operator's incessant answer, plug and call.

A woman came out of an office, a woman in smart black which accentuated the red gold of her hair. From the threshold she flung back;

"I shall peteetion the Court here and I shall not gif up eef I haf to carry the case to the Supreme Court."

"American slightly denatured with Spanish," Joan decided. The throaty voice sent little chills sprinting through her veins. The woman's face was as cold and perfect as that of a marble Venus. A face with cruel, greedy, glittering eyes, green as huge emeralds, and scarlet lips.

"Good-afternoon, Mrs. Lamont," the girl at the switchboard murmured as she passed.

The woman looked at her as if she were a

11

revolting specimen in a zoo, drew her silver fox skins with their knot of gardenias about her shoulders and swept by in a wave of perfume. As the outer door closed the operator wrinkled a disdainful nose in its direction and snapped;

"That seems to be that, sugar!"

She plugged in a switch. Spoke into the receiver;

"Mr. Janvers is in the A.D.'s office, Mr. Lamont."

She said to Joan;

"You'll have to wait a few minutes."

Joan waited, interested in the stir and activity about her. An office door banged open. This time it was a man who paused on the threshold to declare angrily;

"I'm through. Because you've built up my business, you think you can go ahead without consulting me, think I ain't got ideas of my own. I'll show you! I'm going to the Bard Agency now. Perhaps there'll be someone in that outfit who'll put over my advertising as I want it done. Good-bye!" He slammed the door.

"Gosh, this seems to be the Lamont Agency's Tabasco day," the switchboard girl snapped.

As the man approached, Joan observed the angry redness of his face, the sheen of his black hair below the rakish brim of his soft hat, the fine lines which radiated from the corners of his protruding glass-marble eyes as if etched with a sharp point; the red carnation in the lapel of his perfectly cut coat, his spats, the polish of his shoes which was only a degree less shining than his hair. He might be forty. More likely fifty. He straightened his tie and threw an oblique glance at her. As the outer door closed behind him, Joan asked in a whisper;

"Was that Mr. Lamont?"

The girl at the switchboard sniffed contempt.

"That eye-roller the boss? Guess again. That was Janvers of the Straight As A Crow Flies Bus Line. He can't pass anything in skirts without throwing back his shoulders and straightening his tie. He started as a taxi driver. His business headquarters are in the Middle West but he spends one month in every three in Boston and we handle all his publicity. He's always flying off the handle like that. Hope we haven't lost his account. It's a big one. I'll try now for the A.D."

She plugged in a switch, spoke into the transmitter. A voice rumbled in reply. She answered;

"He is? You will? Okay, I'll send her in."

Joan was aware that the girl took in every

detail of her tailored blue suit, the sheer blouse with its crisp jabot, her hat, the star sapphire on her third finger, even her blue shoes before she sniffed and approved bitterly;

"Don't be jittery. You'll make the grade. You've got what it takes. Art directors like 'em good-looking even if they can't draw. Third door on the left."

"I don't like to talk about myself, but I can draw," Joan assured with a smile.

It seemed to her that she traveled miles before she entered a room the walls of which were hung with original sketches, some in black and white, more in color. A tall man standing at the window turned.

As his eyes met hers they seemed to lift her heart and drop it. It was the breath-snatching sensation she had when an elevator shot down suddenly, it was like having nerves she hadn't known were there, shocked alive by a surge of excitement. His black hair had one rebellious kink, two straight lines cut deep between his amazingly brilliant wide-set hazel eyes, eyes clear, clean, compelling, the line of his finely modeled, sensitive mouth was tense, his skin was bronzed.

In a mirror behind him she appraised herself as she might the drawing of a head.

Chestnut hair, natural wave, nice hairline, area from cheekbone to ear commended by artists, a bit of slant to deep blue eyes alight with warmth and sparkle, lashes long, dark, gold-tipped, plenty of color in cheeks and lips — she was glad now that she had decided against make up. On the whole, clean-cut type. Not too bad if this art director "liked 'em good-looking" and she could draw. Lucky that an inner voice had urged her to wear her most swanky hat. Early in her business career she had discovered that the average man is susceptible to feminine headgear and shoes. She choked back a laugh as she thought of the shimmering rubbers left, as it were, outside the door of this temple of advertising. How could she be so flippant when this interview meant so much to her?

She opened her portfolio.

"I brought these proofs in the hope that you would like them and give me a chance at some roughs."

"Won't you sit down?"

"Nice voice, rich and deep, but tense," Joan thought.

He pulled out a chair for her before he sat on a corner of the desk. She had the feeling that he was forcing his attention to the black pages of the portfolio on which were pasted samples of her work.

15

"All these have been published?"

"Yes."

"Where have you sold your stuff?"

She named several New York advertising agencies.

"Why desert the Big Town for this city?"

"My family moved to a small town — not a suburb — near Boston. I was needed so I came along."

"I'll bet you hated coming."

"At first I did, but, now I like it. I suspect I'm a dyed-in-the-wool New Englander at heart, my father's people were Massachusetts settlers back in Colonial days."

"You realize, of course, that you won't get the prices here that the New York agencies pay?"

"So I have been told, but, one can do more satisfactory work if one can talk a layout over with an art director than if one attempts to carry on by mail. As I am nearer Boston than New York, I shall try for work here."

He frowned at a page, tapped a proof pasted on it. It was a colorful picture of a girl and two dogs.

"I like this. Sure it's yours?"

Joan sprang to her feet. The disconcertingly cool tone of his voice, the suspicion in his eyes which were no longer hazel but keenly black, sent color to her hair.

"What do you mean, 'Sure it's yours'? Do you think I would show that if it were not my design?"

A man with a boyish round face, round blue eyes and sleek fair hair, dashed into the room. He stopped and grinned a greeting to Joan as the man on the desk said;

"Take a look at this International Dog-Soap Company proof, Tony."

The blue-eyed man leaned over his shoulder, looked at the proof, winked at Joan.

"It's a good try, sister, and a good piece of designing. There's a beautiful balance of weight in the figure. The only trouble is you're the third person this week who has shown it as his work. Spotted it, didn't you, Craig?"

"I did."

Surprise dashed with anger choked off Joan's voice. "Craig!" The man to whom she had been talking was not the art director, he was the 'boss'! Craig Lamont. The switchboard operator had said that he had come in with a grouch. Apparently his wife's visit, the girl had called the red-haired woman Mrs. Lamont — with her threat to carry a case to the Supreme Court had increased the gloom. And he was taking it out

17

on her. The realization was like a handful of fat pine flung on fire on her smoldering anger. She blazed;

"What do you mean by 'good try'? I designed that drawing for the Dog-Soap Company. I'm Joan Crofton. Turn a few more pages and you'll find three others for the same firm. I wouldn't be likely to show four not my own, would I? You'll find my initials J.C. on the last one and on some of the other proofs. Perhaps you think I've stolen them all. You've discovered it, have you? Then that's that."

She caught up the portfolio and tied it. At the door she flung over her shoulder a crisp "Good-morning."

"Hold on." The blond man who had been addressed as Tony caught the door-knob before she could turn it. "You mustn't go like this, Miss Crofton, mistakes occur in the best regulated firms, you know."

Joan regarded him disdainfully.

"Are you suggesting that this by any stretch of imagination may be called a best regulated firm?"

"Br-r-r right off the ice!" He turned up his coat collar. "Don't shoot the man at the piano, he's doing the best he can." Joan bit her lips to keep back a smile in response to the boyish mischief in his eyes.

18

"I'll take care of this, Tony." Craig Lamont opened a door to the adjoining room. "It was my blunder. Sorry, Miss Crofton. Come into my office and let's get this straightened out. Forgive us won't you? There have been artists who have shown the work of others as their own."

As if she had to be told that. He must think her a novice in the advertising game. Her angry eyes met his. Was a smile lurking in their depths? Was he amused at her indignation? She'd show him.

"How do you know that I'm not dishonestly claiming all that work signed J.C.? I won't go into your office. I wouldn't work for such an agency. I'll leave this priceless thought with you. They not only pay more in New York, they know more about art. A whole lot more. Good-morning."

"Good-m-morning." There was a gulp in the voice of the art director.

"That will keep you in your place for a while, Tony," Lamont observed crisply. "Allow me —"

He opened the door. To Joan's angry dismay he accompanied her through the large room. She was aware of cautiously turned heads, of an instant's cessation of the click of typewriters. She stole a glance in the direction of her rubbers. The toes coyly

19

peeked from beneath the seat where she had left them. Could she retrieve those glittering belongings in her present aloof and disdainful mood? She could not. It would be anticlimax. The man beside her might act the perfect gentleman and insist upon putting them on. Then what?

"Someone on the line for you, Mr. Lamont," the girl at the switchboard said as he passed.

"Hold the call, Miss Gould. I'll be back in a moment."

In the corridor he rang for the elevator. As they waited he suggested;

"Not too late to let us have another look at your work, Miss Crofton. Won't you come back? I liked your proofs. There's a new slant to them and we're keen for a new slant. We may be able to talk business."

"I'll never talk business with your agency," Joan declared.

As the elevator door clanged open he suggested;

"You're something of a fire-eater, aren't you? Never is a long time. Good-morning."

He was smiling as the car dropped out of sight.

Back in his office Craig Lamont answered the telephone. He gazed unseeingly at his art director perched on the corner of his desk.

"Lamont speaking — Mother! How are you? Sorry I was in New York when you arrived at Silver Birches. Got back on the job this morning. Have been waiting for a chance to call you. Who? — You sent Joan Crofton here? Why didn't you give her a letter to me? — She came. She didn't like the reception we gave her and beat it for another agency, probably Bard's — He has? Of course you'll be nice to him, Sally Shaw, why not? Tony and I'll be out for dinner tomorrow night. Why not invite Phil to Silver Birches and get it over — quick. You'll do it sooner or later, you know you will. — Okay. Good-bye."

He spoke to Tony Crane.

"The Crofton family has inherited The Mansion, that corking old 1800 brick house, the land adjoins Silver Birches. Joan Crofton showed Mother the list of Boston agencies she had been told to visit. Mother steered her here though the girl was strong for trying Bard Inc. first, had planned to take the agencies alphabetically. Nadja had been here threatening to petition the Probate Court, when she left Gould phoned that Janvers was waiting for me in your office and I had a set-to with him. He was so darn cocky that I saw red. He was all het up because we'd gone ahead with that last ad without waiting until he reached town. I told him that we'd paid out two hundred dollars on it and reminded him that we'd done it before. The real reason he blew up was because I won't let him go on the air."

"That lad had better learn that b e e n isn't pronounced ben, and cut ain't from his vocabulary before he talks on the radio."

"I tried to make him realize that. After Nadja's threat I was fit to tie and didn't tackle the ex-taxi driver right."

"I thought she was anchored in Hollywood."

"She made two pictures. Recently I've heard that they didn't click. That's why she's back here to make life merry for Mother and me. We can take it. Apparently this isn't my tactful day. I shouldn't have seen Miss Crofton, her sort of work isn't my job until it comes up for the final decision, and I don't like dealing with women, but I wanted to get Janvers and Nadja out of my mind, and told Gould to send the girl to your office. When she came into the room I didn't really see her. I was seeing Nadja's green eyes. I got off on the wrong foot with her too."

"You would. Your first reaction to any girl is to doubt her honesty."

"I admit it, Tony. I've heard of Joan Crofton's work. She's good and I've been thinking that the feminine angle in the Bus Line ads would help. The majority of bus passengers are women and a woman would know how to appeal to their sense of comfort and adventure. After our blundering reception she probably has shot straight for the Bard Agency."

Tony Crane's blue eyes blazed with anger.

"I go fighting mad when Phil Bard's name is mentioned. You took him in here when he was walking the streets, jobless. I'll bet you did it because when you two were boys he lived, figuratively speaking, on the wrong side of the track."

Craig Lamont crossed his arms and his knees and gazed at the wall as if he were watching a picture unfold on a screen.

"I can see now the tumble-down house in which the Bardonis lived. It was sordid. You'll have to hand it to Phil for Anglicizing his name and climbing out of shantyville. He led the high school class in studies and athletics —"

"He wouldn't have if you and Carl hadn't been sent off to Prep School," Crane reminded.

"You've been listening to Mother. She never liked Phil even as a boy when he delivered groceries after school hours."

"Your mother has the right hunch. That lad's a bad egg and I'll bet 'you ain't seen nothin' yet.' That's a quotation, in case you care. Didn't he hang round Nadja? Any man who will play tame cat to a married woman has a screw loose. You taught him all he knows, then when he's worth something to you he walks out and tries to take your accounts with him. Sometimes when he looked at you, his eyes would give me the shivers. I always hung round for fear he'd stick a knife in your back."

"You've been seeing too many gangster pictures, Tony. Phil may have been jealous of what I had and have — natural enough, isn't it — but he's a sniper, he wouldn't attack in the open. If he hadn't had what it takes to make an advertising man, he wouldn't have made good, and he has built up a business. Janvers was friendly with him when he worked for us, that's why he is on his way there now."

"And so is Joan Crofton! What do you know about that! He's looking for something new and that girl has it. I liked the dark, decisive strokes in her drawings. Did you notice her hands? Graceful, sensitive, capable, with beautifully cared for shining pale pink nails?"

"I did. I noticed also the whopping star sapphire on her finger. That doesn't look as if we had turned down a girl who needs work."

"You can't tell by that. May have been inherited or a present from a boy friend. Sapphire or no sapphire we need the gal. Suppose I could head her off?"

Craig Lamont remembered the glint in Joan Crofton's eyes and the edge in her voice as she said;

"I'll never talk business with your agency."

"Heading her off is out, Tony. We'll try diplomacy. Better drop in for lunch at T Wharf tomorrow. Janvers always lunches there when he's in town. Says the water and the boats remind him of his gob days."

"If you ask me, I'll bet he was a snappy sailor lad. Kind of queer that with his eye for the female of the species, he isn't married."

"We don't know that he isn't. He likes

25

you, Tony. He'll probably rave at you, then admit that we've made his bus line tick and be a good boy. We'll get the girl artist and we'll keep the Janvers account too — unless —"

"Unless what —"

"Mother phoned that Phil Bard had taken rooms at the Inn in Carsfield for the summer, there's a chance that he may become Joan Crofton's heart interest, girls like him. Then where would we be?"

"Well, we'll be in Carsfield too, won't we? You'll move out to your mother's house next week and I'll settle down at the Country Club. If you weren't such a darn girl skeptic, you might cut in there, the way he cut in on your business," Crane reminded belligerently.

Craig Lamont laughed.

"Curious that you and I should have had the same idea, Tony. It will take some cutting in, though, after my bad break this afternoon. Joan Crofton's temper is a powder-magazine that needs only a spark to set it off."

"Let's pray that the Bard Agency will supply a spark, and that the powder-magazine will blow the tricky Phil off the map," declared Tony Crane fervently.

Meanwhile dampness seeping through

Joan's smart blue shoes as she crossed slushy streets begrimed by soot from belching chimneys and washed by rivulets rushing along the gutters, was reducing the temperature of her anger. How like her quick temper to flare and burn the bridges behind her, she brooded. As an apology for his suspicion, Craig Lamont would have given her a chance to submit sketches. Experience told her that Tony Crane would have smoothed the way for her. She had met any number of art directors of his type who had proved to be helpful without falling in love with her — at least most of them had stopped at friendship. It would serve her right and give her a much needed lesson in controlling her temper if she didn't get a chance to show what she could do for weeks.

She doggedly resisted the urge to call it a day. She wouldn't go home and admit to her father and mother that she had lost out on her first try for work. They had enough on their minds following the closing up of his business and their move from New York, which they loved, to a small town to say nothing of their consternation and concern when their younger daughter Vivian, had announced her determination to try her fortune in Hollywood. Now that Uncle Mark

27

Crofton had left her five thousand dollars, she would not bury herself in a stuffy village, she had insisted. She would stay in New York while she prepared for her journey to the coast.

Joan winced as she visualized her father's white face, her mother's wistful eyes as she had asked;

"You had a legacy too, Joan. Are you off on your own or will you go to Carsfield with us?"

"Of course I'm going with you!" she had answered fervently. As she watched the color come back into their faces, her conscience pricked. She wasn't going entirely on their account, it would be heavenly to escape Jerry Slade's weekly proposal that she marry him. She had added gaily;

"You don't think I'd let you two babes wander into the deep dark woods alone, do you?"

Babes was hardly the word for them, she thought as she picked her way across a slushy street. Her parents were charming, with an up to the minute knowledge of world happenings, politics, books, music, art and sports. They had hosts of friends. They were so good-looking that eyes turned to gaze at them as they passed, they were generous to a fault. Their love of the social

28

side of life, the beautiful and the choice had trapped them after her father's business had developed chills and fever. She couldn't remember a time during the last few years, when Monday morning hadn't found her mother figuring bills and her father shaking his white head over them. When his brother had died and left him the life tenancy of The Mansion and an income from a trust fund, he had closed out his business. With his arm about his wife he had said;

"Joan, your mother and I have a chance to live without the pressing anxiety of debts. Now that we know to a penny what we will have to spend, we intend to budget our income and keep within the budget if it kills us. We know our failings, don't we, Patty?"

Her mother's dark eyes had flashed with laughter as settling herself closer within her husband's arm she had flouted in her soft southern voice;

"Speak for yourself, David. I haven't any failings. I've just got artistic temperament."

They were like that, always taking life on the chin. They were dears. Joan blinked moisture from her lashes.

She lingered in front of a flower shop. Behind the glass were trays of deep purple Parma violets; waxy gardenias, a flat dish of rosy camellias against a background of tall-stemmed crimson roses; bowls of freesia, yellow, white and lavender; sprays of white lilac, and slim wands of pussy-willow. Outside, stands and benches displayed pots of tall red tulips, creamy daffodils and pale yellow jonquils. Huge green terra-cotta jars flanked the door. The blossoms on the branches of forsythia, which filled them, were like a shower of golden rain. Blue and pink and white hyacinths outlined the curb of the sidewalk.

"All you need is a robin hopping and chirping in the window to make this real spring," she said to the swarthy faced woman from whom she bought an exquisite gardenia. She would have preferred violets but the sight of the lovely purple bunches flashed Jerry Slade's face and his weekly offering on the screen of her mind. She didn't want to think of him. She hadn't realized what a nightmare his persistence had been, until she had left him behind forever.

She returned to the street with mind and heart full of color and hope. Proprietors of flower shops like the one she had left were more than business men, they were public benefactors purveying beauty, she told herself as she sniffed the fragrance of the blossom pinned on the lapel of her coat.

Here she was. The Bard Agency. With

what brand of reception would she meet? Would her honesty be questioned? She visualized Craig Lamont's eyes as he had asked, "Sure it's yours?" and burned with resentment.

She opened the door. She had planned to make her first call here but when she had shown Mrs. Shaw — at her request — samples of her work, and the list of advertising agencies which she intended to visit, her neighbor had been courteously insistent that she try the Lamont Agency first, said that she had gone to school with the mother of the man who headed the corporation and that he was making a spectacular success of his business.

"Who do you want to see?"

The crisp voice of the girl at the switchboard snapped Joan out of her reflections. This operator was young, pretty, with lips the color of orange peel. If her costume erred on the side of appropriateness it made up in color and line.

"The art director, please."

The girl thrust in a plug, spoke into the receiver waved an indefinite hand;

"He'll see you. Scott Rand is the man you want."

Joan passed a door marked Philip Bard, another which proclaimed to an inquiring world that the Production Manager did business within, before she opened one marked Art Director. Two greenish eyes regarded her gloomily as she entered. The desk behind which sat the man in shirt-sleeves was strewn with colorful sketches.

She promptly untied her portfolio and announced;

"I'm Joan Crofton. I'm after work. Will you look at these proofs?"

Scott Rand, she supposed it was he, ran thick-jointed fingers through tousled red hair and brought his tipped-back chair down on all fours. He grinned encouragement.

"Sure, Joan Crofton. Say, I've heard of you. You did that big dog-soap campaign, didn't you? 'Soap. Soap! Be-u-ti-ful soap,' or words to that effect."

She nodded eagerly. Recognition at last. This interview promised to be fun. She watched the art director's face as he turned the pages of her portfolio.

"I like these. No over-elaboration. You've got something. A new slant — for the love of Pete —"

He spoke into the telephone in a guarded voice;

"Janvers still there, boss? Cook up an excuse and leave him a minute — I think I've found something."

It seemed but an instant before a slight, foreign looking man entered and closed the door behind him.

"What's the rush —" he saw Joan and brushed up the corners of a small black moustache with the invincible-male gesture she particularly hated.

Scott Rand was on his feet. His hair reared as he tapped a page of the portfolio with one hand and waved the other in the direction of Joan.

"Miss Crofton, the boss. She did that Soap, Soap, Be-u-ti-ful soap ad that had us all ga-ga. Look at these proofs. Notice the simplicity and strength of the group settings. I'll bet we could land Janvers with her and that new copy-writer we've taken on, especially if we sneaked her up on the taxi-baron for an interview. He likes 'em good-looking."

Under the reproving glare of his boss, Rand subsided into his chair. Bard, of Bard's Agency, turned the pages of the portfolio. His voice was noncommittal as he asked;

"What do you know about bus travel, Miss Crofton?"

"Not much. I've never traveled in one."

"Ever heard of the Straight As A Crow Flies Bus Line?"

"Yes."

"Get some dope on it, will you? I want to show half a dozen folders for use in the terminal. My client's going out of town for forty-eight hours. Can you work up six roughs and show them to us day after tomorrow?"

"I can," Joan assented. She hoped with not too much eagerness.

"Don't think it would help for Janvers to meet Miss Crofton now, do you?" Scott Rand suggested eagerly.

"I do not. I'll expect you day after tomorrow, Miss Crofton. Good afternoon."

As Bard left the room, Scott Rand glared at his back and growled;

"The trouble with that lad is, you can't tell him anything. We want Janvers and Janvers is girl-conscious." As he met Joan's surprised eyes he added hastily; "The boss is a crack-a-jack ad man just the same. Drop in at the terminal and look over the folders they're using now. Bring us some roughs that will knock our prospect all in a heap, Miss Crofton. Good-bye."

He opened the door for her, a courtesy Joan had not expected from the man who had remained tilted back in his chair when she entered.

She went out into the street with her head high and an all's-right-with-the-world glow in her heart. She felt tinglingly, exquisitely alive. She had a chance to submit through a rival agency, some roughs for one of Craig Lamont's "big accounts." If only she could come face to face with him this minute she would look through him as if he were a wraith.

How blue the sky was. How high. How cloudless. The air was sweet. She drew a deep breath. God was in His heaven and Jerry Slade was far away. She laughed. Her reception at the Bard Agency had changed her outlook on the world.

III

Joan spent the next two hours in the terminal of the Straight As A Crow Flies Bus Line. At judicious intervals she asked questions at the different desks, collected folders; listened to the amplified announcements of the destination of busses; watched passengers arrive and depart; the porters off and on duty; caught some of their remarks. She bought a magazine at the newsstand. Perched on a high stool at the lunch counter and ordered tea and toast.

As she drove home, over roads filled with glazed pools, deep ruts and slush, past ponds honeycombed with ice, her mind seethed with ideas. It was almost dusk when she reached The Mansion, the brick house, with its white columned portico, its long windows in the lower story and curved dormers above. It dated back to 1800 and was considered one of the finest examples of Federal architecture in the country. Her uncle had bought it as a background for his collection of rare furniture and china.

The springlike day had thawed some of the snow heaped on the lawn beside the drive. A red-winged blackbird which had outdistanced its flock on the northward migration swung on the brown tip of a branch. The sun had set but the afterglow tinted white houses pink, turned skeleton trees to claret, pools in the road to crimson mirrors, grotesquely distorted shadows, and drew its color brush lightly over untrodden snow fields till they looked like spreads of rosy plush tucked over the land beneath. A sliver of moon like the paring of a gold coin hung in the darkening sky. One brilliant star kept it company for all the world like a lady-in-waiting. There was a hint of the fragrance of swelling red buds.

"Spring in the air, all the time there is, heaps of interesting work — and play — ahead, and no Jerry Slade telling me his life is in my hands and that he can't live without me," Joan exulted as she drove into the garage.

She entered the house by the rear door. Stopped to listen. Voices. The tinkle of silver on china. The scent of toast. There would be at this time of day. Were her mother and father marooned on a desert island, an aviator, perhaps a native from some remote continent, would be sure to drop in for a cup of tea.

She caught the gleam of the shell-shaped fire-screen of wrought brass, the pale greenish blue of the paneling, the reflection of her father's white hair in the mirror above the Adam mantel in the drawing room as she stole by the door. She didn't want to break her train of thought by talking with anyone.

She snapped on the light as she entered her work room. Fortunately the late owner's love for the antique hadn't dulled his sense of the comforts of contemporary living. The rose-color chintz at the windows picked up the glow from the lamp. She sniffed at the gardenia before she thrust the stem into a vase of water. She hung up her coat, pulled off her hat and glanced at the old clock on the mantel ticking off the minutes. Had she time before dinner to make rough sketches of a few of the ideas which had pelted through her mind on the way home? If her parents had heard her come in she would be summoned to meet their guests, if not she was safe from interruption.

Perched on a high stool before her drawing table with its cargo of T squares, rulers, brushes, pencils and paints, she made a start.

She sketched a radio sending forth zig-zag lines and clear-cut letters.

"Old stuff," she told herself and commenced again.

CALLING ALL TRAVELERS! CALL-
ING ALL TRAVELERS! she printed in
heavy sans-serif lettering. That was better.

She became absorbed in her work. Once
she chuckled. Her ideas were developing
with the speed of the immortal Mr. Finney's
celebrated turnip.

" 'It grew and it grew
And it grew behind the barn' " she
chanted under her breath.

She frowned as she regarded the sketch.
In her thrilled realization that she was being
given a chance to show what she could do,
she hadn't thought to ask friendly Scott
Rand how much the prospective client was
willing to spend. Even if the girl-conscious
Janvers wouldn't finance four-ink printing,
he might like to see how color improved a
folder. She would submit roughs in full
color and as carefully done as finished work
would be. She would put the best work of
her life into them, if for no other reason than
to help the Bard Agency get the Janvers account. She'd show the head of Craig
Lamont, Inc. that "never is a long time."
She'd better stop being vindictive and con-
centrate. She would have to work every day-
time minute between now and day after
tomorrow to have six roughs ready.

Voices in the hall. The front door closing.

The tea-party was over. Evidently her father and mother had not heard her come in. They would be anxious until they knew she was at home. The country after dark was to them a wilderness fraught with danger from lurking wild animals and predatory tramps. In comparison the city was a haven of refuge and safety.

She started her bath. They would know when they heard the water running that she was at home. She pulled out the drawer of the filing cabinet to make sure that in the confusion of moving she hadn't mislaid the folder of clippings about bus travel. It was there.

She checked up on the jars of show-card colors on a shelf, glanced approvingly at the stacks of pamphlets and books she had acquired since she began to study for her work. Living in a small town had some advantages. Her workshop in the New York apartment had been a corner of her bedroom, here she had two rooms and a bath for her very own.

She was slipping into a georgette frock spattered with huge pink roses and hyacinths blue as her eyes, when her mother knocked and inquired in her soft voice with its hint of southern drawl;

"Safe and happy, honey?"

40

"Quite safe and gorgeously happy, Mother. I'll tell you about it when I come down."

She still glowed with the excitement of the Bard Agency interview when she entered the candle-lighted dining room. Had she ever really appreciated its charm before? The ivory paneled walls, gold cornices, blue damask hangings, the arched cupboards, their open doors revealing priceless blue-bordered Lowestoft were beautiful. So were the blown-glass hurricane shades over the candles on the mantel.

Pity Uncle Mark had lived such a short time after he bought The Mansion for his antiques, but, what a background it made for Patty and David Crofton, Joan thought as she looked at her parents. Her mother's dark hair was dressed to show the lovely shape of her head. The brilliancy of her brown eyes and the satin texture of her magnolia tinted skin were accentuated by a green frock. She had been the belle of her county when dashing young David Crofton had snatched her from a dozen adorers, she was still vividly beautiful. As to her father — Joan's throat tightened — there wasn't anyone in the world with such soft, white hair, such kindly blue eyes, so good-looking, so tall and straight, so

41

sporting — so companionable.

"Why are you looking at us as if you'd never seen us before, honey?" her mother inquired. She laughed and waved her hand in the direction of her husband. "Miss Crofton, allow me to present the distinguished Mr. David Crofton, in case you've forgotten that you've met him."

"Catch her forgetting her best boyfriend," David Crofton flouted. He drew out Joan's chair at the table while whitecoated Lopez, the Filipino they had brought from New York to be man-of-all-work, performed a similar service for her mother. She felt her father's light kiss on the top of her head before he seated himself.

"Your mother tells me you had a successful day, Joan," he remarked as he helped himself lavishly to the hors-d'œuvres Lopez was passing.

"A gorgeous day, in spite of the fact that I was — figuratively speaking — flogged from the first temple of advertising I entered."

"Did they know who you were, honey?" Patty Crofton's voice was flatteringly incredulous.

"Even after I told them they seemed able to bear up under the honor of my visit. But at the next place, boy, oh boy, oh boy, I was received with practically open arms. They

42

gave me a chance to submit some roughs for an important account. Already I have slathers of ideas — which of course may or may not jell — and I'll have to work every minute to have them ready day after tomorrow, but, believe it or not, I'll be sitting on the Bard Agency steps when the office door opens. That's why I slipped by the drawing room when I came in. Who were your callers?"

Patty Crofton glanced at the door Lopez had closed behind him before she answered;

"Only one, a Miss Dodd. Lives next door to the post-office in the village. She's the town loud-speaker, I'm willing to guess. She told me more about the residents of Carsfield in the half hour she was here than I have heard in the month since we came. You should have seen your father's face, honey. You know how he hates gossip. It seems that our delightful neighbor at Silver Birches, Mrs. Shaw, was a young widow with small twin sons when she married a rich lawyer from the west, Daniel Shaw, he's now a Senator. One of the sons married when a senior at college. His wife was a torch-singer, Mexican, I believe. Had a string of male followers. The husband died two years ago. He had tied up their child's share of his property — from what Miss

43

Dodd intimated, I judge the little girl is a terror — and left her guardianship to his mother and brother. Miss Dodd fairly licked her lips when she informed us that the will read 'for reasons my wife will understand.' "

"That's as accurate as a stenographic report would be, Patty Crofton. What became of the other son?" Joan asked. Not that she cared, but she loved to watch the sparkle in her mother's eyes as she talked.

"According to Miss Dodd, because of his brother's unfortunate marriage, he's cynical about women. Not the hermit brand, on the contrary, he is asked everywhere and goes. His approval of a girl boosts her at once into popularity. He's good-looking, successful in business, was called the Singing Halfback in college — she says he has a remarkable voice — has a small private fortune and social prestige."

"In short, a glamour-man. How I hate 'em," Joan declared fervently. "I hope he doesn't live with his mother at Silver Birches. It would be boring to keep tripping over such a paragon."

"The talkative Miss Dodd informed us that the 'paragon' has a penthouse apartment in town. May I suggest, Miss Crofton, that it is barely possible that the gentleman

44

under discussion might not keep so near that you would trip over him?" David Crofton suggested smoothly.

Joan laughed and wrinkled her nose at her father.

"Man to the defense of man! That's putting me in my place. You sat me down so hard, Davy Crofton, that my teeth rattled like castanets from the jar. Did the communicative Miss Dodd tell all that over one cup of tea, Mother? I'm glad I side-stepped her, her chatter would have swept my mind clean of all my thrilling ideas for the folders. I must keep my thoughts exclusively on my work for the next forty-eight hours."

"Oh, honey!" Mrs. Crofton drooped in her chair, the picture of dejection. Her husband interposed quickly;

"Let Joan have her dinner first, Patty."

"Never mind my dinner. What's happened? Uncle Mark hasn't materialized from the everywhere to snatch back the trust fund, the legacies and the star sapphire, has he?" Joan demanded breathlessly and instinctively clasped a hand tight over her ring.

"No, honey. Worse than that."

Her mother waited until Lopez had finished passing the vegetables and the pantry door had swung behind him before she

45

nodded toward it and whispered;

"He's given notice. Can't stand the country. Must be near night school. He's leaving 'queek' tomorrow."

"Tomorrow!"

The vision of herself as kitchen-maid, washing innumerable dishes — after her mother's cooking — and dusting instead of drawing, drenched Joan's voice with dismay.

"Now that we've started, we'd better tell the truth, Patty, 'the whole truth and nothing but the truth — so help us,' " David Crofton carried on jocularly. "Vivian wired that she would arrive tomorrow."

Joan sighed relief.

"Nothing so horrible about that. Viv can help with the housework while I finish my roughs."

"Sorry to puncture your balloon of hope, Jo, but, as she's returning to New York in the early afternoon, she'll be here for luncheon and tea only." David Crofton paused for dramatic effect before he added;

"Jerry Slade is planing her on from New York. He's been transferred to Boston and made sales manager of the New England branch of the airplane business."

"Oh, no!" Joan protested. "Why, one of the reasons I was glad to come here was to get away from him. If I don't, some day he'll tie my life up in a hard knot. I know it. That isn't premonition, it's plain common sense. I won't see him tomorrow. I won't. I'm too busy to see him," she declared furiously.

IV

Lopez's week was up after breakfast but Joan had shamelessly and lavishly bribed him to stay until he had cooked and served luncheon. He might leave the dishes for her to wash, she had told him.

She had risen while the indigo sky was still twinkling with stars, while Venus was shining at her brightest and a rose-color dawn was stealing up on the eastern horizon to the accompaniment of the sleepy twitter of birds. From then on, she had worked at white heat on the roughs for the Straight As A Crow Flies Bus Line folders. She had attempted to beg-off coming to the table for luncheon but her mother had been hurt by the suggestion.

"How can you think of it when your only sister is going away for months — perhaps forever," she had protested with a break in her soft voice. "We must stand by Vivian even if we disapprove of this attack of Hollywooditis. She picked up the germ when she made a hit in the Charity Club dramatics. Then your Uncle Mark's legacy supplied funds for the experiment. We've tried but we can't make her realize that there are thousands with more experience in acting than she has had battering at the doors of motion-picture producers."

"You and father could have stopped her going," Joan reminded.

"We didn't try. She won't suffer from privation while her money lasts, when that's gone, she can come home. We stated our reasons against the experiment then left the decision to her. Vivian is twenty-two years old. Under her external sophistication she's a warm-hearted, emotional little girl, but, she knows what she wants and goes after it. You're like that too, honey. Your father and I have put the best of ourselves into our daughters. We stand for honor, integrity, loyalty and ideals, with a heavy accent on ideals, but we can't live your lives for you — we won't even try."

"I don't want to see Jerry Slade," Joan persisted stubbornly. "Why couldn't Viv come to say good-bye without bringing him in her pocket."

"I suspect that beneath her in-again-out-again love affairs, Vivian cares more for Jerry than any of us realize. Life forms amazing patterns. Turns hearts inside out. Why couldn't Jerry have cared for her? But I don't wonder he loves you, honey. Davy and I agree that when we are with you, our hearts are warmed through and through as if we had been sitting in the sun. You will come to luncheon, won't you?"

Of course she had answered "yes" and equally, of course, after that tribute she would have walked over red-hot coals had her mother asked it, Joan told herself that afternoon as in the kitchen she lightly rolled and cut dough for scones. She glanced furtively at the sink piled with dishes. Lopez had taken her at her word and left them for her to wash. Looked as if she wouldn't get back to the roughs for the Bus Line folders for hours. That was the trouble with having a home studio. The members of her family didn't take her work seriously. They were always accepting invitations for her and then appearing deeply grieved when she refused to go. Argue as convincingly as she could, that if she were to make good, she must keep to working hours as strictly as if she were in an office, she couldn't make them realize it.

She glanced at the clock as she slipped a pan of scones into the oven. Time was flying. That minute hand must be bewitched. If only she could hold it back. Instead of finishing the work on her drawing table which she had promised for tomorrow, she was preparing tea, with one of the big white chef aprons provided for Lopez over her turquoise blue knit frock while Jerry Slade drove Vivian around the village, that when she was far away she might be able to visualize the surroundings in which her family was living.

As she sliced bread, she thought of her sister. She had been vivid with excitement when she arrived, but as the day wore on, she had grown more and more subdued.

Jerry Slade had been devotedly attentive to her. Joan had drawn a breath of relief as she decided that his heart-storm over herself had blown out and passed on. Then she had looked up suddenly and her bubble of satisfaction had burst. His large dark eyes, which were in startling contrast to his fair hair — were fixed on her with the expression of adoration she dreaded. What could she do about it? There must be some way of convincing him that she didn't, wouldn't, never could love him.

She'd better stop thinking of him and keep her mind on what she was doing. Lopez had been such a treasure that it was a long time since she had fussed around a kitchen. Unless a maid were secured quickly she might have to do considerable more fussing.

Thank heaven, the kitchen was super-modern, she exulted, as she regarded the electrical equipment which had been installed in the opposite end of the long room from the original brick ovens and their shining copper equipments.

A car stopping! She glanced at the clock again. Vivian and Jerry Slade had returned from their sight-seeing tour. She checked up on her preparations. The huge silver tray with the mellon-pattern tea service, which her mother had brought from her southern home, was already established in the drawing room. She would take in the massive hot-water kettle, cinnamon toast and anchovy canapés and tea would be ready. She would come back for the scones.

As she slipped off her apron, Vivian swung open the pantry door.

"What are you doing, Jo? Where's Lopez?"

Joan gave an excellent imitation of the Filipino's shrug, his expressive hands.

"The late Lopez, you mean, 'Too lonesome. No night-school. He go — queek.' "

Even as she imitated the voice of the departed houseman, Joan was thinking how really lovely her sister was, with her dark hair, her brilliant eyes that had just enough of an Oriental slant to make them fascinating, her perfect nose, her red lips curved like a cupid's bow. The big emerald Uncle Mark had left her accentuated the long slender modeling of her exotic hand with its pointed, rosy nails. Her pale gray wool frock was the latest word in fashion. That was what came from living in what Craig Lamont called the Big Town. Just why had that disagreeable person popped into her mind, she demanded of herself indignantly.

"Mother didn't tell me that Lopez had deserted." Vivian nibbled at a wafer of cinnamon toast. She sniffed — and demanded theatrically;

"Do I smell scones or doth my nose deceive me? I love 'em with little wells of strawberry jam in each one. It's dear of you to prepare tea for Jerry and me, Jo, but — but you won't have to do it again for — a while."

All suggestion of drama had left her voice. Tears welled in the dark eyes so like her mother's. Joan patted her shoulder.

"Buck up, Viv. You don't have to go, you know."

Vivian swallowed hard and brushed a slender hand across her lashes.

"But I want to go — most of the time. You've made good in New York, I want to be somebody. I can't draw but I can act —

53

believe it or not, and if I don't get a chance at that I can model. Think of the times I have slinked around fashion-shows displaying frocks for charity. I'd die in a place like this. The sight of those distant hills gave me the shivers. The great silent spaces are not for me. Jerry asked a native son what the building on top of the highest mountain was and he said an abandoned Inn. Abandoned! I don't wonder. Someone must have had a pipe dream when he built that and expected people to pay to live there. I couldn't believe my ears when Dad began to talk garden. He of all persons in the world going in for the simple life. It's a joke. What do you do with your evenings? What will you do for men?"

"I get around. There's a grand country club for dancing, and theatres and concerts in town if I feel the urge. I don't need men to make me happy. I like them but I've never met one yet who was as unfailingly interesting as my work."

"You don't know what you're talking about. You make me think of a Dresden china figurine, lovely to look at but as unresponsive. It isn't as if men didn't fall for you, they're goofy about you. Do you think if Jerry Slade loved me I'd go to Hollywood? I don't understand you. Love is so wonderful." Vivian pressed her hand over her heart, drew a sigh of ecstasy and raised and dropped her long lashes.

Joan laughed, though she was troubled. Of course Viv was acting, but, there was enough truth in what she said to make the cinema world a doubtful experiment for her. She agreed practically;

"Love may be all you say it is, but at present I'm too busy to take a fling at it. I have a chance at a crack-a-jack ad campaign. You've got this town wrong. To listen to you one would think that the Croftons had landed on an uninhabited planet. Life may be simple, but you'd be surprised if you knew how many families here could splurge if they wanted to." She stopped, cautiously opened the oven door and peeked in. She shut it gently and went on;

"To date we've been too busy getting settled to care to go out much, but the people we have met are delightful. Our neighbor at Silver Birches, Mrs. Shaw, wife of a Senator, returned a few days ago from Washington and opened her beautiful home. It would please you. It's ivory white and looks as if it had grown out of the land. It's the last word in modern architecture and furnishings. Visitors come from miles away to see the gardens. Her tulips are famous. She called at once. She is an up to the minute person — if ever there were one — though she's a grandmother. We hear that her home is a Mecca for artists, scientists, writers, politicians, for persons who think, persons who do things. Mah jong has swept back into fashion and —"

"Don't tell me you spend your evenings playing mah jong with a grandmother, Jo! You, with your flair for smart clothes, you, who were the best tap-dancer and the wickedest tennis player in our set! It makes me more determined than ever to go to Hollywood."

"You may have some dull evenings there when you'll fall on your knees in thankfulness to have a chance at a game of mah jong. Life won't be all glamour there any more than it is anywhere, Viv."

"Of course it won't. Don't think for a minute that I expect a band and a flock of directors to meet me when I arrive on the Coast, or that I'll be signed up after my second test — I had one in New York — and shot up among the stars. I expect to work like a slave, but — it will be at something I'm crazy about. Jerry has promised to fly out and buck me up if I get terribly homesick. I didn't mean to turn sob-sister a minute ago. It's just when I think of M-mother and Dad and you — you're such thoroughbreds and — and you know I a-adore thoroughbreds." She bit her lips to control their quiver.

"Then watch out that you don't fall below a thoroughbred standard of living," Joan warned tenderly. "Do your best to live up to it and try, everlastingly try to make that best better. I'm talking like a pre-war grandmother. Sorry, I didn't mean to preach. Wipe your eyes. Your lashes look like drenched black fringes. You'll have to hustle, my girl, if you and Jerry intend to get to Boston in time to make the New York train."

"Jerry isn't going back."

"He hasn't come to stay now, has he?"

"Don't go jittery, Jo. He's only going as far as Boston to put me on the train, he will live at his University Club there. I wish he'd give you the air, then perhaps you would appreciate him."

"You don't wish that half so hard as I do, my hearty," Joan responded fervently. "As has been said before, unless you intend to miss that train, you'd better hustle. Take the muffin stand into the drawing room and I'll fill the kettle and bring it in."

Vivian caught Joan's arm. Her eyes were wet again, her voice uneven as she implored;

"You'll keep me posted about Mother and Dad, won't you? If anything were to happen to either of them and I wasn't —"

She was not acting now. Joan managed a laugh even though her throat had tightened at her sister's suggestion.

"Nothing will happen to them, silly. How can you look at those two vivid, alive creatures and think it? You may hear that they have fled from this small town to their adored New York, but that wouldn't surprise you, would it? Father was dead tired from the strain of bills and figuring ledgers exclusively in red ink when news came of Uncle Mark's will and he couldn't wait to drop his burden. But when he is thoroughly rested, it's my best bet he'll take command of his life again and sink his teeth into something, if it is only town affairs here. Go along with that muffin stand. As you may have heard somewhere, 'Time Marches On!' "

Vivian turned and smiled before the pantry door swung behind her, a smile that made Joan think of sun shining through a mist. Apparently the conflict between love of home and determination to have a career was tearing her heart wide open. Should she have tried to influence her to remain? No. If a mother and father could let their child choose her own way at the crossroads, surely a sister should not interfere.

She was filling the big silver kettle with boiling water when Jerry Slade swung open the pantry door.

"Viv suggested that I might help you take in things," he said.

Joan struggled to keep from registering exasperation. She appraised his wavy light hair, his brown eyes, his general effect of a blond Viking, his fair clipped mustache above a stubborn mouth, above a super-stubborn chin. Why did she have the uneasy feeling that some day his persistent devotion would make trouble for her? She hadn't felt so about other men who had asked her to marry them. Why couldn't she love him? He was companionable, his standard of living was jeered at by some as verging on the Puritanic — it was her standard too — he was successful in business, he was an ace pilot. He was —

"Well, what's the answer?" Slade demanded and tugged at the end of his mustache.

"I'll trust you to carry in the kettle, Jerry."

"You know I wasn't referring to that. I know what you were thinking. I'm a master mind-reader."

He picked up the kettle and paused in the doorway. He laughed.

"If at first you don't succeed, try, try again, is blazoned on my banner. Think that over, darling."

"If you want to help go along with that kettle, Jerry Slade, and don't call me darling," Joan dictated before she followed him to the drawing room.

Trees were waving crackling, brittle, brown branches against a background of crimsoning sky, a few vagrant, scuttling clouds were copper edged, three crows with raucous calls flapped away into the purple dusk which was stealing over the snowy fields, as Vivian leaned from the sedan and threw kisses to her mother and Joan standing on the porch. Jerry Slade waved and called; "I'll be seeing you!" and the car shot down the street. Two tears like huge diamonds rolled down Patty Crofton's cheeks.

"That child is so — so young to be starting off by herself. It seems only yesterday that she was beating her spoon against her silver porringer and howling when she wanted anything."

"And getting it," Joan reminded. "Viv always has gotten what she wanted and if you ask me, she always will get it. She has that indefinable something, perhaps it is vitality, perhaps it's will-power, it may be luck

— which fights and overcomes obstacles in her path."

"I wonder. I'm afraid she wants Jerry Slade. Are you sure you don't love him, honey?"

"I wish I were as sure I'd land that Bus Line assignment," Joan responded practically. "Don't worry about Viv, mother. If she really cares for Jerry, he'll wake up some morning to find she's the light of his eyes. Men are like that. She will be in and out of love a dozen times before we see her again. Her heart affairs are as impermanent as frost under a spring sun. That's why I feel so safe about her. She doesn't know it, but she measures every man by Davy Crofton, and when one doesn't come up to measurement, she tries another."

"Who could measure up to Davy Crofton?" her mother demanded fervently. "Whenever I think of him I think of that saying of St. Francis de Sales;

" 'Nothing is so strong as gentleness. Nothing so gentle as real strength.' " Two more tears welled and coasted.

Joan put an arm about her.

"Don't watch the car out of sight. Come into the house. We've got things to do. Lopez, the dear departed, left a sink full of dishes and we have dinner to get —"

"I'd forgotten to tell you, Joan, Mrs. Shaw phoned and asked us all to dine with her."

"That's a help. I may be able to get the roughs of the folders finished after all."

"You needn't do another thing in the kitchen, honey. Go back to your drawing. I'll take care of the dishes. We'll put on our swankiest frocks for dinner. They will help keep up our spirits." She sniffed as they entered the house. "Do I smell something burning?"

"Burning? Oh boy! Oh boy, the scones! Darn Jerry Slade! If he had kept out of the kitchen, I wouldn't have forgotten them," Joan's wail floated back as she dashed through the hall.

The kitchen was thick with haze. Coughing and sneezing she opened the oven and let out a blast of black smoke. She couldn't see much through her smarting, watering eyes, but made out the two large pans full of crisp, black objects edged with sparks which once had been scones. The kitchen sink was full of dishes, she'd have to chuck them out on the snow before they got ablaze.

She seized a holder. Drew out the hot pan. She coughed and sneezed as she pulled open the porch door and with all her

62

strength flung out the pan. She heard it land. Something crashed on the doorstep.

"Hey! Look out! What in thunder —"

A man's voice broke in a cross between a yell and a groan.

V

"What's happened? Did I hit someone?" Joan called distractedly. "This smoke is so thick —" She snapped on the porch light.

There was no one in sight. Burned crisps, which once had been scones, dotted the snow, the pan lay on its back in the midst of them. On the stone step at Joan's feet was something that resembled an uncooked omelette mixture garnished with broken glass and eggshells.

She stared at the mess before she dashed through the smoky kitchen to the hall.

"Mother! Mother!" she called.

"Coming, honey." The soft southern voice drifted from upstairs. "I'm getting into a smock so I can wash the dishes. Was something burning?"

Was something burning? Joan savagely strangled the gurgle in her throat. How could she even want to laugh when she might have maimed a man for life? The boy who delivered groceries from the store, perhaps?

Her mother leaned over the bannister.

"I still smell smoke, Joan. Sure nothing's

a-fire in the kitchen?"

"I'm sure. Did you order eggs and cream today?

"No, honey, did eggs and cream come? It must be a mistake. We'll send them back to the store in the morning."

"We won't send those eggs back," Joan giggled nervously.

The air had cleared when she returned to the kitchen. The remaining pan of scones smoked sociably in the oven. The omelette in embryo added a splash of yellow to the stone step. She winced as she remembered the stifled groan that had followed that hoarse —

"What in thunder —"

Perhaps the man or boy was lying unconscious somewhere. Awful thought. She tramped around the house in the snow. Slipped and slid along the drive which the dropping temperature had iced. Looked down the street. No one in sight. Apparently her victim had been able to limp away. She picked up the blackened scones and dropped them into the still warm pan. She brushed a lock of hair back from her eyes as she entered the kitchen.

Her mother, in a lilac smock, was valiantly attacking the dishes in the sink with rubber-gloved hands. She frowned incredulously.

"Your face looks as if you'd come out of a coal-mine, honey! Your shoes are soaking wet. What have you done to yourself?"

"Never mind what I've done to myself. It's what I've done to the other fellow that has me worried," Joan answered gloomily. "Look at that door-step! Someone dropped eggs and cream when I hit him with a hot pan of burning scones. Don't wait for me when you and father are ready to go to Mrs. Shaw's. I'll come later. They'll spend half an hour or more over cocktails, probably. As I don't drink them, I'll use that thirty minutes here on my work. I'll be at Silver Birches in time for dinner."

"Dress first, honey girl. You know when you get interested you don't think of time," her mother warned.

"I promise I won't be late."

With a smock over her evening gown, Joan worked at the roughs. After fifteen minutes at the drawing table she flung down her brush and accused aloud;

"Thanks to keeping one eye on the clock and one ear on a voice shouting;

" 'Hey! Look out! What in thunder —' you're making a mess of this drawing, Joan Crofton. The Bard Agency will think you're slipping when it sees that sample of your work."

She tore the sketch into bits. Time to stop anyway. She pulled off her smock. Went to the window. Moonlit fields swept away to foothills which in turn crouched at the base of shadowy purple mountains. The three brilliant stars in the Warrior's belt were horizontal now that Orion had moved to the southwest. How peaceful. It was hard to believe that across the ocean General Trouble was marshalling his dangerous forces and stalking like a war lord from country to country, his heavy tread shaking the hearts of people everywhere. The river coiled through the valley like a silvery serpent. Espaliered fruit trees stretched like skeletons on the brick walls of the garden. Box-edged paths, which the day's sun had cleared of the last vestige of snow, criss-crossed between flower beds covered with evergreen boughs to protect the bulbs set there in preparation for a spring riot of color. An elaborate iron grille gate in one wall provided a vista of Silver Birches. Uncle Mark and the Shaws had been warm friends, Joan remembered as she looked at it.

How the stars shone! Their reflections sprinkled the platinum sheen of the river with golden coins. Years and years and years ago those same stars had twinkled above the Indians who roamed the valley. Curious how purple shadows turned at night. Shadows! That was a queer shadow in the garden. It skulked. Was it a man? Had he been near the house? She pushed up the window.

"What do you want?" she called.

No sound but the creak of dry branches as they waved in the breeze. No motion in the garden except swaying vines. She must have imagined she saw someone. Since the crash at the door —

That was a thought. The boy who had dropped the eggs perhaps had brought others to replace them. Could she catch him and assure herself that he was not seriously injured?

She flew down the stairs. Dashed through hall and kitchen. Snapped on the porch light. Stared at the stone step incredulously. It had been washed and was as clean as when Lopez had departed. In the middle of it was a basket containing a jar of cream entirely surrounded by brown eggs.

It had been the grocer's boy, Joan thought as she deposited the basket on the kitchen table. The poor fellow had made good still believing that the order he had to deliver belonged at this house. She would stop at the store on the way to town in the morning, ask if she had hurt him and tell him of the mistake.

"Oh, Jo."

She snapped out the kitchen light and ran into the hall in answer to her father's call. He stood at the open front door.

"Why have you come back?" she demanded.

"For you. Didn't think I'd let my second-best girl walk in this icy slush to a party, did you? Get a hustle on, or you'll be late for dinner."

"Watch my smoke!" she suggested slangily and ran up the stairs.

"Do you think Viv is seriously in love with Jerry Slade?" David Crofton asked as cloaked and hooded in a green velvet evening wrap, Joan sat beside him in the sedan. He added;

"If she isn't she gave a masterly imitation today. She couldn't keep her eyes away from him — and he couldn't keep his from you, Jo."

"What can I do about it? I've told him time and time again that I don't love him, but it makes no more impression than a finger pressed on a rubber ball. He bounces right back for another refusal."

"Perhaps you'll see someone soon whom you will love. You might tell Slade that you're in love, that will convince him, for when you fall in love, Jo, you'll plunge in up to your neck, my dear. Hope I won't be jealous when it happens," David Crofton added gruffly.

Joan tucked her hand under his arm and pressed her cheek against his sleeve.

"You won't be jealous when the right man comes along. You'll be glad to have your girl as happy as you and Mother are."

"Your mother! The first time my eyes met hers I said to myself;

" 'As long as I live, I'll love you,' and I will."

"As long as I live."

Her father's impassioned declaration dropped into Joan's heart and glowed like an imprisoned star. She said fervently;

"I won't marry until I can say that to myself about a man. Your marriage comes pretty near being a collector's item. I wish there were more husbands and wives in the world like you and Mother."

"Don't be cynical about marriage, Jo. Don't let what you read in fiction and newspapers fool you. Of course there are marriages that should be dissolved, but there are so many like your mother's and mine that they never make the headlines."

"Haven't you and she ever seriously disagreed?"

"Of course we have. Do you think a man and woman could live together twenty-six years without disagreeing? They'd be a spineless pair if they could. Can you visualize your mother and still ask that question? You're like her, Jo. You both flare when you're angry, but you both have the same spiritual integrity. A promise is a promise to you."

"You and she are such grand friends. When you go out together you seem to be on top of the world."

"We are. Patty and I started out with the conviction that marriage is a high adventure, not an obstacle race. We haven't changed our belief, though we've had some tough, gruelling experiences along an often times rough and rocky road. However, we've pulled through. We still think this is a great old world and look forward to the future with a tingling sense of more adventure to come.

"Your mother and I were lavishly endowed with a sense of humor, and while love may make the world go round, it is a sense of humor that keeps the engine oiled. I don't wonder you are pessimistic about marriage, that was a 'change partners' set you ran around with in New York, but the majority is not like that. You'll see a great change in personal values in a few years. Already the writing has appeared on the wall.

Materialism, realism and skepticism have had their day and a bitter day it has been. Man will become again conscious of a soul and spirituality, and ideals and romance are handmaids of the soul. I hope you'll marry. I want grandchildren."

"Just imagine you a grandfather, Davy Crofton," Joan teased. She felt him straighten as he declared;

"I bet I'll make a good one."

"I bet you will," she agreed fervently and felt a queer little catch in her throat at the thought.

The famed Lamp of Aladdin wasn't a patch on the modern Money Lamp for results. Beauty was its slave. Rub it and all sorts of wonderful things materialized, Joan reflected as she descended the curved stairway at Silver Birches. Butler in impeccable dark livery. Black silk frocked maid. Up-to-the-minute white drawing-room. Crimson accents. Shaded lamps. Long windows. A vista of star-spangled sky. Silver bowls of freesias. Tongues of scarlet, green, purple and yellow flames in the fireplace. Above it a priceless Van Dyke. Before it the hostess, a snowy-haired woman. Smart coiffure. Brilliant blue eyes. Firm skin. Delicate make-up. Symmetrical figure. Not too slim. Black lace frock straight from a fashion flash. Pearls. A rope of them. Sparkling rings. Not too many. Poise. Charm. Indubitably Mrs. Shaw was a woman who had known what she wanted and had gone after it through the years.

She was talking with David Crofton. Joan's heart glowed with love and admiration. She adored the hint of elegance in her father's dress and manner. Her eyes traveled on to her mother. A dark blue net frock with a flame color flower at the breast, accentuated the magnolia perfection of her neck and arms. She was talking animatedly to a tall man whose back was toward the room. A big man with slightly stooped shoulders and a shaggy mane of gray hair was peering through a monocle at a photograph in a silver frame. Beyond him a sleek straw-color head was bent toward the laughing, uptilted face of a dark-haired girl.

Joan caught a reassuring glimpse of herself in a mirrored side of the room as she approached her hostess. She was glad she had worn her newest evening frock printed with enormous yellow and blue pansies on a white ground. Her sandals and bag were the blue of the star sapphire on her finger. Not too bad. A house like Silver Birches deserved one's best.

Mrs. Shaw extended both hands and welcomed her in her slightly husky voice;

"Now, here you are, my dear! When your father and mother arrived without you, I suspected you had side-stepped coming until they explained that you had stayed behind to finish some work. Dan, come and meet Joan Crofton. She is now a resident. You may be able to convert her to your political views."

If Senator Dan Shaw smiled at everyone as he smiled at her, no wonder his constituents had sent him to Washington, Joan decided, as she met his dark eyes twinkling with amusement under shaggy brows.

"Now I know why my wife has returned from Washington a month earlier than usual, Miss Crofton. Already she is beginning to campaign for my party in the next election." The laughter left his voice as he counseled;

"Whichever way your convictions lead you, don't fail to vote. This country needs every thinking citizen at the polls. Too many ignore the voting privilege. Especially it needs the women. There is a tremendous field opening for them in government house-keeping."

"Now I've started you on a-lack-of-civic-spirit tirade, Dan," Mrs. Shaw protested. "Not but that we all need to be stood in a corner and talked to," she admitted fervently. "You know Babs Shelton, Miss Crofton?"

Joan returned the smile of the dark-haired girl in the white frock, who was the town librarian. She had liked her the first time they met, had had a feeling that they would speak the same language.

"Craig, come here!"

Joan's mind turned a couple of hand-springs and landed right-side-up with a breath-snatching thud as the man talking with her mother turned in response to Mrs. Shaw's summons. It couldn't be! It was! Craig Lamont. Craig Lamont with a dark red bruise encircling one eye.

"I'll bet a commercial artist drew off and hit you when you intimated that he was submitting proofs not his own. Goody! Goody! You deserved it," Joan exulted to herself vindictively.

Mrs. Shaw slipped a lovely hand under Lamont's arm. Her voice dripped pride as she presented him.

"My son, Craig, Miss Crofton."

"The glamour-man!" Joan mocked mentally.

Mrs. Shaw's proud voice went on;

"Remember I said that I was at school with his mother? True, but a slight under-statement, I admit, as I am the mother referred to. Craig, you don't need to be told that this is Joan Crofton, the commercial artist whom I tried to snare for your agency. Why did you let her go? Evidently she was snapped up by the next firm she approached as her mother told me that she has been working for hours on what-you-call-'ems."

"Roughs is the word you want, Sally Shaw," Lamont suggested.

As her hostess apparently expected a response from her, Joan extended her hand and looked up. She experienced again the sensation as if Craig Lamont's eyes had picked up her heart and dropped it, the prickle of nerves. Her voice was slightly breathless as she said;

"Now I know where we've met, Mr. Lamont. Your face bothered me. I thought I had seen you before."

He released her hand.

"At this moment something tells me that we've met not only once, but twice before." The glint in his eyes belied the smoothness of his voice.

"Twice," Joan repeated to herself. What did he mean by that? Had she met him before she walked into his office yesterday and forgotten him? Was that why he had been so snooty? No. Craig Lamont was not a man to be forgotten.

"Tony Crane, come out from hiding behind the Senator and say 'How do you do,' prettily to Joan."

In response to the command of his hostess the round-faced, round-eyed man grinned at the smiling girl, turned up his coat collar, shivered violently and stuttered in a frightened voice;

"H-how d-do you do, prettily-Joan?"

Mrs. Shaw, unaware of the theatrical by-play which had gone on while she gave a direction to the butler, deplored;

"I've never seen a prize-fighter, Craig, but you are giving an excellent imitation of what I think one looks like."

"You're thinking straight, Mother," Lamont confirmed lightly. "I caught what in ring terms would be called 'a left to the eye.' "

Patty Crofton crooned compassion. "How ever did you get it?" she drawled softly.

Her husband laughed.

"Perhaps that's a deep, dark secret Lamont would rather not reveal, Pat."

Mrs. Shaw promptly resented the aspersion.

"Of course it isn't a secret. I had heard that your houseman had departed and told Saxon to have eggs and cream sent to your home, David Crofton. Thought they might help out. Craig heard me and volunteered to take them. He said he had an apology to make to Joan and —"

Joan carefully, very carefully, replaced the crystal glass of tomato juice she had lifted from the silver tray the butler held. Had he seen her hand shake? A cold tide of horror poured through her veins and chilled her blood. Craig Lamont had dropped those eggs! The hot pan of hotter scones had made that angry bruise on his forehead. Had she injured him for life?

Her eyes wide, terrified, questioned him. There was a wicked gleam in his as he demanded in a low voice;

"Now do you believe we have met — twice, fire-eater?"

VI

"I'm sorry, terribly sorry," Joan deplored in a faint voice. "Have I injured you seriously?"

Craig Lamont's eyes were laughing, then suddenly gravely steady.

"Time will tell. If you have, I'll have what the builders call a lien on you for life, won't I? At least, I brought home the egg basket as well as a banged eye. Don't tell All," he warned hurriedly as Mrs. Shaw, who had been talking with Tony Crane explained to the company at large;

"Craig said that as guests were departing from the front of the Crofton house he slipped round to the kitchen and left my neighborly tribute on the doorstep there."

Left it. Joan fought back a combination sob and chuckle as she visualized that doorstep.

"Why, honey, that must have been what you thought the grocer's boy dr—"

Joan flashed a wireless to her father. He intervened promptly;

"I've told you that you spoiled that delivery boy, Patty. You smile at him and he doesn't know what he's leaving."

Mrs. Shaw looked at him sharply and demanded;

"What's the mystery? I believe you know how Craig came by that bruise, David Crofton."

"On my honor, I don't."

"He said he ran into the branch of a tree. If that's the truth, Craig, I advise you to give up the idea of spending the summer in Carsfield and stick to bricks and pavements. There are persons too inexperienced to be turned loose in the country. I see by your pained expression that you agree with me, Joan."

"Forget it, please, Mother," Lamont protested. "My foolish accident has occupied stage centre long enough. Let someone else take the spot-light."

"Mr. Philip Bard."

Joan was grateful for the butler's suave interruption. Had her face betrayed her battling emotions? At one instant she was tempted to laugh at the farcical situation, when she looked at Craig Lamont's darkly encircled eye, her throat tightened unbearably. Eyes had been blinded from a bruise like that. She became aware of a curious stillness. She glanced around the room. Tony Crane's eyes were angrily bright; Babs Shelton's were antagonistic as they looked

80

at the man, who, dressed in midnight blue evening clothes of ultra cut and fashion, was bending over the hand of his hostess. Her manner was cool and courteous. Craig Lamont's eyes were inscrutable, a smile touched his lips as he spoke;

"How are you, Phil?"

His voice snapped the tension, just why should there have been tension, Joan wondered. Couldn't the heads of two advertising firms be in the same room without having the atmosphere become electrically a-tingle?

"What luck to meet you again so soon, Miss Crofton! How do you happen to be in my hometown?" Philip Bard asked as he approached.

"Is it really your hometown? It's mine too now. We are living in my Uncle Mark's house."

"The Mansion? Curious I didn't connect you with it when you were at the office yesterday. It's been my ambition to own that place ever since I was old enough to want anything. I was getting ready to buy it when I heard that it had been sold to a Mr. Crofton."

"Better set your mind on something else. The ownership of that house is tied up for years, and may be forever," Joan suggested gaily.

He brushed up the corners of his small mustache. Smiled enigmatically;

"Don't be too sure. I like taking hurdles. I've taken a big one tonight." He glanced at Mrs. Shaw, at Craig Lamont, before his eyes came back to her.

What had he meant by that cryptic remark, Joan asked herself. Hadn't his present hostess liked him before? She remembered with what earnestness Mrs. Shaw had advised her to try for work at the Craig Lamont Inc. before she visited other agencies.

"Dinner is served, Madam," the butler announced.

At the refectory table, with the white-haired hostess at one end and her leonine headed husband at the other, Joan tried to forget her anxiety about Craig Lamont's bruise by concentrating on the details of the charming dining-room which ran the depth of the house. The wood work was walnut like the chairs and table. Chair seats and damask hangings at the circular lattice window were the exact shade of the pink of the hunters' coats. Azure blue-green candles which matched to a tint the runner of rich brocade on the table burned in four exquisite candelabra. A low silver bowl in the centre held a fragrant mass of sweet peas as pinky-scarlet as the hangings.

"You make me think of one of those demon estate-appraisers the way your eyes are boring into the appointments of this room," accused a voice at her left.

Joan laughed.

"You, an art director, ought to be a keener judge of expression than that. It was admiration, not appraisal, Mr. Crane."

"Don't be so formal to a neighbor. Tony to you."

"A neighbor? Do you live here too?"

"I spend my summers at the Country Club. I grew up in this town and unless Craig is abroad, he lives at Silver Birches with his mother and the Senator while they are here. We both keep our residence in Carsfield. We'll move out next week. How are the roughs coming?"

"What roughs?"

She tried to meet his grin with surprised eyes as she asked the question, but she felt her lips curling up at the corners.

"Good, but not good enough. Those cunning little dents near the corners of your mouth betray you. Beauticians have a word for them, dimples. Think I don't know that you beat it to the Bard Agency and got a chance? My scouts are always on the job."

"Do you mean you had me followed?"

She caught his quick look at Craig Lamont at her right.

"Hey, soft pedal. Of course we didn't. 'Scout' is merely a figure of speech. How about it? Is genius burning?"

"As you insist upon knowing, it's blazing. My brushes smoke like the exhaust-pipe of a racing car."

"Not too busy to do some work for the Lamont Agency, are you?"

Before she could utter a crisp and emphatic "Yes!" he turned to answer Babs Shelton. At the same moment she heard the butler say in a low voice;

"Cannon wished me to tell you that he cleared up at The Mansion and left a fresh lot of eggs and a jar of cream, Mr. Craig."

So it had been one of the Silver Birches men whose shadow she had seen flitting about the garden, Joan thought. She turned to Craig Lamont and impulsively regretted;

"I'm sorry you bothered about the cream and eggs and broken glass mixture on the step. I would have taken care of it."

"Is it your custom to throw hot pans at a person who approaches your door waving a white flag for a peace parley? Have you never been taught that little girls shouldn't give way to temper?"

Why did he have the power to make her so

fighting mad? Joan asked herself. She looked at the bruise that ringed his eye and bit back the angry retort on the tip of her tongue. She contradicted;

"It wasn't temper. I wouldn't have seen your white flag had it been as big as a sheet. I had put scones in the oven to bake for tea. In the excitement of my sister's departure, I forgot them. Mother and I smelled something burning. I rushed to the kitchen. I could hardly see for the smoke. I pulled a pan from the oven, saw that the scones were on fire, jerked open the porch door and flung them out pan and all. You are so tall I can't understand how I could have hit you in the eye."

His laugh was boyish. "It was the kid in me. I was leaning down arranging the eggs to form the word Welcome, it was a problem in technique, when the door opened with a bang. I looked up just in time to receive a face full of hot pan. Shock sent the rest of the eggs and cream crashing to the step. That's my side of the story."

"I'm on my knees in apology." Joan's voice was a bit unsteady.

"Forget it. Let my black eye cancel my doubt that you were showing your own work yesterday, will you?"

"Agreed. I hate quarreling."

Later in the playroom while the butler and black-frocked maid set out tables and opened curiously carved mah jong cases to show the decorative tiles within, Philip Bard blockaded the corner where Joan was examining the choice old cabinet which concealed the radio. From it drifted the music of the Beethoven sextet.

"Great effect, isn't it?" Bard waved his hand in an inclusive gesture.

Joan nodded. She listened to the bright string tones of violins against the smooth, mellow beauty of the horns as her eyes followed his on a tour of the room which was a reproduction of an old Normandy kitchen. Brick walls. Copper and brass on the wide hearth. Russet chintz on inviting chairs. Raftered ceiling. Braided rug on the flagged floor.

"You didn't expect to meet me here tonight, did you?" There was a hint of exultation in Bard's question.

"You'd be surprised but I haven't given you, personally, a moment's thought since I left your office." Joan's smile robbed the words of a possible sting.

"Is that so? I'll have to do something about that," he declared with an assurance that fired Joan with a desire to stick a pin into him, preferably one of hat dimensions.

"Here comes Carl's daughter!"

He nodded toward a girl of perhaps ten years in an exquisite rose-pink frock with a Peter Pan collar of delicate lace, who was curtsying and shaking hands with the guests to whom Mrs. Shaw was presenting her. Her wavy black hair was beautiful. She would have been pretty had her blue eyes and her mouth not been petulant.

"I hear that the kid's mother is starting a fight to get her," Philip Bard continued. "Apparently Nadja's had a change of heart since she agreed to her husband's will that left the child and her property to the guardianship of Mrs. Shaw and Craig Lamont. She had a contract with a picture concern then. Believe it or not, it will be some fight with Senator Dan Shaw on the side of the guardians the father appointed. Besides being one of the upper bracket boys, the man's granite when he gets his back up."

His tone was bitter. Had he contracted the Senator's granite resistance? Joan wondered. She had thought Craig Lamont married to the woman who, from the threshold of his office, had threatened to petition the court. Evidently she was his brother's widow. The child flung herself on her uncle.

"Hello Uncle Craigy! Do you think my dress is pretty? Granny let me choose the color. I love it. I'm glad you've come. I'm crazy to run a roadside stand at our front gate — hundreds of autos go by to see the view — but Granny said I'd have to ask you."

She stopped for breath and tilted her head back as his arm encircled her.

"How'd you get the black eye?" she demanded.

He grinned at her and rumpled her dark curls.

"Miss Lamont, your lack of manners surprises me. Aren't you taught not to ask personal questions?"

"Okay Toots! I guess I can ask you anything, can't I? I love you more than anybody in the world, don't I? Have you seen the girl who's moved into The Mansion? Drucilla Dodd was here for lunch. She says she bets that girl will be another female on your trail and —" she mumbled the rest of the sentence beneath the fingers he had clapped over her mouth. She kicked at his shin as with arm about her he forcibly propelled her from the room.

Mrs. Shaw followed them with her eyes as she said;

"You've heard of *l'enfant terrible*. We have one in the family. For years the child's mother allowed her to 'develop' — as she

88

called it — in her own way. She had no time to devote to training her. I'd like to tell her what I call allowing a bright child to grow up like a weed. As for Drucilla — the less said about her the better."

Would she get through this terrible evening without burning up with fury? Joan demanded of herself. Of course that horrid child had referred to her. Wasn't she the girl who had moved into The Mansion? So Drucilla Dodd, the town loud-speaker, thought that Joan Crofton would be on Craig Lamont's trail. Pity she couldn't let her know how thoroughly she disliked him. Her angry eyes met her father's alight with laughter. Of course he had heard and equally, of course, he was telling her to be a sport and forget it.

"If I know my onions — and I do — that kid's in for the licking of her young life," Phil Bard observed beside her. "It's common knowledge that the marriage of her parents was a flop, though there was no divorce. Her father died — cracked up in a plane — and his unhappiness turned Craig into a woman-hater. Carl was his twin and his idol and he blamed the wife for what happened to him. Nadja isn't a bad sort — when she gets what she wants — just modern, that's all. How are the folders for the Bus Line account coming?"

"They will be ready in the morning."

"Fine! If I land Janvers with them, I will have achieved two of my ambitions within twenty-four hours; the Straight As A Crow Flies Bus Line account, Janvers came to me, I didn't go after him, and —"

"What is the other?" Joan asked as he abruptly cut off the sentence.

"To be a guest in this home. Sometime I'll tell you why."

He pointed the last sentence by a smile straight into her eyes. "I'm to be at the Inn this summer. Being a resident of Carsfield, I have decided to be a model citizen and try for the State Legislature. Having you to play around with will add pep to small-town life."

Philip Bard was taking a lot for granted, Joan thought indignantly. She opened her lips to protest. Closed them. After all, a benign Providence might have projected him into the foreground of her life. First, he would be useful in holding off Jerry Slade; second, it wouldn't take long with his assistance to prove that "the girl who had moved into The Mansion" was not trying to annex Craig Lamont. If he distrusted women why had he seen her when she called at his office? It wasn't his job to pass on the art side of his business. She inquired demurely;

"If we are to play around together, I hope you're good at tennis?"

"I'm a wow." She disliked his self-satisfied laugh. "There are dandy courts at the Country Club, they'll be dried out soon. Here's Craig back again. He looks as if he could chew nails. How do you suppose he got that black eye? It's a humdinger. His story sounded fishy to me. Babs Shelton is that way about him."

"Please! Not so loud! Miss Shelton will hear you. She's coming this way."

"She wouldn't mind if she did, she knows me. She and Craig and Carl and I were in grade-school together. What can he see in her? Pretty little number but no what-have-you. She's every woman's model of a second wife for her husband — a choice rarely ratified by the widowers, I've noticed. You can't fool me. I know the world and human nature."

With an effort Joan disguised her rapidly growing dislike of the man.

"Mrs. Shaw is looking at us. Knowledge of human nature won't help you with her to-night. She's a demon mah jong player, I'm told. You'll stand or fall by the sort of game you play."

"Thought it went out of fashion years ago."

"It did, but the craze has returned."

It was difficult for Joan at the table with Babs Shelton, Crane, Bard and Lamont, to keep her mind on the game and the ivory tiles when every time she looked up she saw a bruised forehead and heard a child's voice declare that the girl who had moved into The Mansion was another female on Craig Lamont's trail.

It seemed as if she had been playing and losing for hours when her mother rose from another table.

"It is almost midnight," she exclaimed, "and I promised Joan that we wouldn't be late going home, that she would have plenty of time to finish her roughs, that's the word, isn't it, honey?"

Involuntarily Joan's eyes flew to Lamont's. Why had she looked at him, she demanded of herself as she quickly averted her gaze. He had smiled. Amused was he? She'd show him.

He was waiting at the door when she came down the stairs in her velvet cloak.

"I'm driving you home," he announced.

She drew back.

"Thanks, thanks very much, but I'm going with father."

"Not this time. He and your mother have gone ahead. I told him I'd see that you

92

reached The Mansion safely. Tony is taking Babs Shelton and —"

"Babs! Mr. Bard said that she — you —"

"He told you that? How like him. Babs is Tony's girl. To return to where we started, I'm taking you home. Don't act as if you were afraid of me."

"Afraid!" She went down the outer steps on that contemptuous note.

"It seems absurd to drive the short distance between these two places," Joan said to break the silence between them.

"Bad walking. Hear the tires crunch on the ice? Are you doing some roughs for the Bard Agency?"

"I never tell for whom I am working."

"Business etiquette. I get you. Think you're going to like living in this small town?"

His quick change of subject caught Joan unaware. She had thought he would persist in his questioning about her work. Apparently he was an adept in shifting conversational gears. She watched the glow of headlights pick out a white house, illumine bare branches of trees, shift quickly to others as she answered;

"Yes. It has charm and friendliness, it has kept its small-town character. I like its independence of the city. Already I know the life histories of most of the store keepers. Babs Shelton lets me help in the library one afternoon a week and believe it or not, that's where you feel as if you were living in a glass house through the walls of which your neighbors see even the wheels of your mind go round."

"Then remember that it is a small town and that gossip rolls up like a snow-ball. I'm sorry that Peg quoted Drucilla Dodd in your hearing. That woman's a pest. She's a sort of in-law graft on Senator Shaw's family tree. She supplies a Boston letter to a chain of country newspapers with astonishing success. You'd be surprised to know how many former New Englanders read it. She commands a certain sort of respect if not liking. Many are the social sops thrown to her sharp pen and sharper tongue."

"How fervently you dislike her. Did Peggy quote Miss Dodd? I missed that gem of gossip. I was talking with Philip Bard when the child came in. He's the most interesting person, so world-minded, if you get what I mean. I really believe he'll keep me from missing New York."

"That's fine. We want you to be contented in Carsfield. Here we are at your door." As he stepped from the roadster, he added; "I'll add my mite to keep you from

94

missing New York."

Joan smiled at him sweetly;

"I wouldn't think of being one more female —" she bit her lips. Too late. He laughed;

"Oh, then you did hear Peg's 'gem of gossip'? Just a minute. Don't sit up tonight to work on those roughs for the Bard Agency, supposing, of course, that they are for the Straight As A Crow Flies Bus Line. They won't be used. Janvers called our office today to say he was sorry he flew off the handle, that he realized that our work had built up his business, that he wouldn't leave us. He's as hard-boiled as a ten-minute egg but taken as a whole he's a darned good egg. Good-night."

VII

With his arm on the mantel, Craig Lamont looked about his mother's boudoir. It was modern, up-to-the-minute. Decorated in delphinium blues and silver with chairs and tables and lamps in the latest designs. His eyes came back to her in the low chair. She was wearing satin lounge pajamas of a lilac shade that accentuated the delicacy of her skin and the snowy whiteness of her hair. She smiled as their eyes met;

"A penny for your thoughts," she bribed.

"I was thinking that you are the most up to date woman I know."

"If you'll add the reservation, 'except in morals and manners,' I shall take your estimate as a compliment. Why not be modern? The government census man came today and when he asked my age, I answered promptly, 'fifty,' and then I added, 'I intend never to be more than fifty, officer.' To which statement he responded heartily;

" 'Good for you, Lady!'

"Nothing irritates me so much as to hear a woman prattle that she can't do this or that because of her age. Age isn't a matter of years, it's a point of view. Why remember birthdays? Not that I wish to play tennis in shorts or model so-called sand and surf costumes which have gone embarrassingly near-nudist, and I'm proud to be a grandmother, but you'll never catch me rocking in a corner with a shawl hugged around my shoulders mumbling how much better the world was in my youth."

Craig laughed.

"In the words of the census-taker, 'Good for you, lady!' I'm with you every inch of the way. 'No more birthdays' should be every person's slogan — after fifty."

Her eyes were like sapphires shining under clear water as she declared fervently;

"Craig, darling, you are the most understanding, heart-warming person. You — you haven't even looked reproach because I begged you to give up flying." She brushed her hand across her lashes and said hastily;

"Here I am, sentimentalizing, when I asked you to stop on your way to bed to tell me what Nadja threatened yesterday. I felt so secure when she went into pictures. I hoped and prayed she would stay in them and keep the continent between herself and Peggy."

He told her of his one-time sister-in-law's call at his office and of her threat to petition the Probate Court to revoke the decree giving custody of Peggy to her guardians.

"Does the Senator know?" he asked in conclusion.

"Yes. Nadja's lawyer has written him. She claims that she was so heart-broken and dazed at the loss of her husband that she didn't realize to what she was agreeing. If she insists upon fighting and we want to keep Peggy, the Senator says we'll have to make public some of Nadja's affairs of the heart — if she has a heart — during her married life with Carl and that will hurt the child's future."

"Not as it would have twenty-five years ago, Mother. Peggy will grow up to see things in their right proportions and to realize that what she makes of herself is what counts in the world. We were plenty foolish to buy Nadja off when she threatened to fight after Carl's will was probated. You and I muddled it. The Senator advised cutting to the bone at her first yelp, but we wanted to spare Peggy. We'll cut now. She'll get no more money. I have a hunch that she's after that and publicity. We'll let her have the last good and plenty this time."

"Why, why couldn't Carl see what she was? She claimed to be of a high-class Mexican family. Family! In all the time she was married we never saw a member of it. Carl said she had a brother whom she helped — but he never had seen him. Remember her description of the luxurious *hacienda* in which she grew up? If you ask me, I think the Spanish words and phrases with which she seasoned her conversation were lifted bodily from a Spanish-English textbook. High-class Mexican! Perhaps. But when in anger she swore — in Spanish of course — at the servants, I would think, 'Lady, the high-class Mexican in you has been denatured with a low-class tenement strain.' Why, why did Carl marry her?"

Sally Shaw's broken question roused the canary in his modernistic cage. He chirped sociably before he again tucked his yellow head under his yellow wing.

How often did mothers ask that question about their sons, Craig wondered as he looked at the woman whose eyes were unseeingly regarding the smoldering embers. Was she thinking of the years when her boys were in college?

His mind turned back and he saw Carl as he had been then. He had been passive, willing to follow when shown the trail.

He, himself, had been the more daring twin always reaching out for adventure, always adventuring into the unexplored. He recalled the night, when with Tony Crane, they had been lost on the mountain, he could see the signal fires they had kept ablaze, could again feel Carl shiver with cold as he had walked him back and forth to get him warm. He thought of the day when with a ball under his arm he had taken an almost impossible chance and had ducked and dodged and leaped across a slimy field churning up mud and raising pandemonium in the stadium as he slid to the goal post and scored the Varsity eleven to victory. Carl had fairly sobbed with pride in him.

He remembered that that same night he had first met Señorita Nadja Donesca, the star torch-singer of a musical show. She had pretended that she had heard his voice praised, had begged him to let her arrange a radio audition. He had laughed at her and told her that he was having all he could do to keep up in his classes and sports without taking on anything more.

Publicity stories credited her with being the daughter of a Mexican who had lost a fabulous fortune. Once or twice she had referred to the luxury of her youth, to the *hacienda*, La Torranca, in which she had grown up. She had touched upon it with just the right amount of foreign accent, of repressed sadness. Why not? She was an actress. She hadn't arrived at stardom because of her beauty alone.

Their paths had crossed repeatedly after that first meeting. He knew now that she had managed that. He had avoided her. She was years older than he. Finally, he had told her curtly that he didn't like her. He remembered the sultry yellow glare in her eyes as she suggested;

"You don' like me? So — is it not luckee that your brother does? I like the name Lamont better than Donesca."

He had been dumb from surprise. He hadn't known that Carl had met Nadja, he hadn't wanted him to meet her. That night he had waited up in their college rooms to warn his brother to look out for her. He had paced the floor for hours. It wasn't like him to stay out. In the morning had come a telegram

Married last night. Love,
                              Carl and Nadja.

He lived over the years following when his mother had valiantly tried to make friends with her son's wife. He remembered her joy when the child was born, her hope that the little girl would make Nadja more sympathetically understanding. He winced as he thought of his sister-in-law's not too subtle pursuit of himself, and the mental strain of thinking one jump ahead of her to block her every move in his direction; of his brother's growing disillusionment; of the eagerness with which Carl had followed him when he took up flying; of his frozen calm when one day shortly before he crashed, he had acknowledged;

"I got what was coming to me, Craig. It was the first time in my life I hadn't talked my plans out with you. I was afraid to. I was insane about Nadja and in my heart I knew you would oppose our marriage, but when her show folded-up and she threatened to shoot herself if I didn't marry her at once, I gave in. I knew, even then, that she wanted you, not me."

Craig's throat ached at the memory. And now two years after his death, Nadja was preparing to fight for the child.

"What does she call herself?"

His mother's voice derailed his train of thought.

"Who, Nadja? She's taken her stage name again, Señorita Nadja Donesca."

"Why has she changed her mind about Peggy? Why does she want her?"

"She doesn't want her. She wants her

daughter's income to spend for herself or a bunch of money from us."

"We won't let the child go, Craig. With the right training she will make a fine woman. Last winter I discovered that that flighty Mam'selle whom Nadja had had for Peggy's governess for years, had filled the child's mind with foolish ideas about herself and wrong values. I discharged her. The French of Miss Hopkins, the present governess, isn't so fluent, but she is sympathetically understanding at the same time that she's a disciplinarian. Peggy is superintelligent for her age and she has a bump of determination the size of yours. At present she has a roadside stand complex and in spite of my patient and reiterated explanations that she is too young to start a business career — I consider that phrase 'business career' a master-stroke of tact — I expect some day when I arrive home to see a stand at our gate. Child that she is, she's a difficult person to combat."

Craig Lamont lighted a cigarette and impatiently flung the match into the smoldering fire.

"Have you ever thought that a sound spanking might assist in putting across your argument? Peg ought to know better than to repeat Drucilla Dodd's gossip as she did in the playroom tonight. She knew that it referred to Joan Crofton. You can't tell me she didn't."

"I'm not telling you she didn't, Craig. Stop walking the floor, please. Do you think Joan heard it?"

"I know she heard it. She was furious at our reception of her at the office. I'll bet after Peggy's quote of Drucilla, she's ready to wipe me off the map."

"Would you care, Craig?"

He opened his lips to make a sharp retort, met his mother's wistful eyes and laughed.

"Yes — and no. What is this? A cross-examination as to whether I am considering going off the deep end?"

"Have I ever cross-examined you?"

"No, Sally Shaw. You are a model for all mothers of grown-up sons. Phil Bard was a snappy number tonight, wasn't he?"

His mother drew a surprised breath at his quick change of subject before she followed his lead.

"He was. I don't like him. I hated him when he hung around Nadja the last year of Carl's life. We know that he is a traitor, hasn't he tried to get your accounts? I wouldn't have had him inside this house had I not thought that if I didn't he would think we resented his leaving you and setting up for himself. You were fortunate to get rid of him. And now — he has announced his candidacy for your seat in the Legislature."

"When did you hear that?"

"I don't wonder you are amazed. Drucilla Dodd told me. She said that because of his background he would have a big following. From newsboy to President stuff. This is an age of boosting the under-dog whether or not the under-dog is worthy of boosting. Those last two sentences are my contribution to the wisdom of the century, not Drucilla's."

"When you remember the sordid Bardonis, you'll have to admit, Mother, that Phil Bard deserves credit."

"I'll give him credit for all he deserves, but, he's a traitor. It was evident tonight that he admires Joan Crofton."

"She's doing some work for him. What do you know about her?"

"Only what Mark Crofton told me at the time he bought The Mansion. The Senator and he were pals in Washington and he used to tell me about 'Davy's girls' whom he loved devotedly. His property goes to them outright after their father is through with it. He left them each five thousand dollars and to one a flawless emerald and to the other a gorgeous star-sapphire."

"So that's where the ring came from."

"What are you mumbling about, Craig?"

"Was I mumbling? Go on about the Crofton girls. Is the sister as good-looking as this one?"

"Mark said that she was beautiful but Joan was his favorite. Adorable, was his word for her. I love her speaking voice, gracious and sweet with a hint of laughter. You know that she draws. She also dances superbly and is an expert at tennis. As if that were not enough, he considered her the balance-wheel of the family."

"A fiery balance wheel, if you get what I mean." Unconsciously Craig put his hand to his bruised forehead. Dark color swept to his hair as his eyes met his mother's.

"Did Joan hit you?" she demanded incredulously.

"Don't be absurd, Sally Shaw. Why should she hit me?"

A smile twitched at Mrs. Shaw's lips before she agreed;

"It was an absurd question, wasn't it? You'd better go to your room and take care of that bruise. It looks ugly."

She rose and kissed him. He put his arm about her. She pressed her head against his sleeve.

"It's wonderful to be back where I can have a heart-to-heart with you often, Craig, and to have you here in the house will be heaven." She steadied her voice. "When are you and Tony Crane planning to move out from town?"

"Next week. Then I start on a whirlwind campaign to pile up votes for my re-nomination to the Great and General Court. I'll have to do some tall campaigning with Phil Bard at my heels. After that — well, I don't intend to live in New England all my life, I mean to get into the political front-line trenches." He laughed. "That's traveling fast, isn't?"

"Not too fast. I believe you can get anything you want out of life — if you want it enough."

"Thanks for the vote of confidence, Mother. After that tribute, I ought to get somewhere."

"You will, Craig, but watch out for Nadja. She and Bard are friendly and both are unscrupulous. She has come to the Village Inn to stay, her lawyer told the Senator, until the court gives her the right to take Peggy away with her. He says also, that she wants to make friends with her child. It has been no secret that she — wants you. If — if you should by chance fall in love — I pray every day that you may — watch out for Nadja. She's fascinating when she wants to be, but she's unscrupulous and she has a barbed tongue. I shudder to think what that tongue could do to a girl you loved, to your political future and to us as a family, if it were let loose. You know Nadja."

Craig whistled softly.

"I do." He laughed and patted his mother's shoulder. "Watch me beat her tongue. I like a fight and I'm still heart whole, so I won't have to worry about what she can do to a girl."

"Sure of that, Craig?"

His eyes opened wide.

"Sure that I'm heart whole? See any symptoms that I'm not?" he demanded.

She laughed.

"Well — yes and no. Go along and take care of that bruise. Good-night, good-night, beloved."

VIII

"Are you awful mad at me?"

Startled, Joan looked up from the seedlings she was planting among the yellow and white and purple crocuses in the border around the cerulean lined pool in the garden of The Mansion. The voice had come from a small lilac-linen clad figure squatted Humpty Dumpty fashion on top of the brick wall. Sunlight behind the little girl brought out the satin sheen of her dark hair. The marking on the black and white dog seated on its haunches beside her, hinted at fox terrier ancestry several times removed. A gray kitten at the adolescent stage with out-of-proportion ears and an absurdly long, painfully thin tail, squatted beside the dog.

Joan smiled and shook her head.

"Mad in this lovely garden where the air is as sweet as a perfume shop and the sun is turning everything to gold? I'm not mad at you, why should I be, Peggy?"

The child hitched along the brick wall toward the iron grille gate. The dog followed hitch by hitch. The gray kitten trailed them. She explained as she moved;

"Uncle Craig said you would be when he talked Dutch to me for repeating what Drucilla Dodd said about you."

A tide of anger swept through Joan as the child's mention of Drucilla Dodd brought back to her memory the woman's prophecy, "Another female on his trail."

Why had she had to hear that just after she and Craig Lamont had agreed to bury the hatchet? That had happened two weeks ago and each time she had met the man since the words had echoed through her mind and turned her to ice.

"I guess you are mad. Your face has got so red," Peggy's voice blocked Joan's trail of thought. "I'm sorry. Uncle Craig told me I'd never be a lady like Granny till I'd learned to consider other people's feelings and to think before I spoke. Who wants to be a lady? I couldn't be one anyway. Mam'selle — she was my governess — Miss Hopkins — I call her 'Hoppy' — looks after me now — used to say that with a mother like mine the cards are stacked against me. I'm a wishbone child," she announced with evident pride.

"Mam'selle" must have been either brainless or vicious to start a little girl in life with the mental twist that the cards were stacked against her. Joan tried to keep her perturbation at the thought out of her voice as she asked;

"What kind of a child did you say, Peggy?"

"A wishbone child."

Joan dropped the trowel. From an old-fashioned wrought-iron seat she looked up at the little girl on the wall.

"And what is a 'wishbone child'?"

"Don't you know?" Peggy's voice was incredulous, her eyes, which reflected the lilac of her frock were wide with disbelief. "That's funny. Drucilla Dodd said she'd bet you knew your way round. I should think anyone who knows her way round ought to know what a wishbone child is."

Peggy's imitation of a fat oozy voice was perfect. Joan's mouth tightened but her eyes continued to smile up at the vivid little face.

"Pretty ignorant of me, I suppose, but I don't know. Won't you tell me?"

Peggy scowled thoughtfully.

"If you don't know perhaps you ought to. You may have a wishbone child yourself some day. Mam'selle said there are a lot of the poor things in the world. You see, right after my father died, there was a fight over who would have me and she said that with my Mother pulling at one leg and arm and Granny and Uncle Craig representing my

111

father, pulling at the other leg and arm, I was like a wishbone and if one or the other didn't stop pulling, I'd be broken in two. What are you crying for?"

Joan forced back the tide of pity which had brimmed to her eyes. She realized, perhaps for the first time, the stability, the self-respect, the love, tolerance and beauty on which her home life was founded. She blinked wet lashes and smiled.

"I'm not crying. The sun going down behind you flashed into my eyes and filled them with tears. Hop down from the wall and have tea with me, will you? I'm alone and I would love company. Here's Seraphina with it now," she added as a trim, pink-frocked, black-faced girl deposited a tray laden with primrose-pattern china on a gay yellow table. The maid lingered.

"I sure hope dey's all right, Miss Jo-an. I fix dem from the paper your mother done wrote out for me."

"The tray looks perfect, Seraphina."

"I'se glad, Miss Jo-an. I sho' forgot to tell you. A man phoned an' said dat he'd come dis afternoon to take you flyin'."

Flying! Jerry again. Joan felt the same urge to smash something she had felt as a child when one of her carefully erected card-houses had fallen over. She'd take

Peggy home and escape before he came.

"Did he say what time?" she asked eagerly.

"No, Mam. He just said he'd come in his car an' take you to de airport. You look like part of de gardin, setting there in de green dress, Miss Jo-an. I'll get dat off you some time. Yes, Mam!"

She showed all her white teeth in a broad grin, grimaced at the child staring at her from the wall, before she entered the house.

"Coming, Peggy?" Joan inquired as she lifted a cover. She would go through with the tea-party, Jerry or no Jerry. "This cinnamon toast looks delicious."

The child hitched nearer the gate.

"Granny and Hoppy will go haywire if I stay. My mother is likely to steal me, you know."

She said it with an air of importance. Joan bit her lips to discipline their twitching. The child was amusing, tragic little thing that she was.

"If you want to stay, Peggy, I'll phone Silver Birches, tell the butler where you are and that I'll bring you home."

"Okay, Toots!"

Joan looked back as she entered the house. Peggy was letting herself down the iron grille gate hand under hand. From the top of the wall the black and white dog watched until she reached the ground. He jumped. The gray kitten clawed its way down an espaliered peach tree.

When Joan returned, Peggy was seated astride a yellow chair beside the table, her arms crossed on top of its back. The dog was squatted on his haunches with his unblinking gaze fixed on the tea-tray. The gray kitten sat primly beside him.

"It's all right for you to stay, Peggy," Joan picked up the sugar tongs. "How many lumps?"

"Three — and one on the side for Straw."

"Straw? Is that your dog's name? Isn't it an unusual one?"

"Perhaps it is but he was lost and most starved an' he followed me home from school one day in Washington, an' when Granny said I might keep him, Mam'selle, she was living with us then, threw up her hands like this an' squealed;

" '*Mon Dieu!* It ees what the Americans call the last straw!' "

Her imitation of the French woman's voice and gesture was perfect. Joan became absorbed in pouring tea to hide her smile.

"So I called him Straw. Think that's a nice name?"

"I do, it's so fitting. His whiskers stick out like straws. Do you like cream in your tea?"

"Lots of it with hot water and not much tea. A little cream in a saucer for Frank, please. Frank's the kitten. I named him for a boy in dancing school who used to sneak candy into my hand." Her eyes narrowed shrewdly as she demanded; "Why are you so nice to me?"

"I like you, Peggy. I like to have little girls come and play with me."

"But, I'm not a little girl, I'm a problem child."

Joan gasped before she said seriously;

"You mustn't get such ideas about yourself, Peggy. You're no different from any number of little girls I know."

"Okay, Toots. Tell me their names? Speak for it, Straw!"

While the black and white dog yelped sharply for the piece of cinnamon toast which his mistress held at a tantalizing distance above his head, and the kitten lapped at the cream, Joan went into a mental huddle to collect the names of the aforementioned little girls, but they only teased at the tip of her tongue without formulating.

"Hmp, I knew you couldn't," Peggy fitted Joan's silence to the purpose of her argument. "I guess I know I'm different. Don't I see people nudge each other when I pass and whisper? I know what they're saying, they're saying 'Poor kid!' "

Pity for the child whose life was being twisted and deformed at its beginning, tightened Joan's throat unbearably. If only she could do something about it. What could she do? She felt helplessly inadequate in the face of Peggy's self-satisfaction. At least she could turn her thoughts. She caught at a wisp of an idea.

"Something tells me that one day when you pass people will nudge each other and whisper;

" 'See that lovely girl? She — she — she's the champion woman tennis player in the country!' "

At the imminent risk of smashing the teacup she held, Peggy brought the iron chair in which she had tipped back, down on all fours. Her eyes were big with incredulity as she demanded;

"Do you mean that or are you just kidding me, Miss Crofton?"

"I mean it. I think you have the makin's of a tennis player. And why not call me Joan? We're going to be grand friends, aren't we?

116

I'll teach you to play tennis, if you want to learn."

What had induced her to make that offer, Joan demanded of herself. With work piling up as it was, what time had she to devote to this rather disagreeable little girl?

"I'm a wishbone child." The words echoed through the corridors of her mind in answer.

"If you can help that child find herself, of course you have time," the watch-dog of her conscience growled.

"Would I have time to run a roadside stand too?" Peggy inquired cautiously.

"Run a roadside stand! What put that idea into your head?"

"What puts ideas into anybody's head? Don't you have a lot, Joan? Do you know where they come from? I bet you don't. I think roadside stands are grand. One time I helped sell at one — I dodged Mam'selle. I sold a lot. I guess I could run one and learn to play tennis too. I heard our gardener, Angus the Scot, tell Saxon, our butler, that even if I was the bane of his life — he gets awful mad if I touch a flower — that I was a terrible smart kid."

Joan disciplined twitching lips.

"Then if you think you can spare the time, I'll teach you to play. No one has said that

I'm 'terrible smart' but I'm rather good at tennis."

"I know you're good," Peggy responded fervently. "I heard Tony Crane tell Uncle Craig that you could lick the pants off Phil Bard at tennis. And then he said, 'When are you going to start pushing that lad off the Crofton map, boss? We need her in our business.' " Peggy imitated Tony Crane's voice to perfection.

So Craig Lamont's courtesy to her that evening at his mother's was explained. He wanted to get her away from the Bard Agency. Anger roughened Joan's voice as she demanded;

"And just what did your uncle reply to that?"

"He didn't say anything but, 'Come out from under that table, Peg.' He was awful cross."

"I can understand that. Little girls shouldn't hide under tables and listen and if they hear what is being said, they shouldn't repeat it," Joan instructed virtuously at the same time that her conscience pricked for encouraging the child to talk.

"Okay, Toots, but I notice you listened — When will we start —"

"Oh, here you are, darling!"

Jerry Slade followed his impassioned

greeting with outstretched hands and a blaze in his brown eyes which brought Joan hastily to her feet. If he kissed her as he had once or twice before after an absence, she would — she would — her nails cut into the palms of her hands as she thrust out clenched fists to ward him off.

"Why do you call Joan 'darling'?" Peggy Lamont inquired.

Joan flashed a now-see-what-you've-done look at Jerry Slade before she said lightly;

"He calls every one 'darling,' Peg. It's a habit. Miss Lamont, this is Jerry Slade."

Jerry grinned and held out his hand.

"Hello, Miss Lamont. Glad to meet you. Joan's wrong about that 'darling.' She's the only person in the world I call that. I like her a lot. I've taken rooms at the Inn for the summer so I may see her every day."

"Okay, Toots! Then I'll bet you're what Mam'selle calls lovers? She says my mother had —"

"Peggy, how would you like to pour a cup of tea for Jerry while I —"

The black and white dog interrupted with a series of short, sharp barks directed at the path. The kitten, which had been avidly watching the goldfish in the pool, whisked around and ran toward him. Joan turned.

Her heart stopped and galloped on furiously. Instinctively she put her arm around Peggy whose only comment was an excited;

"Well, see who's here! Mother!"

Without Peggy's whisper, Joan would have recognized the red-haired woman. Her chiseled features were as clean-cut, her greenish eyes as hard as the day she had seen her in the outer office of the Lamont Agency. The same woman, except that now she was in pale gray instead of black with priceless silver fox skins over her shoulders, as she had been then.

"You make me think of a beetle, a shiny beetle, your shell is so hard," Joan thought. What did one do when a mother from whom the court had taken a child tried to get that child, she asked herself. She had no authority to keep her. If only David and Patty Crofton would return. If only Craig Lamont would have a sudden hunch that he was needed and come.

She tried to make Jerry understand that he was to do something, anything, but he merely frowned with annoyance at the interruption.

The woman dropped to one knee and encircled the little girl with both arms. Her throaty voice was shaken as she implored;

"Say that you are glad to see your mother, say eet, dearest."

Peggy shrugged and twisted free.

"Why are you making a fuss over me now? You thought I was a nuisance when you lived at home. I heard you tell my father that."

The woman rose and looked at Joan.

"Funny leetle person, is she not? She has been taught to hate her mother, her own adoring mother. Perhaps if you would leave us alone together, Mees Crofton — it is Mees Crofton, is eet not?"

"It is," Joan returned curtly.

"I am Meeses Carl Lamont, Señorita Nadja Donesca to my publeek. I'm Peggy's mother and I want to talk to her alone for a few minutes." She abandoned her pose of adoring motherhood and glanced at Jerry Slade with pointed meaning in her green eyes.

"I beg pardon," he said stiffly and stalked along the path to the drive.

Joan opened her lips to call him back and closed them. If the woman had come for her daughter, Jerry had no authority to block her. Neither had she but she would try.

She glanced at the garden gate. It was locked. Peggy couldn't be spirited out that way. If she, herself, stood just within the

121

house door, the child couldn't be taken that way and she might be able to phone Silver Birches.

"*Por Dios,* must I repeat? I said alone, Mees Crofton."

The chill reminder set splinters of ice coasting through Joan's veins. She removed her arm from the child's shoulders and broadcast a mental radio call for the appearance of someone, anyone with authority to stop the woman.

"Sorry. I was wondering if you wouldn't have tea while you and Peggy talked. I'll have Seraphina bring it fresh and hot."

"I have not time for tea. Please leave Peggy and me together. After all, you know, you have no authority to interfere. You are not the child's guardian. Even if you married Craig — as perhaps you are planning to do —"

"Who is planning to do what, Nadja?" inquired a voice from the house door.

Craig Lamont! Her wireless call had been answered. Joan's tense muscles and nerves relaxed till she was as wobbly as a desawdusted doll. With a shout of triumph, Peggy flung herself on her uncle. Her breath came in harsh gasps as she clung to him.

"I thought she was going to steal me," she sobbed.

Lamont held the child close in one arm.

"Hey, what's all this, Peg? Where'd you get that crazy idea?"

"Mam'selle said she knew my mother'd try it someday, she was such a schemer," the child explained breathlessly.

Señorita Nadja Donesca's laugh was brittle.

"So that ees what my own leetle daughter ees being taught to believe about her mother, her own mother! That she ees a schemer. *Por Dios!* No court will uphold you in that infamous course, Craig."

She glanced at Joan, who had resisted the impulse to dash away from this unpleasant family interview. If an attempt were made to snatch Peggy, she might help, she had decided. Señorita Nadja Donesca's smile was as cruel as her eyes as she declared;

"Mees Crofton can testify to having overheard that choice bit of slander. I am going now but when I drag you and your mother into court, Craig, I weel win. Of course you want my child. Her propertee goes to you at her death — and eef anything should happen to her —" she shrugged.

"What an infernal suggestion, Nadja," Craig Lamont's face was livid.

The woman laughed. On the path which led from the garden in the front of the house, she turned and spoke directly to Joan.

"Thanks again, Mees Crofton, for arranging thees meeting for me with my darling daughter. We weel have better luck next time. *Adios!* In Eenglish, I weel see you later."

Joan's eyes, wide with amazement, followed her until she was out of sight. She flamed with protest. The woman had dared intimate that she, Joan Crofton, had deliberately planned to bring her and Peggy together. It was maddening! It was —

"Did you plan this meeting?" demanded Craig Lamont furiously.

The whiteness of his face accentuated the faint discoloration at one temple. Joan looked at his accusing eyes, at Peggy, still held close within his tense arm. Anger turned to ice. So he believed that of her, did he?

The corners of her lips curved in a contemptuous smile; her scornful eyes raked him from head to foot. She derided;

"And I thought I had tuned in at the right station, that you had come as a direct answer to my wireless call for help. My mistake, glamour-man!"

IX

Craig Lamont started to follow Joan as she dashed into the house. Why had he flung that question at her? Hadn't he known Nadja long enough to know that throwing suspicion on the girl was the result for which she had schemed? Could anyone not furious with anger and anxiety — look at Joan Crofton and believe she would lend herself to such a plan? "Adorable was his word for her." His mother's voice echoed through his mind.

He scowled down at Peggy in response to her tug at his arm.

"What is it?"

"You'd better not go after Joan, now," she advised sagely. "She's awful mad."

"Perhaps you're right, Peg."

He looked around the garden. Purple, yellow and white crocuses in battalions; pink, white, bronze and yellow hyacinths, squads of them. Glints of scarlet and flame as goldfish flashed in the pool. His eyes lingered on the tea tray on the yellow table, came back to the child looking up at him.

"Come on home, Peg. Joan won't thank us for bringing our family snarl into this garden. How did you happen to come here?"

The black and white dog squeezed himself under the iron grille and the gray kitten squirmed after him. Peggy pulled her uncle back.

"The gate's locked. We can't go that way."

"Then how did you get in?"

"Climbed up the trellis on our side and shinnied down the gate on this."

"All right. We'll go the way you came."

Something tinkled on the flagged path. Peggy picked it up. She called in the direction of the house:

"Okay, Toots!" She held out her hand to her uncle; "Joan chucked out the key. I guess she wants us to go quick."

"Something tells me you've got the right idea," Craig Lamont admitted with a grim smile.

Before he closed the gate behind him, he looked back. No sign of life at the windows but in the garden the negro maid was plodding toward the pool with her bands full of violets and gardenias. She called over her shoulder;

"Sure, I'se hurryin' Miss Jo-an. You folks up Norf here spec's us pussons from Virginny done got wings."

She lingered at the edge of the pool and sniffed at the flowers.

"Dey smell powerful sweet. Sure you want dem chucked —"

"Seraphina!"

Craig Lamont could hear the imperious reminder from where he lingered. Hadn't he every right to linger? Hadn't he had the rubbers Joan had forgotten and left in his office filled with those flowers? Hadn't he placed them on the hall table in the house when the maid had told him that she was in the garden? He had come to beg her to be friends, to forget whatever had made her dislike him. And now —

Seraphina reluctantly tossed the violets and gardenias into the pool. She watched them bob in the water for an instant. With a shake of her head and a muttered protest, she lifted the tea-tray from the yellow table and plodded toward the house.

"Why did she throw away those flowers?"

Peggy's question crashed into Craig's smoldering resentment. He put his arm about her shoulders and turned his back on the gate.

"Perhaps she has hay-fever and the flowers made her sneeze."

"Hay-fever! Joan never has anything the

matter with her. Her mother told Granny that neither of her girls — except for children's diseases — had had a sick day in their lives. I guess her beau didn't want her to keep them."

"What beau? How do you know she has a beau? What's his name?"

"Gosh, Uncle Craig, don't shout at me. I don't know, only I've got eyes and ears, haven't I? And when the man called her 'darling' I thought he was going to kiss her. I guess she thought so too, for she grew awful red and fussed. His name is Jerry Slade and he's going to live at the Inn this summer. He came to take her flying. My, but he's good-looking. He's almost as good-looking as you are, Uncle Craig."

"Thanks, Peggy."

"Your voice doesn't sound very thankful. It's as cross as when you shouted at Joan, 'Did you plan this meeting?' Who did she mean by glamour-man?"

What had Joan meant by glamour-man? Craig adroitly side-tracked the subject. Stopped and looked toward the west.

"See how the mountains stand out against the sky, Peg. Indians once roamed this valley, and set up their tepees here, and hunted and fished. When they prayed they faced the mountains because they believed that the spirits of their people who had died were there, that they would answer their prayers."

"Suppose that's where my father is? Suppose if I looked over there and said my prayers, he would make my mother stop trying to steal me? I don't want to live with her. She used to make me wear ugly brown dresses and Granny lets me pick out colors I like, and pretty hats to go with them. I love being with her and you and Joan. Do prayers do any good, Craigy? Do you believe in them?"

"I do.

" 'More things are wrought by prayer than this world dreams of.' Never lose your faith in prayer, Peg."

"Okay, Toots, if you say so. My prayers don't get answered much. Perhaps it's because I'm not looking toward the mountains. I'll try it next time."

"There's Tony Crane on the river. See him? See how easily he shoots that canoe through the water? How would you like to learn to paddle, Peg?"

"It would be fine — that is, if I have time," she added patronizingly, "Joan's going to teach me to play tennis. She says that some day people will nudge each other when I pass and whisper;

" 'See that lovely girl? She — she's — the champion woman tennis player of the country.' "

Her voice and inflection were a perfect imitation of Joan Crofton's.

"How did she happen to say that?"

"Oh, I'd told her how people nudged each other and whispered 'Poor kid!' when I passed and I guess she thought —"

Lamont's throat tightened till it ached. Damnable that the child should be conscious of the mess her mother had made of her life. He pulled a short dark curl.

"After all, I think you're a pretty good girl, Peg. What say if we race to the house. A bright silver half dollar to the winner." He smiled down into her eager eyes and qualified; "That is, if the future woman tennis champion doesn't think it beneath her dignity to race with a mere runner-up."

"You bet she doesn't. A half dollar is a half dollar. I need money, a lot of money."

"What do you need money for, Peg?"

"Oh, for business. How much start will you give me? Your legs are twice as long as mine."

"I'll wait till you're halfway to the house."

He watched the fleet little figure, with the black and white dog and the kitten like a gray streak racing after it. If her mother carried her fight for the custody of the child to court, the guardians would have to set forth their reasons for maintaining that she was not a proper person to have the care of her daughter. The evidence would scream in headlines in the newspapers. As much as he and his mother would hate that, it would have to be done if there were no other way to prevent the court — if it had a mother complex — from setting aside the father's disposal of the child.

His mind was still occupied with the problem as in the hall at Silver Birches he paid over the shining half-dollar to his victorious niece.

Saxon, the butler, shook his smooth gray head at the little girl.

"You gave us an awful fright, Miss Peggy, running away like that."

"Miss Crofton phoned didn't she, Saxon?"

"Yes, she did, but not till after you had been away a long time. Your supper is waiting for you in the nursery."

Peggy turned on the stairs and made a gamine face at him.

"Okay, Toots! Supper in the nursery. Wait till I'm tennis champion. Then I guess you and Hoppy won't order me round, Saxon."

The butler's eyes followed her as she ran up the stairs. They were clouded with anxiety as they came back to Lamont.

"We've had a terrible time here this afternoon, Mr. Craig. Mrs. Carl burst in on the Madam who was entertaining friends. Your mother was very cool and invited her into the little reception room off the hall and just then the new parlor maid — who doesn't know about — about our family affairs — stepped up and reported that Miss Peggy was staying at The Mansion for tea. Mrs. Carl was out of the house and into the village taxi before I could stop her. I phoned the Croftons to warn them she might come but the only response I could get was a shouted;

" 'Yass sir. Dis am de Crofton res'dence. Massa an' Missus dey done gone out. Dey done gone out, I say.' That colored maid doesn't need a phone, I could have heard her without it."

"It's all right, Saxon. I happened in at The Mansion just as Mrs. Carl was leaving. Señorita Nadja Donesca, she calls herself now. I brought Peggy home. Where's Mother?"

The butler chuckled;

"Mr. Craig I've been answering that question for you for years and years. When

132

you were little boys you and Mr. Carl would come running in, calling before you'd pulled off your caps — 'Where's Mother?' and she was most always there to answer." He furtively drew his hand across his eyes. "She's dressing for dinner now."

"Then I won't disturb her. Is she expecting guests?"

"No, Mr. Craig. The Senator is in Washington and Madam said she'd have a tray on the terrace."

"Make it dinner for two, Saxon. I'm going on the river for an hour's work-out. Tell Mother I'll be at home to dine with her. Tell her not to invite anyone to join us, that I want to talk business."

"Yes, Mr. Craig."

How much of that set-to with Nadja in the Crofton garden would he tell his mother, Craig Lamont wondered as he followed the path that loped through the orchard with its brown twigs swelling at the tips, to the boat house. His thoughts returned to his outburst to Saxon. Saxon was used to it. The Lamont sons had confided their problems to his sympathetic ears for years. Problems! There were problems to burn now not for Carl but for himself. Between Nadja's threat to drag family affairs into court and Phil Bard working tooth and

133

nail to get his accounts, and Joan hating him — who was Jerry Slade? What right had he to call Joan "darling"? He had come to take her "flying" Peggy had said. Did she like flying? He, himself, had a pilot's license — though he wasn't using it at present.

"Just who are you grinding between your upper and lower molars now, boss?"

Tony Crane's hail relaxed Craig Lamont's tense muscles. He grinned at his friend, who, with paddle over his shoulder, and a crimson cushion dangling from one hand, stepped from the river path.

"You ought to model shorts and running shirts for that new sports-goods account we've taken on. The consumer's reaction to your picture as you are now would be enormous, Tony."

Crane dropped the cushion to tighten the belt about his too, too solid waistline.

"That idea is a honey, Craig. I'll beat it for the Croftons' as is. I'll bet the commercial artist in Joan won't be able to resist my svelte lines. After she's admired me a lot I'll nail her to submit roughs for the new sports-goods account."

"Not this afternoon, you won't. I've just come from there."

Crane smoothed back his sleek hair which shone like gold in the sun, made a staff of his paddle and leaned on it heavily.

"Was that why you looked as if you were biting nails a minute ago? I had it all planned that you and I would take Babs and the Crofton lassie dining and dancing this week. I'll bet you've put the cabosh on that."

He shaded his eyes with his hand and peered melodramatically in the direction of The Mansion. "Me thinks I see the dust of battle still rising yonder."

"You have what psychologists call 'the leaping mind.' Cut out the comedy, Tony and listen."

Craig told of his meeting with Nadja in the Crofton garden, of his suspicion that she was there to take Peggy away, of her intimation that Joan Crofton had arranged the meeting.

"And I'll bet you believed her!" Tony Crane interrupted in a voice drenched with disgust.

"For a minute I did."

"Did Joan know it?"

"Something tells me that she did."

No necessity for going into the matter of the disposal of the violets and gardenias. Craig thrust his hands hard into his coat pockets and frowned at the distant mountain tops veiled now in a soft violet haze.

Crane groaned.

"Now we'll never get the Straight As A Crow Flies Bus Line roughs Joan planned for the Bard Agency and I'll bet they were good. That girl has brains as well as eye-appeal. And can she draw? She can. You've got me worried, Craig. Since Carl — left us — you've been as feverishly responsive to girls and women — unless they're elderly — as an electric refrigerating plant in action, but you've never gone out of your way to fight with them as you have with the Crofton girl. What's the matter with you?"

Craig Lamont shook his head and frowned at his friend.

"I don't know. I honestly don't know why I'm always getting off on the wrong foot with her. You tell me, Tony."

Crane looked at him for a long moment before he grinned and shouldered his paddle.

"Not this afternoon, I won't. I still love life. Believe it or not, boss, you'll feel better — or worse — as time marches on."

X

April had blown away in a gale of biting wind and rain. Followed by two days of golden sunshine and presto, branches and twigs feathered into full leaf. Life was exciting in a world where the trees were brown and bare on Wednesday and were a mist of soft red or a vague, tender green on Sunday.

Now, gardens were a riot of pink, purple, yellow, bronze, blue and scarlet. Fruit trees looked like nothing so much as huge rosy puff balls. Lawns were like emerald velvet. Gold and black Baltimore orioles trilled their hearts out and scarlet tanagers flashed through green trees. In the night sky Mercury appeared for a brief visit, Jupiter glowed as the bright, particular star of the heavens and the Great Dipper was high in the North. May was in the saddle and the country world was a paradise.

Joan threw open the iron grille gate that separated the Crofton garden from the tulip-bordered path which led, brown stone beyond brown stone set in low ferns, to the house at Silver Birches. She loved the vista. Patches of ground phlox, some white as snow, some pink as a rosy dawn, spilled from the borders. She fitted tulips to their names — she had acquired much garden lore since she came to Carsfield. The soft salmon pink with pointed petals were Rosabella. Moonlight was a perfect name for the light yellow. Clear pink was Elizabeth and those gorgeous red ones were —

Her eyes narrowed. What was moving in the tulip border? What was that dark thing bobbing? She took a step forward.

"Peggy!" she exclaimed incredulously. "Peggy Lamont, what are you doing?"

The little girl poked her head above the tulips, muttered something and stepped into the brown stone path. Her face was flushed, her larkspur blue linen frock was crumpled. The black and white dog dashed from somewhere to join her and from among the tulips drifted a shrill meow! A robin, with a piece of string dangling from its bill, paused in the business of home-building and watched with bead-like eyes from the top of the wall.

"I'm — I'm weeding, Joan," Peggy haltingly explained.

"Weeding! Does Angus the Scot know you're weeding among his tulips? They are the pride of his life."

"Well, perhaps he doesn't — but — I'm

not doing any harm. Where you going in that pink dress? You look like strawberry ice-cream."

Peggy's change of subject confirmed Joan in her suspicion that mischief was brewing. But where? The gayly bordered path basked in the afternoon sun. The gray kitten had joined the little girl and the dog. An aura of innocence emanated from the three.

Perhaps she was imagining mischief where there was only innocent fun, Joan told herself before she answered Peggy's question.

"I shall walk to the post-office — time I had a letter from that lazy sister of mine — and then to the Country Club for tennis."

"Going to play tennis in a skirt? Gee, but you'll look funny."

Joan was annoyed with herself that the child's scornful comment should prick, but it did. She answered crisply;

"The skirt comes off. I'm wearing pink linen shorts under it, but, I don't walk on the village street in them."

"You needn't get mad about it. Going to walk all the way to the post-office? You'll be tired."

"If I am it will be because I have flabby muscles from scooting round in the sedan so much. Come with me, won't you?" Joan urged regretting that she had been impatient with the child.

Peggy shook her head until every dark curl bobbed and shone like obsidian in the sunlight.

"I can't. Got to change my dress, this one is rumpled. Besides, Granny is away and doesn't want me to go off the place unless she knows where I'm going."

"We'll ask Miss Hopkins."

"She's away too. Said she would only be gone two hours, and wouldn't I please be a good little girl for just that time?"

Peggy's imitation of a precise voice was perfect.

"I said 'Okay Toots' to her face and 'Good riddance!' to her back. What you waiting for, Joan? If you're going to play tennis, you'd better hustle."

"You're right, Peg. Sure you won't come with me?"

"Nope. Can't. I'm going back to the house."

Joan watched the child as she hopped from one brown stone to another up the path. The black and white dog hopped with her and the gray kitten trailed them.

Peggy's flushed face kept recurring to Joan as tennis racquet under her arm she walked to the post-office. She had an uneasy feeling that her comments about the pink linen skirt had been made to attract attention from herself. Should she have kept the child under her eye? How could she when Peggy so obviously wanted to be off about her own affairs?

Señorita Nadja Donesca was coming down the steps of the post-office as Joan mounted them. She was so intent on the address on a square package in her hand that she passed without looking up.

"Lucky I didn't bring Peggy," Joan thought and ducked into the office. The Señorita had looked as if a ghost were rising from that package like a genie from the sea. Perhaps it was something that would stop her fight for her "own leetle daughter."

The memory of the scene in the brick-walled garden brought with it Craig Lamont's face as he had accused, "Did you plan this?" Why should he think she would connive with that odious Nadja? Since that afternoon she hadn't talked with him for more than five minutes at a time. She had met him often — there was plenty of social life in the town, many charming summer homes, made gay and merry by the younger members of the families. Silver Birches brimmed with life and laughter week-ends when Mrs. Shaw entertained her son's friends, smart, attractive girls and likeable men — but whenever she saw Craig Lamont the Dodd woman's prophecy, "Another female on his trail," burned red as a neon sign in her memory. She was gay and friendly with other men, but when with him her mind seemed to freeze over.

"Air-mail letter for you, Miss Crofton," the postmaster reminded from behind the brass-barred wicket.

Joan felt the blood steal to her hair. How long had she been standing in the middle of the office thinking of Craig Lamont? With an effort she smiled at the man who was regarding her with crossed eyes and an indulgent grin.

"Guess you kinder forgot where you was, didn't you?" he suggested. "You stood there so long I thought perhaps you'd gone to sleep. I suppose that letter's from your sister who's gone out to Hollywood. Hear she's goin' into the movies."

There being no other business before him, he opened the wicket, leaned forward on his crossed arms and settled down for a chat.

Joan glanced at the postmark and back at him.

"It is from Hollywood, isn't it, Mr. Jepson? I'm quite sure my sister isn't in pictures yet. Good-bye."

She left him with mouth open on an outgoing sentence and ran down the steps.

The letter burned in her hand as she walked quickly toward the Country Club. She would find a secluded spot there and read it. It was the first real letter Vivian had written to her. There had been postcards galore and letters for her mother and father, but even those had been exasperatingly bare of details.

When she reached the Club she skirted the crowd watching tennis and hurried on to the swimming pool which shone like a fragment of turquoise sky dropped into an emerald enamel setting. Not a person in sight. She curled up on a seat which was screened from the house by a windbreak of blue spruces and tucked her feet under her.

"Safe from interruption here," she exulted and opened the letter. A soft breeze whispered in the fragrant branches behind her, a rose-breasted grosbeak in a tree across the pool, sang a ravishing accompaniment as she read.

"Well, now, Jo," the letter began;

I have been here weeks and this is really the first day I have had enough of importance to write about to fill a letter to you. Have I

143

now? Just wait till you read.

I have sent a sort of postcard diary. You know that for a while I stayed at the largest hotel here. With Uncle Mark's legacy as my financial backing I don't intend to have anyone think I am in desperate need of a job. Poor policy to look hollow-eyed and eager. No one here knows that I am hoping for a chance in pictures, that I would snatch at a stand-in if I could get it. I'm biding my time and looking and what is more to the point — feeling prosperous.

Last week I moved to this hotel — note the impressive letter-head — because I learned that many of the movies live here — that's what the actors and actresses are called out here — what you see on the screen is a picture. Each time I go up or down in the lift I see one or two. It's thrilling. When I begin to think of home and it gets me down, I dash off somewhere, see a lot of celebrities, and my spirits balloon.

To get back to this hotel. Large grounds and heaps of sunshine, swimming pool, patio where I breakfast out of doors and eats, my dear, the food is marvelous. Thank goodness I don't have to diet. I have hired a roadster by the week. I have driven miles and miles to get glimpses of snow-capped mountains, orchards pink and white with bloom, the Pacific, the bluest water I ever have seen; past motion-picture lots, with hordes of extras waiting at the gates — made me shiver to see their strained faces, but one can't stay depressed in this climate — smart restaurants, glamorous shops.

I waited until I was settled before presenting the letters of introduction father and mother gave me. Their friend, Mrs. Bankton, called at once and invited me to have luncheon with her today at the most ritzy place in Beverly Hills.

She is charming, made me think a little of Mother, you know mother's way of making a person feel that she is tremendously interested in her or him and in her or his life — and she is too. Perhaps that was why I told her about Uncle Mark's legacy, The Mansion at Carsfield, the Shaws at Silver Birches, even mentioned the torch-singer daughter-in-law about whom mother had written. You know me, Jo, when I get started. Like Patty Crofton, I am inclined to tell All.

Mrs. Bankton was sweet. I guess she recognized home-sickness when she heard it. Anyway, I felt better after I had talked about you all and when we came out to the street the sky was so blue and the air so fragrant and the group of autograph hunters around the door so stimulating — I wonder if they'll ever push and crowd for mine — that I was on the crest of the wave again.

Mrs. Bankton wanted to drive me home but I thanked her and told her that after the delicious luncheon — for the good of my figure, I'd better walk. My real reason for declining was that I wanted to loiter and windowshop. I was wearing my smartest navy blue sheer — it does things for my emerald — and felt a satisfied glow each time I saw my reflection in a window.

FLASH TO TITLE.
THE GREAT ADVENTURE.

Every life has at least one that should be set up in capitals — and this was mine, but I had to sketch in the background for it.

The atmosphere shimmered. The sky was cloudless. There were flower-stalls at every corner filling the air with perfume. Shop windows were shaded by awnings. I stopped to look at a display of perfectly divine jade when a man's voice beside me said;

146

"Beg pardon, but you dropped this under the table at the restaurant."

I can hear you sniff and say, "Old stuff!" but it really was my handkerchief he was offering. It was the green and navy chiffon you gave me. I recognized him as one of two men who had sat at the table next to us in the restaurant. I had looked at them surreptitiously and wondered if they were gangsters in pictures. He was good-looking in a rough-neck sort of way. His eyes were slaty but brilliant and boring.

I thanked him, took the handkerchief and turned to look in the window to indicate that the incident was closed.

The next thing I knew a hand grabbed my elbow and a voice hissed;

"S-step along with me! You're my girl, s-see? Talk. Talk fast. If you yip, I'll shoot!"

Now really, Jo, I'm not going to add "and just then I woke up!" It wasn't a nightmare. It was real. It happened in a second. For an instant I stared at the livid face and burning eyes of the man who had returned my handkerchief. Did I yip? I did! I opened by mouth and screamed and screamed and screamed.

If I hadn't been frightened out of my

senses I would have shouted with laughter at the stupefied expression on the man's face before he dashed away.

What followed will always remain a jumble of sounds and people in my mind. It seems that a few moments before at a jeweler's shop up the street, a man had grabbed a handful of gorgeous diamond bracelets from a tray. Perhaps he passed them to a confederate and then lost himself in the crowd. Perhaps they were in the pocket of the man who spoke to me. Evidently he thought if we walked along together talking, no one would suspect him. The first cerebration of the shop proprietors and the police was that I was — they call it, "the finger-girl." The fact that I screamed of course rather shook them in that conclusion. I was personally conducted to the police-station where I told the story of my young life. They showed me some photographs and I had no trouble in picking out the man who had threatened to shoot me.

I hated to drag Mrs. Bankton into it, but I gave her as a reference. She came at once with her son who is a lawyer in Los Angeles, it seems that the family is of great importance in the community. With many apologies, the authorities let me go

— and also the jewel thief. They had been so busy trying to tie me up with the theft that he escaped — the pack is at his heels, I understand. They expect he will be caught with the goods before sundown.

Luckily Mrs. Bankton — the son melted away, I've no idea what he was like — drove me to the hotel. My knees had turned to wax, and melted wax at that. She wanted to take me home with her — but I thanked her and said that I had come to Hollywood on my own and that I wouldn't sob out my sorrow on her shoulder at the first crack of blood-curdling adventure.

She was sweet — so like Mother — I didn't mean to have that tear splash, excuse the blot — when she said;

"My dear, my shoulder is at your disposal whenever you want it. I noticed those two men at the table next to us, and thought they were keenly interested in what you said. Their ears actually stood out they listened so hard. You had courage to scream when the bandit threatened you."

Courage. What else could I do, Jo? I knew from his face that the man had done something terrible. Could I take one step with him? I could not. I'd rather be shot.

Not that I thought that all out then, I didn't. I just opened my mouth and let out my voice. And from what I hear it was some voice. I expect —

I had to stop writing two days ago to answer the telephone. Reporters. Police. More reporters. I drew the line at News Reel men. Scouts from three production units. I am to have tests tomorrow. I was properly reluctant to consent — it took a lot of urging before I said "Oh yes," while all the time I was having the jitters inside for fear they wouldn't persist. I have adopted Mother's southern accent. It's sure fire. I am so shaky from excitement that I can hear my brain cells rattle.

You may read a sensational account in the newspapers of the robbery, though I doubt if ripples from the theft of diamonds in California, even though those bracelets were worth thousands and thousands of dollars, will spread across the continent.

> Love and more love to all,
> Devotedly,
> Viv.

XI

As Joan folded the letter, she felt as if she had been bodily transported from the exciting shimmering world of snow-capped hills, blue Pacific, motion-picture lots, smart restaurants and glamorous shops, to the cool fragrant shade of the blue spruces near the Country Club swimming pool. No wonder Vivian had capitalized the Great Adventure. Suppose the bandit had shot her!

She repressed a shiver. She looked at the date of the letter. The first part had been written more than a week ago. Why get excited now that danger was over? Viv had screamed, the man had run, she was safe and probably already had had the test she was after, not one, but several. Again she had characteristically got what she wanted. She had left out the climax of the story. She hadn't written whether the thief was still at large. From now on Viv's life would be full of color, adventure and achievement. She was bound to make good. In contrast how adventureless seemed the life she herself had chosen. To be sure, she had her work, Philip Bard was giving her plenty, although the folders for the Bus Line, which she considered the best things she ever had done remained in her files. He had been furious at Janvers' temperamental hop from one agency to another and back again.

How could she have stayed in New York and let her father and mother fare forth on an utterly strange manner of living, when they wanted her and relied on her? She couldn't and be herself, that was the answer. She wasn't indulging in self-pity, was she? Didn't she like her life and the stimulating glimpses she had of the business world? She did.

"What a hide-out!"

The exclamation whirled her thoughts back to her surroundings. She glanced up at Craig Lamont, who in white tennis clothes, with a racquet under his arm, was looking down at her. What was it about him that picked her heart up? His brilliant eyes? His smile which disclosed perfect teeth? The determined line of his jaw? The impression he gave of quiet strength and confidence? The consciousness of his ironical eyes on her had a maddening way of lingering long after he had taken himself off to speak to a more responsive girl. Whatever it was, she wouldn't allow it to get her. She felt her face stiffen. He protested quickly;

"Just a minute before you congeal, Joan. Hunting you up wasn't my idea. Babs and Tony want us to take them on at tennis. Come on. Why advertise to the Country Club at large your anti-Lamont fixation?"

Why indeed, Joan asked herself.

"Not the slightest reason in the world," she responded gaily. "I'll play."

She thrust the letter into the pocket of her pink linen skirt and sprang to her feet.

"Ooch! Ooch!" she wailed and clutched Lamont's sleeve.

"What is it? What's the matter?" he demanded and flung his free arm about her shoulders. "Why are you hopping? Have you been stung?"

"I'm not hopping! I'm s-stamping. I've been sitting on my feet! They're asleep! Golly, how they prickle!"

Lamont's boyish, rollicking laugh made him seem like a different person from the grave, restrained man she had seen before.

"I thought you'd stirred up a hornets' nest," he explained between chuckles. "Better now?" he asked as she released his sleeve.

"Quite all right." She stamped each foot before she picked up her racquet. "Let's go."

As they crossed the lawn toward the

tennis court, Joan tried to think of something nonchalant to say, something that would impress the man striding along beside her with the fact that she was so indifferent to him that an anti-Lamont fixation occupied her mind not at all. She wanted to be brilliant, epigrammatic and she succeeded only in being dumb. Why didn't he say something?

A black-haired girl in a green linen frock with her arms full of gorgeous pink tulips hailed them.

"Know where these flowers came from, Craig? Your enterprising niece is selling them at a roadside stand outside the gate at Silver Birches. She's doing a land-office business, scantily attired in yellow shorts with a halter-neck top. Follies effect. She has a nice sense of theatre. Three cars stopped while I was buying. Poor kid. Do you keep her short of pocket-money? Ol' meanie!" she mocked gaily and passed on.

Craig Lamont's incredulous eyes followed her and came back to Joan.

"Was she telling the truth or was she kidding?" he demanded.

Joan remembered the bobbing dark head in the tulip border, Peggy's crumpled blue frock, her air of injured innocence.

"I have a horrible conviction that she was

telling the truth," she answered.

Lamont seized her hand.

"Come on! We'll beat it to Silver Birches. Keep your fingers crossed, Joan, and wish hard that we get there before Angus the Scot charges that roadside stand."

Ten minutes later as his low-slung black roadster slid to a stop before the great iron-grille gates at Silver Birches, Lamont exclaimed;

"Too late! Here comes Angus on the run."

A short, squat man in blue overalls and a shirt open at the neck thudded toward them frantically brandishing pruning shears. His toes turned far out, almost at right angles with his ankles. A tuft of red hair in the middle of his bald head stood up like the few remaining bristles in a worn-out shaving-brush. His face was purple. His heavy jaw wobbled as he tried to shout to the little girl, who at his approach, shrank behind a wooden packing-box, on the top of which were a small black and white dog, a gray kitten, a dozen empty tin cans and one full of brilliant red tulips whose heavy blossoms drooped on their green stems like the heads of sleepy children.

As Lamont jumped from his roadster, Peggy dodged from behind the box and grabbed his hand. The black and white dog leaped to the ground and barked furiously at the gardener. The gray kitten indifferently gave herself a facial massage with a silvery paw.

"Hello, Uncle Craig! Hello, Jo-an," Peggy called in a voice slightly breathless.

"Mr. Craig! Mr. Craig!" Angus the Scot had found his voice. "You know what — that bane of me life's done now?" He swallowed a sob. "She's — she's cut me tulips — me prize tulips. Me Brilliants and me Rosabellas and — look at her — h-half dressed, with that bare back and those n-naked legs. She —"

"You sound just like a frog, ch-chunking, Angus," Peggy interrupted in a voice which proclaimed her cold distaste for a ch-chunking frog. "I'm not half-dressed, either. I'm wearing my new sun-suit."

"Will you hear that, Mr. Craig. That — that hard-hearted —"

"Just a minute, Angus. Let's get this straight. Did you cut the tulips, Peg?"

She twisted on one foot in incriminating hesitation, looked down at her uncle's hand which gripped hers, then at Joan leaning forward in the roadster. She stuck out her tongue.

"Tattle-tale!" she accused.

156

"Stop that, Peg!" Lamont caught her shoulder and turned her to face the angry gardener. "Did you cut the tulips?"

"Yes, I did. I don't see what Angus is making such a fuss about. They're not his tulips."

"N-not my t-tulips!"

Lamont interrupted the Scot's furious splutter.

"What did you do with them, Peg?"

Peggy drew a circle in the drive with the tip of a soiled white sneaker above which wrinkled a yellow sock, and fixed her eyes on the toes she was wriggling within it.

"Sold 'em."

"Where's the money?"

She pointed at a tin can on top of the packing box.

"Bring it to me."

She pouted, swung her bare shoulders and arms to register indifference, picked up the can and brought it to Lamont. He turned the money into the palm of his hand.

"Fifty cents! Is that all, Peg?"

"Of course it's all! I sold ten dozen tulips for five cents a dozen and —"

"Do ye hear that, Mister Craig? Me prize tulips that cost the Madam one to five dollars the bulb —"

Tears welled to the Scot's green eyes, his

Adam's apple worked furiously, he brandished the pruning shears at the child.

"Wait till yer grandmother gets hold of yer," he warned. "I hope she'll lambast yer till that bare back of yours is black and blue. I'm going to her now and show her."

He gulped down a sob, seized the drooping red tulips from the tin can and plodded up the driveway shaking his head and muttering to himself.

"I guess it's lucky he went. I guess he'd have blown up if he'd stayed round much longer, he was so mad," observed Peggy unfeelingly.

Lamont caught her under the arms and swung her toward the roadster.

"You're going to the house now. Your grandmother will know what to do to you," he warned.

Peggy planted her feet.

"Granny isn't there. I'm not going. I won't sit beside Joan, and if you marry her, as my mother said you would — I'll run away from Silver Birches. She told tales."

"I did not, Peggy," Joan denied and was furious that she had allowed the child to anger her. She stepped from the roadster.

"You won't have to sit beside me. I don't care to ride beside a little girl who steals. I'm walking home."

"Joan! Come here!" Lamont's voice was peremptory.

She turned and answered;

"As has been said before — I'm walking."

She was aware that Peggy and her uncle stood for an instant looking after her. She could feel their eyes boring into the back of her head. Then she heard the grind of gears and the diminishing purr of the roadster's engine.

"That is that!" she told herself. "Good riddance!" Why had Peggy accused her of telling tales? The girl in green with the bunch of pink tulips at the country Club had told Craig about the roadside stand.

"Because Peg knew that I had seen her in the tulip border," Joan answered her own question.

Had she lost the child's friendship, she wondered, as she walked on, only subconsciously aware of passing cars and blossoming fruit trees and twittering birds. She hated to lose a friend, even a little girl friend. Perhaps it was just as well. Thanks to Drucilla Dodd and that poisonous Nadja Donesca, Peggy was completely sold on the silly idea that she, Joan Crofton, wanted to marry Craig Lamont. Craig had heard that often enough to believe it true. From now on she'd show him. She shrugged disdain.

159

Scoffed to herself;

"I wouldn't marry Craig Lamont if he were the only man in the world. Marry him! Never!"

"Never is a long time."

She shivered. Craig Lamont's words echoing through her mind had sent little premonitory chills skittering along her nerves.

XII

As Joan approached The Mansion the beauty of the old house, with its white portico against the brick, was like a cool hand on her smarting consciousness.

She followed the path around the garden to what the townspeople called Indian Rock from which one could get an uninterrupted view of the country.

She held her breath at the sheer beauty of it. Fields upon russet gold fields basked in the afternoon sunlight; hills upon violet hills, crests upon crests rolled and rolled to meet the infinite heavens. The few clouds in the sky made her think of snowy icebergs sailing swiftly along a sapphire sea. The atmosphere was so clear that she could see the glitter of windows reflecting the sun in the abandoned Inn on top of the mountain. From the valley rose the enchanting song of a hermit thrush.

She sat on the rock, rested her elbow on one knee, cupped her chin in her palm, and watched the clouds fall into different patterns and drift in fluffs of pink swansdown dripping gold fringes across a purpling sky.

In contrast to the glory of earth, sky, wind and sun how trivial seemed her anger at Peggy's repetition of a silly remark, her consternation that Vivian had brushed shoulders with crime. It was not an uncommon experience in these melodrama drenched days. Davy Crofton had said that man was again becoming soul conscious. She could feel hers expanding. She would not allow herself to get furious again with Jerry Slade or with — with Craig Lamont. One might just as well pour a potion of poison through one's veins as to let anger sweep through one.

Spiritual serenity enfolded her in soft, cool wings. She sat so motionless that a rusty-breasted robin hopped nearer to regard her with a bead-like eye in its tip-tilted head. "Phoebe! Phoebe! Phoebe!" called a bird in a near-by tree.

The purr of a motor broke the fragrant silence. Followed Seraphina's voice from the front of the house.

"You want Miss Jo-an? She went out to de big rock — Indian Rock folks call it. I see her pass de window 'bout five minutes ago."

Joan felt as if she had been pulled forcibly from a spirit world as she looked at the tall, thin man striding purposefully toward her. His beak-like nose made her think of the figure-head of a ship. It dwarfed his other features. He had a paper in his hand. She slid from the rock. She had a curious feeling that she would better take what was coming standing. He touched the brim of a hat which looked as if it had seen many summers come and go. One corner of his mouth twitched constantly.

"Are you Joan Crofton?" His voice was deep and solemn.

Joan tore her fascinated gaze from the folded paper he was tapping against one hand.

"I am."

"I'm the sheriff of this county."

The sheriff! Why had a sheriff come to see her? Her heart went into a nose-dive, zoomed and looped the loop. Had her mother and father had an accident with the car? She caught the man's slazy sleeve.

"What's happened? My mother — father?"

The man administered a paternal pat on her fingers.

"No, no, tain't nothing like that, Miss. Sorry if I frightened you. Your eyes are most poppin' from your head and you're white as a sheet. I have a summons to serve on you. Now you've been subpoenaed, that's all."

Joan strangled an urge to laugh. Was relief making her hysterical?

"Sub — sub — what did you say I'd been, Mr. Sheriff?" she asked shakily. If only his mouth would stop twitching. Hers threatened to develop a sympathetic quiver.

"Subpoenaed."

"And what might that be? Is it like being x-rayed or finger-printed or what is it?"

"No, it ain't none of those things. You've been summoned as a witness. Open this and you'll understand."

Joan unfolded the paper with the caution she would have used in opening a package she suspected might conceal a bomb.

She read aloud;

COMMONWEALTH OF MASSACHUSETTS

Suffolk County   *To Joan Crofton*
YOU ARE HEREBY REQUIRED, in the name of the COMMONWEALTH OF MASSACHUSETTS, to appear before the PROBATE COURT on the twentieth day of May current — to give evidence of what you know relating to an action — then and there to be heard between

Mrs. Carl Lamont	Plaintiff and
Mrs. Sally Shaw and	
Craig Lamont	Defendants

HEREOF FAIL NOT, as you will answer your default under the pains and penalties in the law in that behalf made and provided —

Joan stopped reading. She frowned at the date and demanded;

"What does this mean?"

She looked up as she asked the question but the sheriff was not in sight. She exclaimed;

"He gumshoed away. I don't wonder he wanted to escape! He might have waited to explain. Davy Crofton will know. Hope he's at home. I'll ask him."

Her father was standing at the open grille gate in the garden frowning at the brownstone path which led to the house at Silver Birches. As she stepped from the terrace he called;

"Come here, Jo. Are my old eyes playing tricks or does the tulip-border which was a riot of bloom this morning look slightly moth eaten?"

"Nothing the matter with your eyes, Davy Crofton," Joan assured as she stood beside him. "Peggy Lamont felt the prick of sprouting business wings and cut a lot of those gorgeous red Brilliants and the exquisite pink Rosabellas. The lovely pale yellow Moonlights have been thinned too."

She told him of the roadside stand, of Angus the Scot's fury — she omitted the child's accusation of her — of her own suspicion earlier in the afternoon that mischief was brewing when she had seen Peggy's dark curls bob up from the tulip border. She added,

"But she seemed so innocent I concluded that my imagination had broken loose and forgot about her. Why have we wasted all this time on Peggy Lamont when I have troubles of my own?"

"Troubles! What do you mean, Jo?" her father demanded sharply. "What trouble?"

"I've been sub— subpoenaed."

"Subpoenaed! Why?"

She thrust the summons into his hand.

"Take it. Read it! Did you ever know of anything so maddening?"

David Crofton ran his eyes over the printed lines.

"I don't understand, Jo. Why should you be summoned as a witness in the Lamont widow's fight for her child?"

"You tell me."

"Have you ever talked with the woman?"

"Once when she came into this garden. I told you about it. I told you that I suspected she had come for Peggy. Peggy did too, for she sobbed to her uncle;

" 'I thought she was going to steal me,' " and then she added; 'Mam'selle said she knew my mother'd try it some day, she was such a schemer.' "

"And what did Mrs. Lamont reply to that?"

"Oh, a lot of drivel about what her own 'leetle' daughter was being taught to believe about her own mother. And then she warned Craig Lamont throatily and theatrically that no court would uphold him in that 'infamous course.' Now I ask you what has that family row to do with me?"

David Crofton reread the paper and shook his head.

"The family row has nothing to do with you, but the fact that you heard Peggy repeat what Mam'selle said may give Mrs. Lamont a legal right to have you summoned as a witness. The Law moves in a mysterious way its wonders to perform. Looks as if you'll have to testify that you heard the child quote the governess."

"What a mess! I was feeling so happy and peaceful out there on Indian Rock, thinking

167

that I'd never get fussed over anything again, when along comes that sheriff and blows my good resolutions to smithereens. Testify for that poisonous woman. I won't do it."

"You'll have to. That last line of the summons warns;

" 'Hereof fail not, as you will answer your default under the pains and penalties in the law in that behalf' which stilted phraseology means in every day language 'You've got to go.' Here comes Lamont down the path from Silver Birches. I like his free stride. Nothing blurred about his face. Clean-cut. Better get him to pose for you, Jo. The firm brown column of his throat above the open-neck of his polo shirt would sell sports clothes by the gross. We'll ask him —"

"Don't tell him —"

Craig Lamont entered the garden.

"How are you, Mr. Crofton?" He smiled at Joan. "Thought you'd be glad to know that the way of our young transgressor is to be made hard. The Department of Justice has considered her case, and she is to wear the khaki-colored dresses she hates until there is not a petal left on a tulip in the garden. You know how that child loves colored clothes. I'll say that's fitting the punishment to the crime. Much to her surprise and consternation her grandmother had returned. What's the matter? What's happened?"

He looked from daughter to father and back to Joan.

"What is it?" he asked again sharply.

Joan thrust the paper toward him.

"Look at this and you'll know what's the matter." She saw the dark color steal to his hair as he read. He folded the paper and returned it.

"Nadja thought up this infernal trick the day she came into this garden. It is so like her. I'm sorry, Joan. Terribly sorry, but you'll have to testify to what you heard."

"I won't. I don't care a snap of my fingers for you and Peggy, but I love your mother and I won't help anyone hurt her."

"Easy, Jo, easy," her father warned. "You don't mean that about not caring a snap of your fingers about Craig and —"

"Oh yes, she does, Mr. Crofton. I'm her particular blind spot," Craig Lamont interrupted coolly, "but she's going to change her mind and like me."

"Never," Joan defied.

His eyes were steady and controlled as they met hers.

"That word is almost a slogan of yours, isn't it? As has been said before, you are going to change your mind about me. I'll make you."

Joan shrugged.

"Make me like you! You can't."

He laughed.

"Can't I? 'You ain't seen nothing yet.' Your lilacs are way ahead of ours at Silver Birches, Mr. Crofton," Joan heard him remark lightly as she turned to make a dramatically silent exit from the garden.

XIII

"Just a minute, Miss Crofton, till I get this nailed up and I'll be with you. There's a registered package that was too large for your box you've got to sign for," Jepson the postmaster called as Joan entered the office with the box-key in her hand.

"I'll wait."

She watched him as he tacked up a white poster on the wall beside the door. She read aloud the printed description under the photograph on it.

" 'WANTED
" 'FOR THEFT
" 'AL DAWN'

"What a lot of aliases the man has, Mr. Jepson.

" 'Height 6 feet, weight 175; color of hair, black; black clipped mustache; eyes gray; about 35; unmarried; rough voice; educated; race-course and confidence-man.' "

Head slightly tipped she thoughtfully appraised the photograph on the poster.

"Not a vicious face, weak, though, isn't it,

Mr. Jepson? Curious eyes. Pale for that dark hair. Confidence-man and thief. It's hard to believe that a person with lips that sag at the corners and as chinless as a cod fish would have the courage to steal."

Jepson administered a final whack to the poster and retreated to his lair behind the barricade of letter boxes. He opened the brass wicket and thrust forward a package and a slip of paper.

"Sign here."

Joan smiled response to the eye that was fixed on her — the other seemed to be engaged with the poster on the opposite wall — and explained;

"I'm on my way to Boston. The package is too large to carry around. I'll leave it here, and stop and sign for it on my way home. Will that be all right with you, Mr. Jepson?"

"Sure, but ain't you anxious to see what's in it? It's postmarked Hollywood. Guess your sister's sent you a present."

"Looks like it. Can't be for my birthday, that isn't due until September. I'm all excited to know what is in it, but I must catch the train to Boston. Sometime I hope this town will be put on the map sufficiently to climb out of the two-a-day class. One train to town in the morning, one out in the afternoon."

"Say, why are you rushing for trains? You got a car, ain't you?"

"Yes, but my mother and father need it today."

"Has your sister got a job in the movies yet?"

Joan pulled on her string gloves that were the exact shade of her pale beige knit frock.

"I haven't heard, Mr. Jepson."

"You go to Boston an awful lot, don't you? They tell me you're sort of an artist."

Joan steadied twitching lips.

" 'Sort of' about expresses it. I'm what is called a commercial artist."

"You don't say. And what may that be?"

"I draw pictures to advertise things, to make people want to buy them. I'm going to the Boston Public Library now to look up some material. That is — I'm going if I don't lose the train. I'll stop for the package on my way home. Good morning."

She turned from the window. Señorita Nadja Donesca stood directly behind her. Except for a film of rouge on each cheek, her face was as colorless as her white linen suit.

The sight of her sent the memory of the court summons surging and smarting to the top of Joan's mind. She snapped a curt "Good morning!" but either the woman was too preoccupied to hear, or didn't want to

173

answer for she made no reply.

She looks as if she were walking up to the firing line. Perhaps she's heard something that will block her case. Here's hoping — Joan thought as she ran down the steps of the post-office.

Two hours later, seated at one of the tables in Bates Hall in the Boston Public Library, she snapped the rubber band about her note-book and for the first time since she had sat down regarded the other persons at the table under the green-shaded lights. Four men. One had his book close to his near-sighted eyes. Another with a regiment of heavy volumes deployed in front of him had a good-looking face weakened by a prim, sanctimonious mouth. There were deep lines about the sunken eyes of the third, who was not reading, but was staring into space. The head of the fourth man was bent over a book. His chin rested in his cupped hand as he frowned at the printed page. He looked up quickly as if Joan's intent gaze had penetrated his aura. His eyes, a surprisingly light gray, were as brilliant as the spectacular diamond in his hectic tie. They bored into hers then shifted quickly to the man beside him.

She hurriedly picked up the books from which she had been making notes. Had she been staring? He had looked resentful. On the way to the desk, she puzzled over his face. There was a suggestion about him of someone she had seen before. Identification eluded her. She would think she had it, then it would dodge around a corner of her memory.

She stopped on the landing of the grand stairway to look down into the court. Above it the sky was pure turquoise. The spray of a fountain turned to diamonds where sunlight caught it. The iridescent necks of pigeons glistened as they dipped and shook their feathers in the silver pool at its base. Benches along the stone walls of the cloister glowed with the color of the frocks of women and girls who sat reading and smoking. Palms rattled fronds in a light breeze.

She leaned forward. Was that Señorita Nadja Donesca sitting down? It was. In the same white linen suit she had worn in the Carsfield post-office this morning. What was she doing in a Public Library? One couldn't think of her as being there for study or a book. Perhaps she had come to meet her lawyer, or a witness in her fight for Peggy. She was looking at her wrist watch.

She, herself, had better watch the time. Philip Bard had invited her to lunch with him at T Wharf. "In the interest of your seeing-Boston education," he had suggested.

She glanced at the bronze clock set in one wall of the court.

If you don't get a move on, my hearty, you'll be late for lunch and you know you're pretty smug about being on time to the minute, she reminded herself.

She tucked her note-book into the green bag which matched her hat, passed the noble lions of St. Gaudens guarding the landing, ran down the broad yellow-marble stairway and fared forth into the street. She hailed a taxi.

An advertisement on a passing truck switched her thoughts to Craig Lamont. His face flashed on the screen of her mind and set her pulses quick-stepping. Two weeks had passed since he had warned her that he would make her change her mind about him. For days she had had a breathless sense that something thrilling was about to happen, but nothing had. She hadn't even seen him. She had motored and dined and danced as usual. She had acquired a maddening habit of glancing quickly at the door when a man entered a room.

Just looking for trouble, aren't you? she scoffed at herself.

A dark-haired little girl on the street reminded her of Peggy Lamont. Since the roadside-stand episode the child had haunted the garden of The Mansion when she was in it. A face would pop above the wall like a Jack-in-the-box and grimace at her.

The first few times the head appeared, she had called pleasantly, "Hello, Peggy," but as an out-thrust tongue was the only answer, she had ignored the child's recent appearances. They were getting to be something of a nightmare.

Apparently Peggy felt that she was responsible for her punishment, Joan's disturbed thoughts surged on. What about her own grievance? Wasn't it the child's fault that she, a totally disinterested person, had been dragged into Nadja Donesca's legal fight? Day after tomorrow she would have to appear in Court to testify that Peggy had said that Mam'selle had said — It made her furious whenever she thought of it.

"Don't think of it," her father had counseled. "Learn to control your thoughts, Joan, be captain of your mind. Don't spoil today by what you may have to meet in the future and remember that today is yesterday's tomorrow."

David Crofton would think her a weak

sister if he knew that at this moment, instead of watching the passing show in the crowded streets, she was dreading an appearance in court. She should consider it a rather exciting experience. If only she could side-step Craig Lamont.

For goodness sake stop thinking about that man! He's getting to be an obsession, she scolded herself. I presume he sticks in your mind because never before in your life have you so thoroughly disliked a person. Forget him.

She looked from the taxi window. She loved the hum and life of the city. She loved the life in a small town too, loved the neighborliness and friendliness of it. She liked having Jepson, the postmaster, ask if her sister were in pictures yet. He wasn't curious about her family affairs. He was interested. Probably Drucilla Dodd was curious. She hadn't yet met the woman whom Patty Crofton had dubbed the loudspeaker. She had dodged her when she had heard her voice in the drawing room of The Mansion.

To her surprise her mother and father were reveling in small-town life. In spite of the fact that before the advent of Seraphina a procession of maids had drifted through the kitchen and she had had to buckle down to cooking and housework between the visitations, Patty Crofton had made her home a centre of hospitality with perhaps a snack party after the local dramatics, or a Sunday buffet luncheon for Mrs. Shaw's young guests, or a tea for someone. David Crofton had laughed and confided to Joan in his wife's hearing;

"If this house were to float down river in a flood your mother would manage a tea-party on the roof."

"Here you are, Miss," the driver's voice startled her out of her reflections.

Philip Bard was at the taxi door before the man could open it. His gray flannel suit was immensely becoming. Joan tried to define the glow in his eyes. It might be triumph, but what was there about taking her to lunch to suggest that? He waved away her change and paid the cab charge.

"You're late," he said as she walked beside him on the rough planks of T Wharf. "Have you been in this part of the city before?"

"No, I'm thrilled. Isn't it interesting? Smell the sea! I love it."

"We'll walk around before we have luncheon."

Joan drew a long breath of the salt, tar, fish, old-ship seasoned air. Automobiles

179

crawled past. Curtains flapped at open windows in the dull yellow buildings that extended almost to the end of the wharf. Gray gulls, white gulls, soared into a dazzle of sunshine, dove into thick green water. Squatty tug boats whistled and scooted past like fussy, stout women crossing a crowded street. Pigeons strutted and pecked at the oats which a big gray horse was scattering from a nose bag. Here was a row of anchored guinea-boats with red, blue, yellow and green location flags dangling from long bamboo poles; there a line of fishing-schooners with nets stretched from mainmast to deck to dry. Color everywhere. Color captured and transferred to the canvases of a group of students, crouched or seated or kneeling on the rough planks. Color in the pink shells and ivory claws which girls in blue smocks were stripping from crabs heaped in brown kegs in an open shed. Color in the piles of lobster-pots. Color in the turquoise sky. Color, streaks of it, in the thick green water. Color in the islands in the harbor. Color in the purple horizon beyond them.

"Shall we eat?" Philip Bard suggested.

They were standing at the end of the wharf. Joan looked off to sea, said dreamily;

"If you close your eyes, can't you imagine

clipper ships back in 1840 or thereabouts, sailing up and unloading teas and spices and silks from China?"

"I can't. I'm too hungry. Come on."

Joan's eyes glowed like stars as she seated herself in a bright blue chair at a chrome yellow table in the low-ceilinged crowded room which was redolent of frying fish and coffee. Through the haze from an incredible number of cigarettes, she saw a dull-toned old map of Clipper Ship Days in Boston Harbor, another of Colonial Boston. Dusty murals presented ships and sail boats going in different directions under billowing sail, presumably in the same wind, against impossible blue sky and luridly green water.

Voices flowed or rasped according to the mood of the owners. Through the open windows, framed in ship-printed chintz curtains, drifted the scream of gulls, the whistle of tug-boats and the melody *O Sole Mio* wheezed from a hurdy-gurdy. Joan's eyes came back from an inspection of a blackboard beside the cashier's desk on which was chalked the names, ports and arrival hours of expected vessels, and met Philip Bard's.

"I never can thank you enough for bringing me here," she said earnestly. "I'll come back some day with my canvas and paints —"

"Hello, Bard. Mind if I join you? This place is jammed. Getting altogether too popular. I can't find a table."

Joan looked up at the man speaking. Where had she seen him before? The shining black hair, the red carnation in the lapel of his perfectly cut tweed coat? The prominent eyes? He threw an oblique glance at her. She had seen that before, too. She had it. In the Lamont Agency.

"Sure, glad to have you," Philip Bard responded cordially. "Miss Crofton, Mr. Janvers of the Straight As A Crow Flies Bus Line. Miss Crofton is the first-string artist on our staff. Drop in some day and I'll show you some of her work."

As she listened, Joan suddenly knew that this was not a chance meeting, that Philip Bard had planned it. Why? In answer memory broadcast Scott Rand's eager question;

"Don't think it would help for Janvers to meet Miss Crofton now, do you?" and later, "Janvers is girl conscious."

Philip Bard wanted the Straight As A Crow Flies Bus Line account. While they had luncheon he would tactfully steer the conversation to the folders she had prepared. If Janvers wanted to see them would she let Philip Bard show them? They were good. The best work she had done. If Janvers liked them, it might mean that he would transfer his account to the Bard Agency. Suppose he did? Was there any reason why she should give up an assignment to help Craig Lamont Inc.? To help a man she cordially disliked?

She smiled radiantly at the owner of the Straight As A Crow Flies Bus Line.

"Do sit with us, Mr. Janvers. I can recommend this fresh crab meat salad. I've never tasted anything more delicious. The coffee is wonderful."

She encouraged him to talk about himself, to tell his onward and upward saga. She rather liked him. He was rough and ready and boomingly proud of his business success, a man of hard fibre, he was not ashamed of the fact that he had started as a taxi-driver. She admired him for that.

She felt her eyes warm and her cheeks flush with interest as she listened. Nothing so thrilled and stimulated her as did real-life success stories. When she could get them at first hand, she had the Ancient Mariner's Wedding Guest beaten to a frazzle as a listener.

Janvers expanded under the glow of her

absorbed attention. As they finished luncheon he burst out;

"Say, Miss Crofton, I bet you're good at your job. I wish you would do some work for me."

"It might be arranged," Philip Bard conceded smugly.

Joan was aware of Janvers' wary look at him before he agreed noncommitally;

"Perhaps. Well, I've got to hot-foot it. Pleased to have met you, Miss Crofton. You'll hear from me about the ads. You live in Carsfield, don't you? How are you going out this afternoon?"

"I'm taking the last train. Alas, the Straight As A Crow Flies Bus Line doesn't connect with that part of the country."

"Tell me where it can pick you up and I'll send you home in a special bus," Janvers offered eagerly.

Joan laughed.

"You're magnificent. Thanks ever so much, but I prefer to go by train."

"Sure?"

"Sure."

"Sorry, I'd like to do it for you. Perhaps some other time. Good-bye."

Joan watched him thoughtfully as he stopped at the desk to pay his check. Her eyes came back to Philip Bard who with head back was watching the smoke rings rising from his cigarette. She asked;

"What did Janvers mean, that I would hear from him about the ads?"

"That he'll chuck the Lamont Agency and come to us. If he does — if he does I will have pulled off one of the ambitions of my life. I will have snitched Craig Lamont's best account. How I hate him."

His hands twitched, his eyes glared fanatically, his voice was low and hoarse.

"Why do you hate him?" Joan asked in amazement. "Didn't he give you your start in advertising?"

"He did. What does that prove? I've hated him since we were kids in the same town. He had everything *I* hadn't. Fine clothes. A grand home. Manners. A slim mother in beautiful dresses and a string of pearls about her white throat. Mine was fat and red and oily and took in washing. Once he and another fellow caught me hectoring Carl, his twin, and beat me up. Crown Prince, stuff. I told myself then that if ever I got where I could, I'd grind him under my heel. That's why I'm after his seat in the Legislature. I'll get it, too. Now I've hooked Janvers with you and Janvers is his white-headed boy."

Joan had been angry in her life but she knew now that she never before had known how angry she could be. Philip Bard was using her as a "hook." She had thought when Janvers sat down at table that it would be rather amusing and a nice little revenge to do work for Craig Lamont's best account through Philip Bard. All that was out. Philip Bard's mind was twisted. He was mad with envy and malice. She would refuse to submit roughs for the Straight As A Crow Flies Bus Line.

She opened her lips to forcibly decline to work for Janvers, saw the sinister glow in Bard's eyes, and closed them. This was neither the place nor the moment to discuss the subject. She rose and said in as light a voice as she could manage;

"I'm sitting here as if I were a lady of leisure. I'm twenty minutes late for an appointment with your art director now. Let's go."

XIV

Tilted back in his office chair, Craig Lamont frowned thoughtfully at the single yellow rose in a slim crystal vase on his desk and then at Janvers, seated opposite, whose face was as red as the carnation in his lapel, whose prominent eyes made him think of the glassies with which he and Carl had played as boys. Now they snapped with excitement. He answered the Bus Line owner's question;

"Sure, we know Miss Crofton's work. It's good."

"Then why don't you put her on my stuff?"

"We haven't needed her, have we? You've said yourself that our copy was bringing home the bacon, and it will bring more. I've been traveling about the country the last two weeks solely on your business. What's started you after her? Wait a minute."

He answered the phone.

"All right, Miss Otis. Tell him I'll be at liberty soon." He said to the man scowling at him. "My secretary just reported that there's a space-salesman waiting to talk over your new ad with me."

"Tell him to wait. I want to settle this question now. Do I get the commercial artist I want on my stuff, or don't I?"

"Sure, you get whoever you want." Craig Lamont's eyes narrowed. "How did you hear of Joan Crofton?"

Janvers straightened his tie and threw back his shoulders.

"Just lunched with her at T Wharf."

"Lunched with J— her? Alone?"

"Now I ask you — what chance would I have to meet a girl like that? She's class. Bard phoned me that he was taking her there to lunch — seeing-Boston stuff, and wouldn't I happen along. He knew she'd be interested to meet a man who'd made good."

So Phil Bard was the nigger in the woodpile, Lamont thought. He was hell-bent to get the Janvers account and he was using the lure of Joan's vital charm to snare the taxi driver whose yen for youth and beauty was common talk.

Janvers rested his chin on his hands clasped on the crook of his cane and confessed bitterly;

"I got my faith in the loyalty of women knocked out of me years ago, but I'll bet that girl's the type who'd stand by a man she married even if she thought he never would rise in the world. What eyes!"

Lustrous, was the word for them, Craig told himself then was furious that he had let his thoughts stray from the subject at hand. He suggested crisply;

"Meanwhile the space-salesman is waiting."

Janvers rose with a sheepish grin.

"Oh, all right, all right. But you're to get Miss Crofton on my ads — see? If you can't," he threatened darkly — "Well, she's the first-string artist at the Bard Agency. I'll take my business there."

Lamont disciplined a furious urge to crack the head of his best-paying account against the wall and agreed suavely;

"We can fix that. Of course I don't know how much work Miss Crofton has on hand nor how much she knows about bus travel."

"She doesn't know anything about it, she says, but she's going to."

Janvers brought his fist down on the desk with a force that set its brass fittings tapping.

"When we get her on our job I'll throw a party for her, de luxe bus, two drivers in livery and all the trimmings. It will be a corker and you'll plan the passengers and the supper, Lamont. We'll find out where she'd like to go. Meanwhile, she's going home this afternoon by train. I offered her a special bus, but she wouldn't have it, said she could make the last train easily. I saw that I'd ben friendly too quick, and let it go."

He scowled as Lamont answered the phone.

"Why do you let them interrupt when I'm here?"

Craig Lamont fought a primitive urge to seize him by the collar and hustle him to the corridor while he shook into him the realization that his was not their only account. Common-sense nudged his elbow and reminded him that if it were not the only one it was biggest, best and busiest. He laughed, and admitted;

"I have a feeling, Janvers, that a lot of the copywriters and space-salesmen pop in when they know you're here to get a look at you. You're something of a celebrity, you know."

His client hooked his stick over his arm, threw out his chest, strutted to the door and paused.

"Why shouldn't they want to see me? I done my duty in the war, got an honorable discharge and because there was no other job, drove a taxi. Now look at me! I'm Janvers, sole owner of the Straight As A

Crow Flies Bus Line. I'm tops financially."

His manner connoted, "I'm something to see." He paused on the threshold to fling over his shoulder;

"Remember, I want Miss Crofton on my ads. If you can't get her, the Bard Agency can."

After which pronunciamento he closed the door behind him.

The threat roused the fighter in Craig Lamont. He'd be darned if he'd let Phil Bard put across such a cheap deal. If he, himself, hadn't started off on the wrong foot with Joan this wouldn't have happened. That evening at Silver Birches she had agreed to bury the hatchet, but she hadn't, the frost in her manner chilled him to the marrow whenever they were together. His intimation that she was showing proofs that weren't hers that day here in the office didn't account for all of her antagonism, neither did the accusation that she was conspiring with Nadja, he had flung at her in her own garden. Peggy's repetition in the play room and at the roadside stand of Nadja's and Drucilla Dodd's silly gossip had done the trick. Well, he had told her that he would make her change her attitude toward him and he would if he did nothing else during the summer.

The door behind him opened and closed softly. He wheeled from the window from which he had been staring unseeingly at the roofs. His jaw tightened. His eyes narrowed as he demanded of the woman leaning against the closed door;

"How did you get in, Nadja?"

"Walked. *Por Dios!* You do not see a wheel chair concealed about my person, do you? Who was the man I passed in the corridor? I deed not notice his face, but I felt he turned queek to look after me." She preened and pulled her white hat a bit lower over one green eye. She was unusually pale, Craig Lamont noticed, and her eyes were restless.

"That man always turns to look after a pretty woman. What do you want?"

She seated herself on the corner of the flat desk, pulled the yellow rose from the vase and drew the stem through the buttonhole in the lapel of her white linen coat.

"Eet looks rather well, yes?"

She laid her hand with its pointed, blood-red nails on his sleeve.

"Don't freeze, Craig. I want to talk to you. My case comes up in court day after to-morrow. If you weel listen to reason you and your mother may be saved a lot of money, time and perhaps unpleasant publicity —

that might hurt your chance for re-election."

She waited for the implication to sink in before she cajoled;

"I do not want to take the fight for the child to court. Puf! She ees nothing in my life. I want you. Can we not — compromise — it is the word, yes? *Dios!* But I would make a good wife — for you."

She was close to him now, leaning heavily against his arm, looking up at him.

How he hated the perfume she used! He shook her off and stepped back.

"Our lawyer is handling the matter, Nadja. Any proposition or settlement out of court should be made to him."

Color rushed to her hair, receded. In the livid whiteness of her face, her green eyes burned with yellow lights. She challenged furiously;

"Afraid of me, are you? Yes?"

Craig Lamont laughed and took a step toward the desk.

"Oh no, I can always yell for help."

Fuse to dynamite. The woman clenched and unclenched her red-tipped fingers.

"I know why you won't listen to me! You are in lof with the Crofton girl. I knew it that afternoon in her garden. That is why I had her summoned as a weetness to testify that

Peggy said that her governess called the child's mother a schemer. I know it would mak' you mad. She weel not have —"

Tony Crane flung open his door.

"Did you ring?"

His glance swept over the woman as if she were part of the office furniture before he apologized.

"Sorry to interrupt, boss, but that copy-writer has been waiting an hour to see you and begs to remind you of the old but still true adage that time is money." He grinned at the woman who was glaring at him.

"Hello, Señorita Nadja Donesca. You were so quiet I didn't see you before. How's tricks?"

She turned her back and drew on her gloves. Crane cocked one eye at Lamont who answered the look.

"You're not interrupting, Tony. Señorita Donesca was just going. Escort her to the elevator, will you? On your way out tell the copy-writer I'll see him at once."

He picked up a bunch of letters and walked to the window high above the street. He was aware that the woman took a step toward him before Tony Crane protested;

"Hey, that's not the way out, Nadja. Here's the door."

"*Muchas gracias, gracias, señor* Tony."

Crane ignored her sarcasm.

"Don't mind, gal, if the boss is a bit grouchy. He's got a lot on his mind. They tell me politics raises the deuce with a man's disposition."

"*Adios,* Señor Lamont. I weel —"

The quickly closed door cut off the menacing voice.

"A lot on my mind," Craig repeated, and set his jaw hard. He'd say he had. What a mess. What an infernal mess. Nadja had dragged Joan into it. He had begged the Senator to think up a way to keep her from that hearing. The woman didn't want her child — she had acknowledged that — she would trade a court fight for — the bargain was too sickening to put into words. Did she think that anything she might threaten would change his loathing for her?

His eyes were on the people passing on the street below, on the ceaseless procession of trucks and automobiles as his thoughts trooped on.

Nadja had threatened publicity that would block him in his campaign for re-election to the State Legislature. There was nothing true that she could say. What lies had she up her sleeve? No matter how untrue her charges were, they would be headlined and half the persons who read them never would see the retractions. That was the trouble with newspaper stories. Phil Bard was working tooth and nail to defeat him at the polls.

His eyes followed the smoke spiralling from innumerable chimneys, came back to the pigeons cooing and strutting on a roof. Why, why should a woman like Nadja have the power to thrust into the spot-light of notoriety a family which as far back as he knew had had a rigid code of honor which had kept its reputation unblemished through countless years of family loyalty and public service.

She was vindictive. Why should she be? While she was Carl's wife she had been treated with every consideration — even by himself — who mentally and physically loathed her. She knew that. That was the cause of her hatred of the whole family. She would be ruthless now that he had made her understand his attitude.

"You are in lof with the Crofton girl."

Her low, furious voice echoed through his mind. He smiled grimly. In the garden of The Mansion she had accused Joan of wanting to marry him. Where had she picked up that crazy idea? He'd hate to have her know how much Joan detested him.

"In lof with the Crofton girl." Why in thunder did that sentence keep merry-go-rounding? She was the last person —

Joan's face flashed on the screen of his mind. Her eyes, deeply, angrily blue, her lovely generous mouth set in a defiant line, her cheeks as pink as roses. The silent picture went sound. He heard her defiant;

"Make me like you! You can't."

The memory of her voice and face sent the blood racing through his veins! In love with Joan! So that was it. That was the reason he had determined to make her like him! He had so consistently distrusted girls since Carl's disastrous marriage that he hadn't recognized love when it had crept up on him. Now it had him shackled for sure, and for the good of his soul it had happened none too soon. He had allowed his life to be distorted by his fierce, burning inner protest against the tragedy of Carl's marriage. Instead of dwelling on it he should have thrust the memory behind him with all his might, when his brother died.

Curious that the awareness of his love for Joan should bring with it the swift realization of the futility and senseless wastefulness of brooding on the past. He couldn't see her going on in life looking back over her shoulder. She was too valiant, too full of zest to spend a moment in vain regret. Zest! He'd say she had it and a quick flashing temper too.

He laughed as he remembered her eyes on that first — and to date — last call at the Lamont Agency when she had declared furiously;

"Are you suggesting that this by any stretch of the imagination may be called a 'best regulated firm'?"

Which memory brought him back to the fact that he was desperately, irrevocably in love with her.

He visualized her face again, said to that defiant mouth;

"Never is a long time — adorable."

His mother's warning recurred to him.

"If you should fall in love with a charming girl — I pray every day that you may — watch out for Nadja. I shudder to think of what she would try to do to a girl for whom you cared."

Her grave voice was so real that it sent prickles through his veins. Nadja hurt Joan! Was the opening wedge the summons to appear in court day after tomorrow?

He wheeled from the window as Tony Crane entered and collapsed in a chair.

"Did you see Nadja off the premises?"

"I went one better than instructions,

Boss. I landed her in a taxi. Ready to bite, wasn't she?"

"She was. The foot-bell we had put in to connect with your office, that I might ring when I wanted to get rid of a talker with no terminal facilities, was a brilliant idea of yours, Tony, only the next time you burst in, don't give it away by asking if I rang."

"My mistake. It was a break. Now that that is nicely washed up, what next?"

"Where's the copy-writer who's been waiting to see me?"

"Couldn't wait any longer. That was only my excuse for barging in. What was Janvers laying down the law about?"

"He wants Joan Crofton on his ads."

"Well, for the love of Mike! Where did he get wise to her?"

"Bard invited him to meet her at lunch today."

"The dirty sneak. He knew that ex-taxi driver would fall for her."

"He did. Hard. For the first time since he has been our client, Janvers gave me a hint of his views on life unconnected with business. Evidently a woman turned him down because she thought he'd never rise in the world."

"So the old blow-hard twanged a melancholy note on his past love-life, did he? Can you beat it? What else did he say?"

"He threatened to leave us for Bard if we don't get Joan Crofton on his ads. I'm darned near fed-up with his histrionics. I restrained my urge to knock his head off and told him smoothly that I'd see what we could do about it."

"Well, what can we do about it? You and Joan fight every time you get together. What are you grinning about? You make me think of the cat that swallowed the canary."

"Cheerio, Tony. All is not lost. Among other choice bits scattered like crumbs from Janvers' vast store of information was the fact that Joan is taking the last train to Carsfield this afternoon."

He spoke into the transmitter;

"Miss Otis. Send in the space-salesman. Make sure that the Carter Starch campaign is released to the newspapers for morning publication. Don't make appointments for me this afternoon. — No, I haven't forgotten that I'm to talk at the Advertising Club luncheon tomorrow. Phone the Motor Mart to have my roadster sent round at once. I shan't be back to the office again today."

XV

Joan glanced at her wrist watch as the door of the Bard Advertising Agency closed behind her. She drew a little sigh of relief. Scott Rand had kept her for hours talking over and planning work he wanted her to do for him.

She dashed into the descending elevator. The door clanged behind her just as Philip Bard stepped from an up-car. She was in luck. After luncheon he had told her to bring the Bus Line folders to the Agency in the morning. When she had protested that she would be too busy — she wanted time to frame her refusal to submit them — he had suggested driving her home this afternoon that he might get them, but she had told him she had other plans. The more she thought of it the more she disliked that meeting with Janvers at luncheon. She smiled as she remembered his offer of a private bus. She chuckled as she pictured herself arriving in lonely state at the front door of The Mansion.

Her smile faded as she visualized his wary eyes. She hoped he hadn't thought her a party to the account-stealing scheme. She had been glad of the work the Bard Agency had given her, but, she didn't like Philip Bard. He was making social life at Carsfield something of a nightmare. In spite of his rather sordid background he was invited everywhere in the small town. His friends claimed that he had a fifty-fifty chance of succeeding Craig Lamont in the Legislature.

Life was getting complicated to say the least. She had fought and died several times before she had made Jerry Slade realize that she did not want to see him. The final battle had occurred after Peggy's mother and Craig Lamont had taken themselves out of her garden. She had ordered Seraphina to throw away the flowers with which Craig had filled the rubbers she had left in his office. Lovely things, the violets and gardenias, not the rubbers. It had hurt so to give them up that she had turned on Jerry and furiously told him that she never, never, never wanted to see him again. Evidently she had at last impressed him, for he had neither called nor phoned since. It looked as if she might enjoy life after that maddening appearance in court was behind her.

She consulted her watch again. She could make the train if she were not held up by traffic.

She glanced at shop windows as she passed. Valiantly resisted the temptation to stop. Ravishing frocks. Up-to-the-minute furnishings. Flower stalls at every corner. Rose-tinted aqueous clouds. Sidewalks crowded. Tramp, tramp of countless feet. Tap, tap of countless heels. Music. March tempo. A voice, "You have been listening to the United States Marine Band." A loud radio warning, "Wait for the green light. Avoid accidents. Traffic officer your best friend." Automobiles crawling forward. Stopping. Forward again at the shrill of a whistle.

The station clock. Two minutes before the train left. Could she make it?

"Taxi, lady?"

She turned toward the voice. She might make it in a taxi — she stopped. Craig Lamont was holding open the door of a black roadster. She caught her breath. What was it about his eyes that —

"No thanks," she declined frigidly.

"You can't make that train. It's the last for the day."

As if she didn't know that. Automobile horns tooted furiously, sirens wailed.

"You're blocking traffic. Be a sport. Forget you don't like me and come along." He caught her elbow to emphasize his suggestion.

"Step on it, lady," shouted the driver of a truck. "The boy-friend won't eat you."

Joan stepped on it — into the roadster with its thrown-back top. She felt as if thousands of eyes were looking at her, as if thousands of lips were laughing in sympathy with the truckman's sally.

Her cheeks were burning as the car started. Without taking his intent gaze from the jam of automobiles ahead, Craig Lamont agreed;

"You do look good enough to eat in that knit dress. It's the exact shade of coffee ice-cream and I'm strong for coffee ice-cream."

She glanced at him from under her lashes. There was not the slightest trace of a bruise about his eye now. Two sharp little lines which she remembered deepened between his brows as he concentrated on threading a way through traffic.

Workmen-laden trucks waited for the changing light side by side with luxurious limousines. Grime and sweat. Elegance and perfume. Loud voices. Soft laughter. Music from a radio. Glint of dinner pails. Gleam of jewels. Drone of tires on black pavement. Smell of gas. Throb of motors. The end of the day. Homeward bound. To tenement. To cottage. To country estate. All homeward bound.

When they reached the river, Joan rejoiced that the top of the roadster was down. She could see the white sails of boat-models being raced on the lagoon which was as blue as the sky it reflected. The sun rested on the horizon like a huge crimson ball dropped by a giant at play. Above it one brilliant star hung like a Christmas-tree ornament. Against the crimson glow an electric clock burned palely. A salty east wind sprang up. It rippled the river into a shimmering mass of rubies and emeralds. It frothed it with lacy white. A line of pale lights flashed along the Esplanade. Another hung like a girdle of brilliants between sky and water where a bridge spanned the river. From far away drifted the faint chimes of a steeple clock.

"How the lights glorify Harvard Bridge," Joan exclaimed impulsively. "They transform it from a dingy highway to a fairy cable of brilliance."

"Curious that you should have used that comparison. When Harvard College was founded, the other side of the river now called the Back Bay, was lined with marshes. There was no bridge in those days, only a cable-ferry which charged a small fee to carry passengers across. Those fees were the chief source of revenue for the College. Look behind you."

The departing sun was flooding the Esplanade with rose-color. It shot a crimson-spiked challenge to the sickle of moon dangling on a church spire like a silver crescent on a Turkish Minaret; it transmuted the dome of the State House to rich red-gold and set every window in the brick houses which rose tier upon tier on the Hill to gleaming till they looked like the brass breastplates of an advancing army; it set aflame the sweeps that dipped and rose as two slim shells skimmed the water; it tinted the wings of soaring, diving gulls and turned to mother of pearl the airplane high above the Basin.

Joan released a soft rapturous breath.

"Makes me think of 'that great city — descending out of heaven from God.' Beautiful in this light, isn't it?"

"Yes. It's a pity that another line of St. John's doesn't fit, 'and there shall in no wise enter into it anything that defileth.' "

Joan glanced at him from under her lashes. The men with whom she had played round before she left New York wouldn't have known that she was quoting from the Book of Revelations. She asked;

"Is it worse than any city?"

"No, better than many, I presume. But, years and years ago, there was a Massachu-

206

setts Governor in our family. His portrait hung in our living room when I was a boy and my twin brother and I were brought up to feel a great pride in the State, that we had a fine tradition to carry on, that we must never disgrace our ancestor, His Excellency, the Governor. When mother married Senator Dan Shaw, we became more and more aware of what we owe the community in which we live."

"Then why don't you do something to better conditions?"

"I'm trying to. I'm a representative from our county — I keep my residence in the town in which I was born — to the Great and General Court — in other words the Legislature of Massachusetts. I'm up for re-election. Time and the voters will tell whether I get it."

"Of course you'll be re-elected. Is anyone opposing you?"

"Yes. See the purple iris in that garden? Gigantic isn't it? Beginning to feel at home in our city?"

He doesn't want to talk about Philip Bard's fight for his place, Joan thought, before she answered.

"Yes. I love it. I've always wanted to know the Boston of Paul Revere, the Tea Party, Longfellow, Emerson and the Alcotts. I had a feeling that the atmosphere of this city would be rarefied, different from others. I expected the average citizen to look as if he were interested only in heaven, hell and the Evening Transcript. Instead he is just as money-conscious, as swing-band and speed-mad, as cinema-hungry as the rest of the world."

He laughed;

"All of us are not like that all of the time. What have you seen?"

"Your mother gave me a reading-privilege at the Athenaeum. The place drips culture. Shelf after shelf of books, floors of them. Rows upon rows of plaster busts. Whiteness. Stillness. Flowers on all the service desks, bowls of them. A portion of Washington's library. Sun streaming in at long plant-filled windows. Iron-railed balconies from which one looks down on the peace of the old Granary Burying Ground with pigeons flitting round its slate headstones."

"Go on. I am rediscovering Boston through your eyes. Been to the Public Library?"

"Yes. This morning for the first time. The atmosphere there is as different from the Athenaeum as the plate glass windows of the shops are different from the violet-panes in houses on the Hill. It stimulated my imagination. It glows with color, swarms with people of all races. Within its yellow marble walls one can fairly hear the melting pot bubble."

"I haven't been inside the Library for years. Does Sir Harry Vane still stand guard near the door in his bronze clothes which neither rust may destroy nor moth corrupt?"

"Yes. I made a sketch of him and of those brass Zodiac signs on the floor. Everything's grist which comes to this commercial-artist's mill. I know just how I'll use those signs of the Zodiac in a lay—" she stopped. She could have cheerfully bitten out her tongue for leading up to her work.

He laughed and looked at her from the corners of his eyes.

"Why chop off the sentence? Lay-out was the word, wasn't it? How's the work going? Does the Bard Agency keep you busy?"

"Fairly. I'm doing some roughs for two other firms — one is fashion drawing which I eat up — besides carrying on for the International Dog-Soap people. I was terribly pleased when they wrote asking me to send some roughs."

"I don't wonder. It is a feather in your cap. You made another conquest today.

Janvers of the Straight As A Crow Flies Bus Line wants you to do some work for him."

"Did he come to you about it?"

"He did. Does that emphasis on the you mean that you're still determined not to work for me?"

Something in his eyes caught up her heart and dropped it. Whatever it was also tightened her throat before she evaded his question and acknowledged;

"That 'you' was relief. I met him at luncheon today and something told me that Phil Bard was using me — not my work — to snitch your client. I was pretty mad about it. Even if you do think that I would help Peggy's mother steal her, you can't believe that I would help Phil Bard steal your business."

"I don't believe it, Joan. I was wild with fury that afternoon to think that Nadja had brought her sordid self into your lovely garden. And when she thanked you for helping her, it hurt so intolerably that for a second I went haywire. I've talked myself hoarse to the Senator trying to persuade him to pull wires to get you excused from that hearing day after tomorrow."

"Will Senator Dan Shaw appear for you and your mother? I thought the office of his law firm was in the middle west."

"It is, but a lawyer is permitted by courtesy to appear for a client in a state not his own. The Senator insists that you will have to appear but predicts that the judge will strike out your testimony on the ground that hearsay evidence is not admissible. I'm terribly sorry you were dragged into the mess. Meanwhile, believe me when I say that I think you the straightest, sweetest, most wonderful girl in the world."

His husky voice jerked Joan's heart to her throat. She promptly swallowed it. She said lightly;

"Thanks for those kind words. We ought to get on better together after that orchid."

XVI

Craig Lamont shot the black roadster ahead. He drove some way in silence before he said grimly;

"All right, take my 'orchid' as a joke if you prefer, but you're going to learn a lot from now on. I don't know why you think we don't get on together — but we'll let that go for the present. Will you show us some roughs for the Bus Line?"

Joan straightened with a little bounce of exuberance.

"I will. I have six finished folders ready and if you can believe me, they are grand."

She looked up at him with a laughing challenge in her eyes and boasted with gay bravado.

"Even if you turn me down, there's always Mr. Janvers as a court of last resort. Believe it or not, I'm quite sure he will like anything I do."

"I'll never turn you down, adorable."

His voice set her pulses racing. As he met her startled eyes, he laughed, and demanded;

"Now, I ask you, can you see me turning

down your work with the Bard Agency waiting to grab it? Where are the Bus Line folders?"

"In my work-room at home."

"May I come in and see them?"

"You may, if you'll promise to be honest in your criticism."

"I promise."

After that a stretch of silence between them. Joan's animosity to the man beside her magically seeping away and her heart quick-stepping for no reason at all, she told herself. Broad, smooth road. Swish of passing cars. Slanting sun on dazzling chromium trim. White clouds sailing across a turquoise sky. Lengthening shadows. Houses. Spirals of smoke from chimneys. Scent of broiling meat. Young green pushing up in even rows through brown earth. Gardens. A dog barking behind a white gate.

Woods, feathery with leaves of maple and oak, sombre with pine and hemlocks. A pollen-tipsy bee bumping against the windshield. Overhead a company of honking geese heading northeast. A pond. Shrill frog chorus "Deep! Knee-deep! Knee-deep!" Paths worn through fields dotted with the misty white, the golden gleam of flowering shrubs. Birds fluttering, chirping, nest-building. The loud clear "wick, wick, wick, wick," of flickers. The river. Beyond it fields, foothills, and the mountain. Joan drew a long breath and confided;

"I haven't been asleep, really I haven't. It was just that this roadster is so heavenly smooth, and the air so balmy and —"

"Give me a break. Say, and the driver so expert."

"You've said it for me, you're superb. How clear the Inn on the mountain top is in this light. The view of the valley and our ridge must be marvelous from there. Sometime I intend to drive over and see it."

"No time like the present. We'll go tomorrow. It's too early for the low-bush laurel, the mountain will be pink with it in about two weeks, but we can go again then. I'll get a fire permit from the forest warden. If it were to turn cold we would need a fire. We'll start in the early afternoon, take a picnic supper and watch the sun set. It's a great sight."

"It must be but I have a lot of work —"

"You'll do better work after seeing nature's gorgeous lay-out."

Joan considered. Why not go with him? Suppose he did think he had won out on his threat to make her like him? Why not like him? She hated being at odds with anyone.

It seemed so futile when there was so much real trouble in the world.

"Well? Am I to be paroled during good behavior?"

She looked up and then quickly away from his smiling eyes.

"You're right about nature's lay-out. I'll go. I will provide the supper. Shall we cook eggs and bacon and make coffee and —"

"We will not! The last time I picnicked on the mountain we all sat or knelt with our backs to the view while we cooked and choked from the smoke of the fire. When the food was ready to eat the sunset had departed. This is to be my party. I'll have the supper put up at the Club. You'll go? Promise?"

"Cross-my-throat and hope to die. Of course I'll go. Why shouldn't I?"

"No reason why you shouldn't."

He remembered the rough and bubbly road of misunderstandings along which their acquaintance had progressed and reminded;

"Don't forget. You've solemnly promised to keep that date with me tomorrow."

"I never break a promise," Joan asserted with dignity. "Here we are at the village. I love it. I love the two white spires on those Bulfinch churches on each side of the green.

Oh, I'd almost forgotten. I have a registered package at the post-office. Will you stop?"

As Lamont slid the roadster to the curb he asked;

"Can't I get it?"

"No, thanks, I must sign for it."

As Joan turned away from the post-office window with the package in her hand, she saw the poster sent out by the United States Bureau of Investigation. That face! Those curious pale eyes. She had seen them, seen them today. Where? Her heart was pounding with excitement as she ran down the steps.

"What's the matter, Joan!" Lamont demanded. "You're white."

"Let's start, quick, then I'll tell you."

She looked furtively over her shoulder as the roadster shot forward.

"It — it was in there," she said breathlessly. "A picture of a man wanted for theft. I saw him today."

"Saw the thief? Where?"

"In the Public Library. He was sitting at the table where I was working."

"Sure it was the same one?"

"I'm sure. Something about his eyes. What should I do?"

"You! Nothing. Keep out of it. He's miles away by this time. I'll report."

"I don't know why speaking of the wanted man should make me think of her, but I saw Señorita Donesca in the court of the Public Library today."

"Nadja at a library! That's the funniest thing I ever heard. She wouldn't look at a book if it engagingly flapped its pages at her. Let's forget her. Here we are at The Mansion. Am I to see the Bus Line folders?"

"Yes. We'll have tea first. I smell toast burning so I am sure Seraphina is on the job."

"Is Seraphina the dusky maid — who throws away unwanted flowers?"

Joan colored blush-rose pink.

"I'm sorry. They were lovely. But you did accuse me. And —"

"Forget it. My mistake. I should have let sleeping dogs lie. Friends again?" He held out his hand.

Joan laid hers in it. Said with a perfect imitation of Peggy's voice and manner;

"Okay, Toots! I wonder who is here?" she whispered. "I'll say it is someone who has conquered the problem of voice projection. I can hear her through this closed door."

"I'll tell you. I'd recognize that voice were I to hear it oozing from an igloo at the North pole, if I didn't know that shabby sedan in the curve of the drive. It's the Shaw family pest, Drucilla Dodd."

Patty Crofton, in a dashing black hat and brilliant green print frock, greeted them from behind the tea-table as Joan and Lamont entered the candle-lighted drawing room. She spoke to the woman humped in a chair.

"Miss Dodd, have you met our daughter, Joan?"

"No, but I've heard a lot about her from Phil Bard and others. I've heard that you were charming, Miss Crofton, now I can confirm the rumor. Craig — dear boy, it's a treat to see you but too amazing to see you with a girl," she cooed ingratiatingly.

"How are you Drucilla?" Lamont rejoined curtly.

He took the cup of tea Mrs. Crofton prepared and stood back to the mantel. Had the presence of Miss Dodd cut the lines deeper between his eyes? Joan wondered. She was unattractive. Whatever color her pasty skin provided had concentrated on the tip of her overlarge nose. Were her quick shifting eyes indicative of her mental processes? Her thick skin looked as if it might be scraped to advantage, her short checked skirt displayed black ankles which puffed above black ground-grippers. Joan remembered what Craig Lamont had said about the sharpness of her pen and tongue and wished that she could warn her mother who was impulsively inclined to tell All.

"Where's Father?" she asked to break a silence which threatened to become permanent.

Her mother's dark eyes were full of little dancing lights as they met hers, the corners of her lips twitched. The soft candlelight set a million iridescent sparks twinkling in the rings on her hands busy about the tea-things.

"Your father has gone plain garden mad, honey. He just said 'How do you do?' to Miss Dodd, and remembered some seedlings — I think he called them — that must be given more air or the 'damping-off' disease would attack them, if you know what that means, I don't. You were speaking about the charity benefit when the young people came in, Miss Dodd. Do tell me more about it."

Joan disciplined a chuckle. Her father had escaped. Was Craig Lamont straining at the leash? He didn't have to stay. She'd never known a man yet who couldn't worm his way out of a boring situation. She switched her attention in time to hear Miss Dodd say;

"There will be a very exclusive list of patronesses, dear Mrs. Crofton. I hope you

219

will allow us to use your name. Sally Shaw has promised her help. Your mother has changed since the last time I saw her, Craig."

"What do you mean, changed?" Lamont's voice was sharp with anxiety.

Miss Dodd sniffed and shrugged heavy shoulders;

"Grown older, of course, even Sally, marvelous youth-preserver that she is, couldn't grow younger, I suppose. It can't be too pleasant for her to have her former daughter-in-law at the Inn — calling herself Señorita Nadja Donesca. And now that the woman has started the fight for possession of her child — she's doing it for the notoriety as well as money if you ask me —"

"But, I didn't ask you," Craig Lamont reminded savagely. "Mrs. Crofton can't possibly be interested in our family affairs."

Miss Dodd smirked and rose.

"How like your mother you are, Craig. She shut me off, too. I happen to know when the case is to be heard. I'll be there. There'll be a lot of splash for headlines. Why shouldn't I get the money for it as well as any other writer?"

Jerry Slade breezed into the room, seized Patty Crofton's hand and lifted it to his lips before he put an arm about Joan's shoulders and grinned at her.

"Here I am, darling. The original bad penny. Kept away as long as I could. Thought you'd be missing me by this time. I'm now a member in good and regular standing of the Country Club here. Glad?"

Joan hastily freed herself from the possessive arm. She saw the Dodd woman's eyes sharpen like the eyes of a stout elderly fox which has glimpsed a plump partridge in the underbrush, heard her gulp, as if she were swallowing a huge chunk of gossip before she cooed;

"How delightful to see such spontaneity in these hard-boiled days." She shook a pudgy finger at Jerry Slade. "You have a charming fiancée, young man."

Joan was too angry to deny the implication. Patty Crofton quickly contradicted;

"You're jumping at conclusions, Miss Dodd. Joan is not engaged. Must you go?"

Drucilla Dodd looked at her before she said suavely;

"I was going before you so hospitably suggested it, Mrs. Crofton. I'm slated to dine with one of the city's socialites tonight. She is to give a series of dinners and has promised me the details for publication. I left my car in your drive. I can make Boston in time if Craig will come out and start it for me. I

221

never know when it will balk."

She shook hands with her hostess. Turned to Joan.

"My dear, how fortunate you are to have two strings to your bow. So far-seeing of your Uncle to set you down next door to a rich, eligible — if stony-hearted — bachelor like Craig." She shook a pudgy finger and intoned like a delphic oracle. "But don't get discouraged, even stone will chip, my dear, even stone will chip, if you keep steadily at it. Good-afternoon, everybody."

Patty Crofton's wide eyes followed her as she preceded Craig Lamont from the room. They sparkled with laughter as they came back to her daughter, her voice simulated terror as she implored;

"Follow them, Joan! There was murder in his eyes! He may do something terrible to her."

"If he doesn't, I will," Joan declared savagely. "Pest! I'd like to swish her in boiling oil and she isn't the only one, either. I've positively no use for a bad penny. I hate 'em, so don't come back again, Jerry. Goodbye!" She flung the last words over her shoulder as she crossed the threshold.

She was still burning with anger as in her work room she opened the package from Hollywood. She read the card enclosed;

"It's supposed to be a good luck bracelet.
It has your birthstone.
Couldn't resist buying it for you.

Love, Viv."

Joan slipped the bracelet on her wrist. It was of heavy carved flowers in green and yellow gold with centres of synthetic sapphires. She nodded approval. Effective. Smart. It would be if Viv selected it.

She answered a knock at the door.

"Who is it?"

"Craig Lamont. Your mother said I might come up and see the Bus Line folders you promised to show me."

The charm of the bracelet had calmed the tempest of anger which had sent her dashing up the stairs, but as Joan crossed the room two sentences which Peggy had quoted popped up in her mind with the unexpectedness and celerity of a Jack-in-the-box.

"When are you going to start pushing that lad off the Crofton map, boss? We need her in our business."

Undoubtedly that had been the reason behind Craig Lamont's invitation to drive her home. He needed her in his business. He had been so friendly and — and heartwarming that she had almost liked him, and all the time he had merely wanted her work.

Hadn't he seen Janvers that day? Hadn't that unbearable Drucilla Dodd said that it was too amazing to see him with a girl? Evidently he didn't object to being with a girl when his business interests were at stake.

"Hello! Gone to sleep in there?"

He could laugh about it. Sure of her wasn't he? She said crisply;

"No. I've changed my mind about showing you the folders."

"Why? Have I lost you again? Look here, you're not foolish enough to be angry at what the Pest said, are you?" The hint of steel in his voice sent a small chill tremor through her veins.

She said briefly that she wasn't.

"Did Slade change your mind for you?"

"Are you intimating that I have no mind of my own?"

"Joan, firing questions and answers back and forth like this is ridiculous. Open the door."

"May I remind you that this is my room and my door?"

There was an instant of silence then a cool clipped voice agreed;

"You're right. I'm going. Good-bye."

Joan took one quick step forward, stopped. The note of finality in his voice tightened her throat. Had he meant that he never would come back? Why were he and she forever quarreling? She had loved the drive home with him, had been blissfully content and happy, had thought;

"I've found a friend."

And then the Dodd woman had intimated that she, Joan Crofton, if she played her cards right could get the glamorous Craig Lamont if she wanted him. Cat! Why had she had to be in the drawing room to spoil everything?

XVII

The troubled query recurred again to the rhythm of strings and horns as several hours later Joan sat on the rail of the Club veranda with her head tipped back against a pillar. She had sent her partner for an ice. Curious how the moment she began to be friendly with Craig Lamont something occurred to re-kindle her dislike of him.

Through a window she could see her mother and father dancing. Their faces were grave. Ever since they had heard of Vivian's mix-up in the diamond theft, they had been anxious about her, had felt that she was in danger while the thief was at large.

David Crofton's arm tightened about his wife, who was lovely in a pale green frock which billowed like waves of the sea. His lips moved. She looked up and met his eyes. In an instant their faces were alight with laughter.

Joan dabbed at suddenly wet lashes. Those two weren't just lovers, they were companions, friends, wonderful friends. How different her mother's life and ideals were from those of Señorita Nadja Donesca, who in a gay flowered frock, which had nothing in the back above the waist but shoulder straps, had just detached herself from a group of men with whom she had been talking and walked away by herself. Apparently her unsavory record as Carl Lamont's wife had not hurt her popularity in some quarters.

"I'll bet we landed Janvers and the Straight As A Crow Flies Bus Line account today, Joan. As a team we're unbeatable."

Philip Bard sent his assured voice ahead of him as he approached. It jolted her out of her reflections. He was smiling as he twisted one end of his small black mustache, his dark eyes were alight with triumph. Sleek was the word for him, sleek from the top of his head to the toes of his shoes, his mind was sleek too, Joan thought with distaste. This was the psychical moment to inform him that she wouldn't be a party to account-snitching.

"I don't intend —"

He interrupted.

"You're a knock-out in that silvery blue gown with the moonlight touching your hair. If Janvers could see you now we'd nail him. Boy, that's an idea! He's here as my guest. He hinted he'd like to swim in the social pond when he comes to this part of the country, and as I'm eating out of his hand till I land him with your bus folders — I brought him along. I'll get him."

Joan waited only for him to enter the Club House before she slipped away to the opposite side of the veranda. She didn't want to meet Janvers and she didn't intend to. Philip Bard had admitted he was using every lure possible to get the man's business. Her Bus Line folders was one of the lures he wouldn't get.

He would find her if she remained here. She ran lightly down the steps and across the dark lawn. Her feet kept time to the music of the orchestra. Faint and far away thunder rumbled. The moonlight was on the other side of the house. She would curl up in the seat, enticingly sequestered behind blue spruces, where she had read Viv's letter. She had a lot to think about. After the battle fought behind the door of her room this afternoon, would Craig Lamont want her to go to the mountain with him tomorrow?

The music had the far-away effect of an off-stage orchestra when she reached the spruces. From the other side of the tree wind-break came a man's tense voice;

"Couldn't meet you. Had a hunch I was

being spotted. I'm in a jam. You know why. Had to come to you. Detectives after me. You've got to hide me and my side-kick."

Joan pressed her hand hard against her pounding heart. What had she stumbled on? What should she do? She heard the murmur of a voice. A woman's? Caught the word "Al." "Al!" Al Dawn was the name on the thief-wanted circular in the village post-office. The man's voice again.

"O.K. Meet you at midnight — What's that? I don't hear a sound. I'll look."

Joan dropped to her knees. Suppose she were caught by a man who was being hunted? There was movement on the other side of the trees. Would he find her? She held her breath. He was coming!

The orchestra crashed in a finale. With laughter and gay voices the dancers spilled from the Club House, ran down the steps, raced across the lawn to secure the seques-tered seats behind the wind-breaks.

"Here comes a crowd!" the man whispered. "Beat it. We'll be waiting. Bring that —"

There was furtive movement the other side of the spruces.

Joan crouched where she was until she joined the tide of dancers surging back to the Club House at the invitation of horns and strings.

Her pulses were quick-stepping as she again perched on the veranda rail. She'd better collect her thoughts before she was claimed for a dance. Was the man who had been behind the blue spruces the thief wanted by the United States Bureau of Investigation? The woman had called him "Al." What should she do about it? Craig had said to do nothing when she had told him that she was sure she had seen in the Library the man whose picture was on the wall of the post-office. Had he a sweetheart among the maid-servants at the Club? She was to meet him at midnight. Where?

"Well, my luck is holding. Think of finding you alone. All over your mad at me, darling?"

Jerry Slade's voice scattered Joan's thoughts. They whirled for an instant like scraps of paper caught in a hurricane before they settled into a now-or-never pattern. Life seemed to be just one problem after another. Apparently her outburst this afternoon had not made a dent in Jerry's assurance. She must be a futile sort of person if she couldn't make a man realize that she meant what she said. She would make one more attempt. She smilingly but inexorably withdrew the hand he had caught in his.

"Jerry, you are one of the most intelligent men I know, but you are dumb where I am concerned. Can't you understand that I don't love you, never will love you? Won't you stop proposing to me every time you see me?"

His face settled into what she had named his "Pilot look." His lips stiffened in a stubborn line, relaxed into a forced smile.

"Sorry not to oblige, darling. I'd like to be big-hearted Jerry, fade away and leave you to these other men, but it isn't my way of doing things. Try, try again is my rule of life. As that fat woman said this afternoon; 'Constant chipping will wear away stone.' I won't stop trying to make you love me till you're married to another man."

Joan met the ardent gleam in his eyes and knew that he was speaking the truth.

"How can I get rid of him, how can I?" she demanded of herself. Once she had asked her father that question and he had answered;

"Tell him that you're in love. That will convince him."

That wouldn't do any good. Jerry had said he wouldn't give up until she was married. Why not tell him she was engaged? It wasn't marriage, but it might help. With sudden determination, she confided;

"Then you'd better strap on your parachute, Jerry. You're on the verge of a crackup. I'm engaged." She dropped her lashes as if to hide the radiance in her eyes. Vivian wasn't the only actress in the family.

"Who is he?"

His voice was rough. He gripped her hands with a force that cut the star-sapphire ring into her finger.

"I shan't tell you his name yet, Jerry. Mother and father will announce my engagement formally at the proper time."

That statement was true, at least, she comforted her pricking conscience. If ever she were engaged they would announce it, wouldn't they? She was appalled at the ease with which the lie had tripped from her lips. If anyone had asked her an hour ago, she would have sworn that she was a truthful person. Why feel guilty? She was improvising for his good as well as her own, wasn't she? The deeper she cut now the quicker his wound would heal.

She saw his white, stunned face. Her eyes were dreamy with simulated rapture as she exulted;

"Jerry, he's wonderful! He's tall and straight and dark and terribly good-looking, he's making his mark in politics, and when I'm with him I think, as Saint somebody or other said;

" 'Nothing is so strong as gentleness. Nothing so gentle as real strength.' "

What had sent the quotation her mother had used in reference to David Crofton surging to the surface of her mind? she asked herself. She was thorough when she started on a campaign.

Jerry Slade regarded her with eyes on fire.

"I recognize him. I don't have to wait for your father and mother to announce the engagement. It's that advertising man, Lamont," he declared vehemently.

"Did I hear my name?" inquired a voice. From the lawn Craig Lamont pulled himself to the porch rail and perched there beside Joan. He looked from the girl's startled eyes to the man's white face before he said lightly;

"I did hear my name, didn't I? I saw you sitting here and came to ask for a dance, Joan. Hope you were saying something nice about the absent."

Slade scowled at him with tragic eyes.

"I'll say it was something nice. Joan was telling me she was engaged to you." He looked at the horrified girl. "I said I wouldn't give up until you were married,

darling, and believe it or not, I won't," he
flung at her and turned on his heel.

"Jerry! Come back! You know —"

Craig Lamont caught her arm.

"Just a minute, Joan. What's it all
about?"

"I didn't mention your name, I didn't,"
she protested frantically. The last word was
submerged in a blare of strings and horns.

In answer Lamont dropped to the lawn,
caught her about the waist and swung her
over the rail. Her protest was stifled against
his shoulder.

"Can't hear a word you say here. Come
on."

He drew her along grass paths bordered
with fragrant flowers which were colorless
in the dim light. In the shadow of a rustic
arbor which was like a dusky island in a
silver wash of moonlight, he stopped. From
a distance drifted the music of the swing orchestra, muted, throbby, the faint rumble of
thunder.

"Now tell me all about it," he com-
manded.

Hands pressed against her breast in an attempt to quiet her pounding heart, Joan
looked at him. She met his eyes, clear,
intent, unsmiling. What could she say? How
explain Jerry Slade's tirade? If he were any

other man in the world she could laugh it off, they would make a joke of it together, but with Craig Lamont —

"Well, what's it all about?" he demanded. "Slade congratulates me on my engagement to you and you look as terrified as if you were being accused of murder. Would it be such a bad break to be engaged to me?"

The low vehemence of his voice beat against her heart. The roof of the rustic arbor seemed to echo it. She stepped out of the seductive shadow into bright moonlight away from the voice. Explained breathlessly;

"It's a mistake, really it is. I — I — Jerry Slade won't believe that I don't love him, never will love him. He said he wouldn't stop proposing to me until I was mar— married. And then — and then —"

"Take your time, adorable," Craig Lamont came close and brushed back a lock of her chestnut hair. "And don't be frightened."

"I'm not frightened, I'm not," Joan protested hotly. "I'm furious with myself. It was so stupid of me and I loathe being stupid. I told Jerry that I was engaged and then my imagination gnawed its rope — it's good when it gets a start — and I described a man and — and he jumped to the conclusion that it was you. As if there isn't more than one man in the world tall and straight and dark and terribly good-looking, who is making his mark in politics."

"I see. And you didn't mean me?" There was a disturbing note of laughter in his low voice.

"Of course I didn't mean you! I'm glad you can take it as a joke, I can't. If you hadn't held me I would have stopped Jerry Slade. You don't know him as I do. He's furious with me. I had no thought of you in my mind when I told him that rigmarole. I'd never fall in love with you, never, if you were the only man in the world."

She caught his sleeve.

"Do something, anything. Find Jerry and stop him from spreading that silly story. Don't you understand? Everyone knows that you don't care for girls. They'll laugh in their sleeves and think that I —"

Footsteps on the gravel path. Joan tried to draw him back to the shadow of the summer house. Too late. Philip Bard called;

"Well, here you are, just where I told Janvers to meet us. I've been hunting everywhere for you, Joan, and all the time you're with my business rival. Trying to steal my No. 1 artist, Lamont?"

Craig Lamont shook his head. His voice

picked up Joan's heart and held it beatless as he said;

"Not trying to steal your artist, Bard. Just talking to Joan. Evidently you haven't heard of our engagement."

XVIII

"What do you mean, engagement?"

Philip Bard's sharp question covered Joan's gasp of surprise. Had Craig Lamont really announced their engagement? It was amazing. It was stupefying. It was incredible. Perhaps she hadn't heard the words. Perhaps it was a nightmare. Perhaps the man's voice behind the blue spruces had been a dream too?

She frowned at the Great Dipper high in the north and followed the curve of the handle around to the southeast. That bright star in the end was Arcturus. Masses of cloud above the hills shimmered with lightning, rumbled as if an embattled army were cannonading. She wouldn't be likely to see and hear all that if she were dreaming, would she? She put her hand to her hair. The lock which Craig had smoothed back a while ago was stirring in the rising wind. The wind was real. She was awake.

Her eyes flashed from face to face. Philip Bard's was mottled with anger. Craig Lamont's was white. He answered Bard's question;

"Is it necessary to have the word engaged explained to you, Phil? Engagements happen every day — I've been told."

"Does this mean that you won't work for me any more, Joan?" Bard demanded furiously.

Joan came out of her coma.

"It isn't true —"

"Joan means that it isn't true that she won't work for you, Phil," Craig Lamont interrupted. "Why shouldn't she? I'm not engaged to the artist, I'm engaged to the girl."

"And who is eet who is engaged to a girl?" inquired Señorita Nadja Donesca as she stepped from the purple shadow of a pine. Even in the dim light, Joan could see that her face was drawn and colorless, that two sharp lines cut between her wide green eyes.

"It's Lamont and Joan. They're engaged," Philip Bard flung the explanatory bomb straight at her.

"Craig! Engaged!"

Had the venom in Señorita Nadja Donesca's eyes been deadly rays, Joan would have dropped where she stood. She shivered. Lamont laid his arm lightly about her shoulders.

"Come on. Let's dance."

Joan thought for an instant that the woman staring at them would spring forward and claw with her clenched fingers. A flash of lightning, nearer now, set her green eyes a-glitter as she reminded maliciously;

"You have turned down my offer to compromise, Craig. Day after tomorrow you weel come to court. Both of you. Watch me fight for Peggy and keep her. My best weeshes, Mees Crofton. *Por Dios!* You weel need them marrying into that familee. Mother-in-law trouble, if you get what I mean. And do not be sure that you have Craig for always. Come wif me, Phileep — I was looking for you. I haf something of great importance to ask you. We weel leave the lofers, yes?"

She slipped her hand under Philip Bard's arm and drew him along the path. The murmur of voices drifted back till the two figures were lost in the green gloom of a grove.

A man appeared from among the trees and stared after them. It was Janvers in the perfection of evening clothes. He breathed as if he had been running. The words halted, rasped as he explained and questioned;

"Bard told me to look him up, that he'd be in this summer house. Who was the woman with him, Lamont? In a tantrum, wasn't she? I've heard that voice before.

Didn't I see her come out of your office today?"

Craig thought quickly. Nadja had said that Janvers had turned to look after her as they passed in the corridor outside the Lamont Agency office. Had he recognized her? He was excited now. Suppose the man knew something about her which would stop her fight for the child? He explained;

"The woman with Bard is my brother Carl's widow. Now she calls herself Señorita Nadja Donesca. She claims to be the daughter of a Mexican general, who at one time was enormously wealthy."

"Little Maggie a rich Mexican general's daughter and a widow!" Janvers' laugh grated. "What do you know about that!"

"What do you know about it?" Lamont demanded.

Janvers smoothed his chin with a well kept hand adorned with a huge intaglio ring.

"You say that woman is your brother's widow?"

"Yes, she is dragging the family — and Miss Crofton as a witness — into court day after tomorrow in a fight to get the custody of her child."

"So, there's a child," Janvers reflected aloud. "Come to my office tomorrow morning, Lamont, and I'll give you a few facts that may help in your fight. I'm leaving here at once. Bard said he'd propose me for membership but if Maggie — my mistake, Señorita what's-her-name — belongs to this Club, it ain't class enough for me. Goodnight, Miss Crofton. I'll be seeing you. Lamont has agreed to get you on my ads."

Joan's sense of nightmare persisted. She was in an agony of bewilderment. She must wake up. She must. What did she care about Nadja Donesca's past life when her own was being snarled by this stupid engagement story? She frowned at Craig Lamont.

"I hoped it was only a hideous dream. Why, why did you do it?" she demanded furiously.

His steady eyes met hers.

"Do what?"

"Do what! Don't be so — so wooden. You know what I mean. Why did you say we were — were —"

"Is engaged the word you're fumbling for?"

"I'm not fumbling for anything. Having landed me in this mix-up —"

"Did I land you in this mix-up?"

"You're not intimating that I told Jerry Slade that you were the man I was going to marry, are you? As I told you before —"

"If I were the only man in the world you

wouldn't fall in love with me. You needn't repeat it. The fact is impressed on my memory."

"I'm glad something I have said this fiendish evening has registered. Now, having told Phil Bard that — that — something that isn't true, what are you going to do next?"

His eyes smiling, reckless, met the scorn in hers. His glance dropped to her mutinous mouth.

"What usually follows an engagement, adorable?"

He caught her in his arms and pressed his lips warm and tender on hers. He released her suddenly.

"I'm sorry," he said huskily.

"Sorry! Sorry! Is that all —" the wild pounding of Joan's heart choked off her voice.

"Jo!"

David Crofton spoke from the path. His wife stood beside him. Joan's face burned with color. How long had they been there? Had they seen — she couldn't say it even to herself. Her father said in a low voice;

"Jerry Slade told us that you and Craig were engaged. It can't be true. You wouldn't tell him before you told your mother and me, would you, dear?"

"I'll explain —"

"You won't! You won't! You've done harm enough," Joan interrupted Craig Lamont. "It's such a mess, Davy. Such a mess. I told you that some day Jerry Slade would tie my life up in a hard knot. He has."

Her voice broke on the last word. David Crofton slipped an arm about his daughter.

"Take it easy, Jo. Take it easy. Tell us what it's all about."

To the accompaniment of distant reverberations of thunder, brokenly, breathlessly, Joan poured out the story of her conversation on the veranda of the Club House with Jerry Slade. She reminded her father of his advice that the next time he made himself objectionable, she'd better tell him of her love for someone else.

"You did suggest that, didn't you, Davy?"

"I did. But, did I advise you to name the object of your passion?"

"Don't laugh about it, don't! Can't you see what a mix-up it all is? I didn't name — anyone, I didn't. I just described an imaginary person. I said the man I was engaged to was wonderful, tall and straight and dark and terribly good-looking, that he was making his mark in politics and then to round out the picture I quoted that bit of Francis de Sales about strength and gentleness, Mother is always saying about you.

Are you listening to me?"

David Crofton shifted his thoughtful eyes from Craig Lamont to his daughter's troubled face.

"You needn't tell me any more, Jo. I know the rest. Jerry Slade jumped to the conclusion that your synthetic sketch — purely synthetic, I understand that — was of Craig Lamont. He came post-haste to your Mother and me with the story. I knew at once what had happened, that you had taken my advice about stopping his pursuit of you. I fixed him with a cold eye and warned;

" 'Slade, Joan doesn't want that known at present. If you let a word of it leak out, I'll break your neck.' He looked as startled as if a favorite dog had bitten him, straightened and gave me back icy glare for icy glare and said stiffly;

" 'I shan't let a word leak, sir. Goodnight!'

"So you see, my dear, there's nothing to worry about. We'll consider the episode closed."

"It isn't closed, Mr. Crofton," Craig Lamont's voice was cool and clear. "Joan had said that Slade would spread the news from one end of the Club to the other. So, the moment I had a chance I confirmed it.

245

You wouldn't have had me deny it, would you?"

"Was consideration for Joan the only reason you confirmed it?"

There was a smile deep in Craig Lamont's eyes as they met David Crofton's.

"It was not, sir."

"Of course it wasn't," Joan broke in angrily. "Janvers wants me to work for him, threatened to take his business to Phil Bard if the Lamont Agency couldn't get me on his account and when Phil appeared suddenly a few minutes ago he — he —"

"Craig is the name," Lamont supplied deftly.

Joan's glance should have withered him before she added;

"Said we — we — were —"

"Engaged," Lamont finished for her.

"What can we do about it, Davy? What can we do, Mother?

"Honey, don't get so excited," the Southern drawl of Patty Crofton's voice was accentuated, a sign of inner excitement. "Look at those masses of dark clouds. There's a tempest coming. Let's go back to our house now, have a snack while we hold a sort of council of war and plan what is to be done. Craig must be considered."

"Craig! Craig! I think I'm the one to be

considered," Joan interrupted furiously. "He got me into this mix-up, didn't he?"

"Well, suppose for purposes of argument, we admit he did. Every accused is innocent until he is proved guilty, isn't he?"

"Davy Crofton — you won't take this seriously. Don't you realize that this last hour has been just one hundred percent nightmare? Don't you care that I feel as if I'd been forcibly fed to a man whose only interest in me is to use me in a business fight? Can't you see that I'm a wishbone commercial artist?"

"Instead of going into a fury about it, you ought to be thankful that you're good enough to be wanted by two rival firms," her father suggested practically. "You're taking this altogether too seriously, Jo. It isn't like you, I don't understand it. Come home, dear. I'll take you along. Craig, bring Mrs. Crofton, will you?"

"If Craig Lamont goes to The Mansion, I won't," Joan warned defiantly.

XIX

Craig Lamont stood with his back to the mantel in his mother's blue and silver boudoir. She was as lovely and wide-eyed as if he hadn't roused her from sleep.

"Sorry to pull you out of bed at midnight, Sally Shaw, but I wanted you to hear the story from me first," he explained.

She tightened the belt of the pale blue satin coat over her matching pajamas, dangled a silver mule from the toes of a bare foot.

"I was awake. I couldn't sleep in this storm, Craig. What a crash! Hear the rain! It's coming down in torrents. It would have been hard to forgive you if you hadn't come directly to your mother. Life is kaleidoscopic, isn't it? One never knows when the pattern will shift. I don't wonder Joan is furious at being railroaded into an engagement. What little demon prompted you to confirm it?"

"What else could I do? Joan had said that Slade would broadcast the news. I couldn't deny it, could I?"

"But, it hadn't been broadcast. Apparently David Crofton was quite capable of scotching the rumor. You didn't by any chance want it to be true, did you?"

"As if you didn't know that I love Joan, Sally Shaw."

"The gods be praised! I thought you never would recognize the symptoms, my boy. I wanted to wake you up, I love her, too. I was afraid you might lose her — but the Senator ordered me to let you alone. You know how afraid of him I am."

"Yes, I know, you and the Senator. You and he make me think of the Croftons. A man and woman who are still grand friends and lovers after years together. You four have restored my faith in marriage, have made me believe in the fairy-story ending 'and they lived happily ever after.' If Joan once loved a man, she wouldn't fail him — ever. I did want the engagement to be true, but I didn't want it to come true that way."

He walked to the window. Hail beat and clamored at the glass. He watched a chain of lightning zig-zag across the sky, waited until the crash which followed had rumbled away among the hills before he admitted gloomily;

"Joan hadn't much use for me before, but she had promised she would go on a picnic to the mountain with me tomorrow —" he glanced at the crystal and silver clock, "it is already to-day. I suppose that's on the toboggan. Hatred pretty nearly expresses her sentiments now. She's furious. Refused to talk the matter over."

"I can't understand why she didn't deny it at once, why she didn't tell Philip Bard that it wasn't true."

"She started to and I stopped her."

"Why? It would have been so much better to have laughed it off as an amusing mistake. There would have been the buzz as of a million bees let loose then the talk would have died down. Now it's a mix-up. Won't Joan agree to let the engagement stand for the present?"

Lamont turned and with hands thrust hard into the pockets of his dinner jacket, faced his mother. Should he tell her that Nadja also knew of the engagement, and of Janvers' recognition of the woman who had been her son's wife? "Maggie," he had called her, nothing Mexican about that name. In her outburst of protest in the boudoir weeks ago, Sally Shaw had said that she suspected that Nadja was not high-class Mexican. How right she had been. If he told her now that her judgment had been confirmed it would bring back the bitterness and pain. He would wait until after he had talked with Janvers before he told her that she had been right in her appraisal of Carl's wife.

"Are you dreaming, Craig? What a crash! It shook the house. You haven't answered my question. I'll repeat it. Won't Joan agree to let the engagement stand?"

"I wasn't dreaming, Mother. Joan insists that she will tell how the misunderstanding arose."

"It would make much less talk if she would let the situation remain as it is for a week or two. Nothing is more easily broken these days than an engagement — unless it is a marriage. I'll talk to her."

"She won't change."

"I'll try to make her see reason. I'll go to The Mansion today. I will have to wait until after lunch."

"Go if you like, but she won't consent," Craig Lamont prophesied.

He had been right — Joan had courteously but firmly refused.

"I can't let it stand, Mrs. Shaw, really I can't. Besides, I've answered a dozen phone congratulations already and denied the engagement. Your son has told you that the mix-up came because of a silly lie I told. How was I to know that the man to whom I confessed an undying passion — I must

251

have been good — would jump to the conclusion that I was talking of Craig Lamont?"

"And of course you weren't?"

The amused question sent hot color to
Joan's hair. She retorted with more heat
than courtesy.

"I should say not. I don't even like him.
Never have liked him. Never will like him.
Sorry if I've hurt your feelings."

She felt gauche and young and crude as
Mrs. Shaw denied lightly;

"Of course my feelings are not hurt, my
dear. You don't think me one of those
foolish mothers who expects all girls to fall
at the feet of her son, do you? I'm only
trying to see this thing through smoothly.
This mix-up — as you call it, is an annoyance to you — but it's more than an annoyance to Craig. It may wreck his happiness."

"What do you mean?"

The gravity of Mrs. Shaw's voice was like
the grip of a steel hand on Joan's heart. Had
her silly story to Jerry Slade hurt Craig
Lamont? His side of it hadn't occurred to
her. But, she hadn't said she loved him, had
she? Jerry had picked his name out of a clear
sky.

"I wonder if I can trust you and tell you
something?" Mrs. Shaw's voice jerked Joan
back to reality.

"I hope I can be trusted," she snapped.

"Of course you can, my dear, of course you can. I was merely thinking out loud. I don't know what Craig would say if he knew I was betraying his confidence — but, you ought to know that he is in love with a charming girl. He's mad about her. It is his first love affair since his freshman days. Carl's unfortunate marriage embittered him. The Senator and I were so pleased. He was about to ask her to marry him when out of pure chivalry, he came to your rescue."

Joan closed her eyes and opened them. The greenish-blue paneled walls of the drawing room hadn't fallen down upon her, the mirror above the Adam mantel still reflected the white-haired woman in her lilac print frock. Something had crashed somewhere. She felt as if she couldn't breathe. Craig Lamont in love? Did he kiss the girl as he had kissed her last night? The memory sent fire licking through her veins, set her heart pounding. She protested passionately;

"But he need not have come to my rescue. I didn't mention his name to Jerry. I just drew a picture with words as I make a sketch on paper. I only said that the man to whom I was engaged was wonderful and tall and straight and dark and terribly good-looking and — and in politics. Isn't there more than one man like that in the world?"

"Of course there is, my dear. Pretty stupid of your friend Jerry to think you were describing Craig. But, men in love aren't noted for clear thinking. Try to drop the annoying thing from your mind. The excitement over the engagement — Craig is so well known and liked that there will be excitement — will blow over. Even in this small town something is bound to happen which will push it from local dinner-table gossip."

She rose and held out her hand.

"Don't let this spoil the friendship between you and me. I like you very, very much, remember."

"And I think you're wonderful. It's maddening that this should have hap—" Joan bit her lips to steady them.

Mrs. Shaw patted her shoulder.

"Never mind, dear, never mind. Things will straighten out. Things have a marvelous, unbelievable way of straightening out."

Seraphina appeared at the door with a long box.

"Dey's for you, Miss Jo-an. Flowers, de boy said. I'll bet you won't make me throw dem in de pond."

"Put the box on the table, Seraphina. That will be all."

As the maid left the room Joan flared;

"See that? Flowers! Phone calls! Mother and father had to go to town today. I'm alone. I have to answer. I can't stand it. I won't. What shall I do?"

The fact that tears welled in her eyes only added to her anger. She hid her face against Mrs. Shaw's shoulder.

"There, there, my dear. You're making a mountain out of a molehill. Go off somewhere this afternoon and leave the flowers and phone calls to Seraphina."

Joan raised her head and blinked wet lashes.

"Sorry. Didn't mean to turn sob-sister. It isn't like me, really it isn't. I — I'm a stranger to myself. That's a grand suggestion of yours to make a get-away, but where can I go? Mother and father have the car."

"Why not keep your date with Craig? He told me that you and he had planned a mountain picnic for this afternoon. Here he is, now. Come in, Craig and advise us. Joan is being flooded with congratulations and flowers. She wants to escape. I suggested that she keep her date with you."

"Did she need the suggestion?"

Was Craig Lamont really as surprised as his voice and eyes indicated? Joan wondered. Was it possible that he had expected her to go after last night? As if he divined her thoughts he reminded;

"You crossed your throat and hoped-to-die promised that you would go with me this afternoon, Joan. I expect you to keep that promise. Better change to something warmer than that linen thing you're wearing. The thermometer dropped thirty degrees after last night's storm. That's our New England climate. It will be cold on top of the mountain after the sun goes down, and we're to see the sun set, remember."

"I don't care if I did promise, some promises are better broken than kept," Joan declared rebelliously. "I'm not —"

Seraphina resembled nothing so much as a grinning black gargoyle as she plodded into the room with a florist's box in her hand.

"More flowers for you, Miss Jo-an. I guess we folks'll have to borrow some vases. Yes, Mam. An' a lady jest telephoned to ask if you was at home, said she was comin' right over to congrat-congeratulate —"

"That will do. Put the boxes on the table, Seraphina."

As the maid left the room, Joan looked at Craig Lamont.

"I'll go. I'll do anything to get away from this terrible house."

The last word floated back from the stairs. Mrs. Shaw smiled at her son.

"So far Victory perches on your banner, Craig. Watch your step, my dear, if you want to keep it there. Sunsets and mountain-tops are heady."

"Think I don't realize that? Cool, calm friendliness is my role — if I can keep in character. Thanks for talking with Joan. It helped."

His mother's eyes shone with laughter.

"Not nearly so much as a little story I told and the flowers I sent. Those were a positive inspiration. I timed them to come while I was here."

"You and your inspirations! Did you send all of those boxes, Sally Shaw?"

"Yes. Without cards. It eases my heart to see you smile, Craig. It hurts me so to have you hurt."

"Hey, no tears." He put his arm about her shoulders and kissed her tenderly. "If I can't straighten out this mix-up to my satisfaction — and Joan's — I'm no good and deserve to be hurt."

"It's an ill wind that blows nobody good. Your engagement story has taken my mind off our appearance in court tomorrow. Before, I couldn't keep it out of my mind. Did you see the Senator?"

"Spent a large portion of the morning with him. He's pulling strings to have the hearing on Nadja's petition behind closed doors. She's all for publicity — slathers of it. Don't worry about tomorrow. I have a hunch — Here's Joan."

Mrs. Shaw smiled as she spoke to the girl.

"You are a quick dresser, my dear. You would please the Senator, he declares that I'm congenitally late. That blue tweed frock with the matching topcoat is just the thing for a mountain picnic. Run along. I'll stay and put the flowers in water."

"Flowers!" Joan frowned at the long boxes. "Don't put them in water, please. Will you look for the cards and have Seraphina take them back to the senders?"

"That would be the simplest thing to do, wouldn't it? Run along — wait a minute! Are you taking anything to eat? You'll be ravenous when you reach the mountain."

"I'd hate to tell you what is in the hamper in the roadster, Sally Shaw, you'd never let it go," her son answered. "Something you like. Come on, Joan. We need every minute if we are to reach the top of the mountain before sunset. Don't expect us till you see us, Mother, but just to add a touch of melodrama to our expedition, if you see two lights on the mountain, rush to our rescue.

Remember that Carl and I worked out that signal? We never used it but once, worse luck." His mother nodded with tears in her eyes.

"I remember. Run along, children," she said gaily.

Joan's heart was lighter than it had been for hours as she looked back from the roadster and called to the white-haired woman on the porch.

"Thanks for helping. Will you leave a note so that Mother and Father will know where I've gone?"

Mrs. Shaw nodded and waved her hand. The car slid smoothly out into the highway just as a boy waving a special delivery letter and a long box dashed into the driveway.

He jerked off his cap with the speed and grace of a monkey on a hurdy-gurdy.

"Hi! Letter and flowers for you, Miss Crofton!" he shouted.

Joan took the letter. "Leave the box at the house," she said and added; "Ooch! More flowers!"

"Forget it. We're off on a party," Craig Lamont reminded lightly. "Let's agree that we won't even think of that confounded engagement until we get back to your house, will you?"

She nodded and slid down in the seat. She

watched the black road, bordered by green shrubs and the feathery foliage of trees, unwind like a spool of motion-picture film. Already her snarled nerves were relaxing under the smooth motion of the car, the rhythm of its wheels on macadam, the fragrant air, the glimpses of lovely gardens where the clear colors of peonies and iris were in bloom. She knew that gossip about herself and the man beside her was rampant in the village but they were leaving it farther and farther behind. After all, what did it matter what people thought who didn't count in her life? Those who really cared would understand. She had a feeling of irresponsibility, as if she had been caught in a swift, serene current and was being swept along without a care as to where it landed her.

They stopped at a crossroads to look at a sign and she heard the rush and splash and tinkle of a brook, which the storm of the night before had swollen. Sunlight set the chromium on passing cars ablaze. She hadn't slept at all last night, she remembered.

She looked up and met Lamont's friendly, smiling, hazel eyes. Of a sudden her world, which had been topsy-turvy, became a right-side up, stabilized world.

She acknowledged thoughtfully;

"Curious, isn't it, what a change of outlook will do to one's point of view? My emotions were tied in hard knots, now in this heavenly air, I realize that I was making an insurmountable mountain out of a silly little molehill."

She laughed;

"In spite of my late emotional spree, I still love life and if you shoot the roadster ahead like that, we're likely to crack-up against a tree, both of us."

"Sorry," Lamont reduced speed. "It was such a relief to find that you were back to normal that I stepped on the gas. Now that we've agreed to forget —"

"There's one thing I want to speak of and then we'll drop last evening into the bottom of our minds. What will the girl you want to marry think when she hears that engagement rumor — notice that I can refer to it with calm now — she's bound to hear of it."

"What do you know of the girl I want to marry?"

"Don't bite! Your mother —"

Joan broke off the sentence. Mrs. Shaw had told her about the girl with whom her son was in love, in confidence.

Craig Lamont laughed.

"So, mother told you about her, did she? I

thought Sally Shaw could keep a secret better than that. Just between you and me, Joan, I love the girl, deeply, tenderly. I wish I had asked her to marry me before — before yesterday — but even if she hears of what happened last evening — she probably won't, you have so consistently denied it today — she will understand when I explain. She has imagination and a flair for the dramatic. She may be a bit difficult at first but she'll see it my way — in time."

"You're magnificent! You must be very sure of her," Joan flouted.

He looked down, as if he were seeing something deep in her eyes. Looked back at the road and conceded;

"I'm sure of myself and that's half the battle."

"You and Jerry Slade," Joan commented crisply. "Well, that's that. The subject is now closed."

XX

Lamont stopped the roadster at a gas station in a small white church-spired village near the base of the mountain. From the open door drifted a radioed baritone voice singing.

"Every street I walk on
Becomes a lover's lane
When I'm with you. When —"

Abruptly the voice ceased. The man who dashed forward to service the car stopped, regarded the driver with incredulous eyes and a glittering gold-tooth grin before he approached with out-stretched hand.

"Shucks, but it's great to see you, Craig. How you been?" He nodded and winked at Joan. "The wife?"

"Miss Crofton, this is my old friend, Johnny Nolan. We fought our way through the eighth grade together."

"Pleased to meet any friend of Craig's," Nolan attested heartily. "He and me and Carl — say, Craig, I was sorry to hear about Carl. I had a queer feelin' that if you an' I'd been round, he wouldn't have had that acci-

263

dent. Remember how we used to pitch into Phil Bardoni or any other guy who gave him a dirty look?"

"I remember, Johnny. He doesn't need us now. Put in ten gallons of gas, will you?"

Nolan returned from filling the roadster's tank and leaned sociably on the door.

"How far you going?"

"To the top of the mountain. How's the road?"

"The town hasn't got to work on it yet and I'll bet last night's rain and wind raised hobs with it. Someone's opened a swell hotel on one of the other peaks — tain't quite so high as this one. Whoever it is has a pull with the Government and there's a big crew making a road."

"And the town fathers have let the road on this mountain go to the dickens. I get you. Have you had any reports on it?"

"Nope, nary a one. Everyone's shooting for the new place. That's human nature. A sedan stopped here for gas — at — well, I'd say 'twas 'bout three o'clock this morning, the storm was over then. Three guys in it. The fella drivin' said they was goin' up the mountain to see the sunrise. Struck me 'twas a cockeyed thing to do, but as I'm not setting out to run the world nor the people in it, I didn't say nothing except to ask 'em

264

to stop and report on the road when they came down."

"What did they say about it?"

"They didn't stop. The goin' may have been so rough it shook up their memories and they forgot. They were back in just about the time I allow for the trip up and down. When I heard their car I stuck my head out the bedroom window and yelled;

" 'How's the road?'

"They didn't stop to answer. I only had time to make out the number — 'twas a Mass license — before the red tail-light shot by. It may not be as bad as I think it is, but you won't find the road like a trottin' park."

Nolan chuckled and winked at Joan.

"I guess you know Craig well enough, Miss, to know that he ain't got it in him to turn back. The young men are getting in the saddle fast. Now that he's started in politics, we fellas that went to school with him expect to see him Governor one of these days."

Lamont laughed but Joan saw color rise under his bronzed skin.

"Is that a wish or a prophecy? Which ever it is you can see that I'm fairly lapping it up. I'll stop when we come back and report on the road. You have a snappy stand here, Johnny."

"It ain't too bad."

Nolan stepped to the door, pressed a button and the outlines of the building flashed with blue, green and red lights.

"How's that for class?"

"It's a smash-hit! I'll be seeing you, Johnny."

As the car shot forward Joan observed;

"If all your constituents are as enthusiastic as your friend, Mister Nolan, I shall look forward to shaking hands with Governor Lamont when he receives the populace in Memorial Hall in the State House on some February the twenty-second. Then I'll be boasting, 'I knew him when —' "

"Johnny's an optimist. He and Carl and I were in the grade school together in Carsfield. Mother believed in public school education — but — when her husband, Dan Shaw, was elected Senator, she wanted us within easy motoring distance and sent us to a Prep school near Washington. Here's the beginning of the mountain road, it winds and winds till it reaches the top. Look at the ruts. The rain must have rushed down in torrents. Think you can take it? If not, we'll turn back and go somewhere to dine and dance."

"Turn back! I never turn back. I'm like a rising young politician of whom I've heard

266

recently. 'Onward Christian Soldiers!' "

"Onward it is. Johnny was wrong about my never turning back. I'd turn back a dozen times before I would take you into danger. Also, I've given up flying."

"Why? Don't you like it? I love it. I have piloted Jerry Slade's plane."

"I think it's the greatest sport in the world, but, after Carl's accident, Mother asked me to give it up. Of course I did. It was so little to do for her who has done so much for me."

"Mothers are wonderful, aren't they?" she said softly.

"I'll say they are," Lamont answered fervently.

After that they were silent till a tremendous jolt bounced Joan out of her seat.

"What a bump," she gasped. "Our progress makes me think of an army tank maneuvering over hill and dale — mostly hill. I thought we wouldn't pull out of that hole."

"The first part of the road wasn't so bad. Hear that crashing of underbrush? It's a deer. There are plenty of them on the mountain. They are a pest to the farmers, they eat the young plants in their gardens. We're getting on. We've passed through the tall timber. The mountaintop is a tableland dotted with rocks and blueberry bushes.

Hear that thrush below us among the trees? Heart-twisting music, isn't it? See the top of the Inn chimney? I'll be glad to get you off this rough road."

The roadster took the last sharp rise like a bird on wings. Joan looked at the shabby building ahead. It was an Inn of another day. Years removed from the throbbing world of automobiles and airplanes. Horses had ploddingly drawn buckboards up the long, laborious mountain road to the wide doors which were shuttered now. Upper windows gazed with glazed lidless eyes at the illimitable stretch of sky and valley. The mountaintop was patched with rocks and low juniper and scraggly blueberry bushes. In a crevice of rock a valiant dandelion flaunted one yellow blossom. The hollow tap, tap, of a woodpecker drifted eerily from the roof.

The sound set Joan's nerves a-creep. Curious that it should affect her like that. She wasn't a jittery person. Resolutely she turned and looked at Craig Lamont who was lifting a hamper from the roadster standing in the curve of the drive before the Inn. Beyond him she could see the chimney of a small log cabin.

He set the hamper down and pulled two cushions from the rumble.

"Take these, Joan and your topcoat. We'll picnic on the other side of the house — the view from there is glorious. A panorama of east, west, north and south. We'll see the sun set and watch the moon come up."

Joan picked up the cushions and followed as he led the way.

"I hope the moon doesn't rise too late. We are a long way from home remember, and as your friend Johnny Nolan suggested, the mountain road is far from being a trotting park."

"Don't worry about getting home. The headlights on the roadster will reveal every crack and cranny. Here we are." He sniffed. "Smell wood smoke? Evidently someone else had our idea. Glad they didn't stay. We'll have the world to ourselves and what a world! Take a look through these."

Joan adjusted the field glasses he handed her. Through them she saw clearly the valley spotted with clumps of big trees, maples, oaks and gracefully spreading elms; fields and foothills; a bridge that hung like a spider's web above the white water of a shimmering river; villages that looked as if they might have been carved from mother-of-pearl; a chain of ponds glittering like polished mirrors and on a distant ridge, two buildings that reared faint and shadowy against the sky like painted houses on a painted back-drop. She recognized Silver Birches and The Mansion.

"The view from here is even more glorious than I dreamed it to be," Joan exclaimed.

"I'm glad. It's about once in a hundred times that experiences turn out better than one's dreams. Help unpack the hamper, will you? Hope I selected something you like."

Joan peeked into a covered thermos dish.

"It looks and smells marvelous. *Filets mignon,* luscious mushrooms, parsley-powdered snowy potato balls, little bunches of asparagus tips tied with gay red pimento ribbons and the last perfect touch a shoulder-knot of watercress and infant carrots. You've made a mistake, Mister, this isn't a picnic supper, it's a banquet."

Lamont laughed.

"I'm a growing boy. I can't live on sandwiches and scrambled eggs."

Iced fruit juice cocktails and an appetizing variety of hors d'oeuvres preceded the *filets* piping hot, with sandwiches, thin and tangy. Followed a dessert of maple eclairs with fragrant coffee, rich with cream.

Lamont produced a silver cigarette case and offered it to Joan. She shook her head.

"Don't you smoke?"

"No. I don't care for it, why acquire the habit? Viv and I decided against it. That reminds me — the special delivery. The letter was from my sister. Mind if I read it?"

"Go ahead. I'll re-pack the hamper."

"Viv's in her element," Joan remarked when a few minutes later he dropped to a cushion beside her and clasped his hands about one knee.

She folded the letter and watched the red-tinted gold of the afterglow spread over fields and turn ponds to a chain of colored beads.

"Mother told me she was making a stab at pictures. Any luck?" Lamont asked.

"Yes." In her pleased excitement over her sister's chance, Joan asked; "Want to hear about it? I'll read you parts. I won't bore you with the whole letter."

"You couldn't bore me." He cleared his voice. "I heard you chuckle once. Must be amusing. Shoot."

Joan ran her eyes over the first page.

"This is what they would call routine stuff, I suppose. About her tests and the directors with whom she talked. She has passed the personality and audition tests. This is the chuckle." She read;

"Last week I dined at the Banktons' gorgeous house. Interesting guests. The lawyer son was there — remember he came to my rescue when I got mixed up with the diamond thief? I told you I didn't notice him then, but I did that night — he's wonderful. Dark and lean with a flashing smile and eyes that see everything. He's like Dad. How did I find out? Listen, my child and you shall hear.

"I had been at the studio for hours. Came home and rushed to dress for dinner. When I entered the Banktons' drawing room I was hollow to my toes. They evidently had been waiting for me so when the butler passed a tray — I seized a glass of what looked like orange juice — you know, mother always serves orange juice on a cocktail tray in case a guest doesn't care for anything stronger — with the desperation of a water-soaked sailor grabbing for a life preserver. I drank it and refused hors d'oeuvres.

"What I had drunk wasn't orange juice I knew the moment it burned down my throat — and by the time I was seated at the table, the darned stuff had set me a-quiver — I presume because I never drink, it had virgin ground on which to work. I was frightened. I looked at the man beside me and whispered hoarsely;

" 'What's happened to me? I'm going to

sing! I've just got to sing.'

"He didn't laugh, though he must have wanted to shout at the country mouse. Instead, he beckoned to the butler, gave an order and before I could finish, 'I'm going to sing,' again he had laid some melba toast beside my plate and whispered;

" 'Eat it. Quick! You'll be all right in a minute.'

"You've heard of the way a starving man wolfs his food? I swallowed that toast at the same rate of speed. I knew that the man was watching me. When the third wafer had disappeared, he whispered;

" 'Better?'

"I looked up and met his smiling eyes, there was a trace of anxiety in them. I whispered back.

" 'All right. My family and hostess have been saved from disgrace. The little songbird in my throat has winged away.'

"We laughed together. 'Do you sing?' he asked. 'Not a note,' I answered, 'it was the cocktail. To whom am I indebted for the life saver?' He grinned. 'Oh, I'm only Mrs. Bankton's little boy.' Then I came to. 'The Crown Prince of the House of Bankton,' I said. 'Imagine my not knowing you after the way you saved me from jail. Now you've helped me again. Hope your fees for res-

cuing lovely ladies in distress aren't too tremendous.'

" 'We'll settle about the fees later. Tell
me what you've been doing since we met.'

"I told him. I hadn't talked long before I
discovered that he didn't approve of a
motion picture career for me. He's wonderful, Jo, and —"

Joan turned a page.

"We'll skip that. Wonderful men appear
in Viv's life at the rate of six a year. I can
imagine her eyes, big, brown, terrified and
irresistible as she gazed up appealingly at
the Crown Prince of the House of Bankton
and whispered;

" 'I've got to sing.' "

Lamont laughed.

"I don't wonder you chuckled over that
description. I'll wager anything you like
Bankton falls in love with her. Go on. Let's
have more of the letter."

"After that," Joan read on, "Neil Bankton
told me that they were still looking for my
diamond thief."

"What diamond thief?"

With her eyes on the red-gold glow
stealing over earth and sky, and tinting the
foam of a cascade frothing down the moun-
tainside, Joan told of Vivian's encounter
with the supposed jewel thief, of his threat

274

to shoot her; of her scream, of her appearance at Police Headquarters. She concluded;

"The story is as melodramatic as a gangster picture, as unbelievable as — My word!" she sprang to her feet.

"What is it, Joan? You're white!"

She looked furtively over her shoulder as she said very low;

"Am I? I don't wonder. Last night I heard a man whisper;

" 'Couldn't meet you. Had a hunch I was being spotted. I'm in a jam. You know why. Detectives after me. You've got to hide me and my sidekick.' "

"Steady, adorable. You're shaking. Where did you hear it?"

"At the Club. I was standing near the blue spruces."

"At the Club! Put on your coat. You're shivering."

"It isn't from cold, it's excitement. I caught the word 'Al' in a woman's low voice and then the man said;

" 'O.K. Meet you at midnight.'

"I must have moved for the woman thought she heard a sound. I dropped to my knees and just then the dancers streamed out of the Club House and I was saved. I know my heart was in my mouth. Do you realize that 'Al' is the name on that circular in the post-office of the man wanted for theft?"

"Did you hear anything more?"

"The man whispered; 'Beat it. We'll be waiting. Bring that —' then they must have mixed with the crowd of dancers."

"Have you told anyone of this?"

"No. I was thinking what I ought to do when Jerry Slade appeared and I — and I, oh, you know the rest," Joan concluded impatiently.

"Yes, I know the rest, that subject is taboo," reminded Lamont gravely. "They were to meet at midnight. That means that the hunted man has at least twenty-four hours' start, and if he is the thief wanted by the Bureau of Investigation, you may trust him to be miles away by this time. However, when we get back to the village, we'll tell your story to the sheriff. Didn't get the woman's name, did you?"

"No."

"But the man is 'Al.' Come on, we'll put the hamper in the roadster, get the robes and my coat. It's growing colder."

He took a few steps and turned.

"Happier than you were when you left home, Joan?"

"Yes. Are you?"

He laughed.

"I'm so happy. 'I'm going to sing. I've just got to sing.' Something about this place always catches me by the throat, fires me with patriotic fervor. Let's sing the Battle Hymn of the Republic. Know it?"

Joan nodded.

"All right. Let's go." He sang in a rich baritone;

" 'Mine eyes have seen the glory of the
    coming of the Lord.
He is trampling out the vintage where the
    grapes of wrath are stored,
He hath loosed the fateful lightning of
    His terrible swift sword,
His truth is marching on!' "

The hills caught up the last words and sent the magic and the music of his voice echoing from top to top till it faded into a soft murmur.

Joan's eyes shone behind tears as they met his.

"That caught me by the throat. I love your voice. Sing something else."

"You love my voice! That's getting on!" he said gruffly.

He thrust his hands hard in his pockets and increased the distance between them. He accused with assumed severity;

"You didn't sing one note of the Battle Hymn. This time do your share. Come on. We'll give 'em 'When I'm With You.' It's been humming through my mind ever since I heard it at the gas station."

He sang two verses of the sentimental little song with caressing gaiety. Joan joined in the chorus and tapped out an accompaniment on the rough ground.

" 'Every street I walk on
Becomes a lover's lane
When I'm with you, when I'm with you.' "

They rendered the finale with operatic fervor. Lamont's eyes were brilliant with laughter as he approved;

"What a team we make! We're great. Let's appear on an amateur hour. I'll bet we'd get a sponsor by wire begging us to go on the air."

"That's an idea. We might broadcast for the Straight As A Crow Flies Bus Line."

"Sold! Joan, you were born for the advertising business."

Laughing they turned the corner of the Inn. Lamont stopped.

"Where in thunder —"

Joan's startled eyes followed his. The black roadster had vanished.

XXl

Joan Crofton and Craig Lamont stared at the place where the roadster had been as if by sheer willpower they could force it to materialize. Their eyes traveled to the log cabin. The door swung slowly, eerily on its hinges. Joan's heart stopped, clicked into gear again. She whispered;

"Someone has stolen it! Must have been hiding in there. Listen!"

From down the mountain rose the purr of a high-power car. The diminishing sound roused Craig from his coma of unbelief.

"I left the key in the ignition lock. Can you believe anyone would be so stupid?"

"It wasn't stupid. Who would expect an automobile thief on this mountaintop?"

"Joan, you're the grandest sport in the world. I'm furious with myself for having been so careless."

"Perhaps it was a break that the key was there. Someone wanted that car the worst way. He might have done something terrible to you — to us — to get it."

"That's a cheering thought. Where did you get that?"

"Oh, I keep a store of them. I got imagination — plus," she boasted and laughed, at the same time that she looked furtively over her shoulder at the swinging door.

"Lucky I reminded mother of that two-fire signal, isn't it? And luckier that I got the fire permit from the forest warden, otherwise we might be pinched and personally escorted to the hoosegow. We'll build the fires. Someone at Silver Birches will see them and send out a rescue-crew."

"We won't wait for a rescue-crew. You may do as you like, but I'm going down the mountain now. It's still light enough to see."

He caught her arm.

"No. It's light up here but already the winding road is black among the tall trees. It was bad enough in the roadster, you'd be all in before you were halfway down. We'll have to wait here."

"I won't. Think of the talk it would start on top of that fake engagement. You have an electric torch in your pocket. That will help light the road. I'm going."

"No, you're not, if I have to tie you. If you stepped into a hole, you might sprain your ankle or break a leg. An injured heroine can be carried for miles by a two-fisted man in fiction, but in real life, that's another thing again. Come on, Joan, be a sport, help start the fires, and trust me, will you?"

She looked at him, at the expanse of sky already darkening, at the precipitous descent of the rough road, and back at him.

"All right, Dictator," she agreed and smiled.

Relief rushed over him in a warm tide. She trusted him. The mountain road was rough at any time but he had noticed as they drove up that it was full of holes and gullies. He had counted on the powerful headlights of the roadster to light the way down. The roadster was now illuminating the road for the thief and there was a chance that he might wait in the dark for them thinking they had money. Joan was safer on the mountain top. Someone at Silver Birches would see their signals, must see them and come to their rescue. It would be dawn before they came, at the earliest. A cold dawn, if he knew the signs, and he did. He reminded;

"Not so long ago you said that your sister had all the adventures. You'll have something to write in your next letter to her, believe it or not. Pick up all the dry wood you can find and I'll start the fires. Don't go out of sight."

"If you knew how the merry-pranks are

playing tag along my nerves, you wouldn't feel that I needed that warning," she responded and commenced to gather wood.

After a sizable pile had been collected and the two fires started, Craig Lamont suggested;

"We'll sit halfway between the fires, Joan. You chuck wood on the one at the right, and I'll take care of the one at the left. Sure you're warm enough?"

She nodded. What could he do if she were not, he asked himself. His top coat and the robes were in the roadster. He glanced at the cabin. The chimney meant that there was either a stove or a fireplace. She could stay in there out of the cold if worse came to worst. He wouldn't consider that yet. The man who had stolen the car must have been hiding there. He —

"Look! Isn't it gorgeous! Like a brilliant set for a ballet!" Joan's thrilled whisper broke the train of disturbing thought. "The beauty of the world stabs at my heart."

He nodded. Hands clasped about one knee, he watched the horizon flame scarlet and crimson. Above it floated fields and islands of clouds, violet, jade, lemon and tender green. The canopy of sky took on a matchless purple. Millions of light-years away a star blinked with pale fire. As if to return the sun's spectacular farewell, the earth glowed with sudden color. Ponds were transformed to purple, emerald and golden mirrors; the valley turned to rust and rose, distant hills to hyacinth and the river looped and rippled like a crimson ribbon. Along the highways a stream of automobile lights, looking in the distance like the lamps of fireflies, flowed unceasingly. The croon of breeze-stirred pines and their fragrance rose from the woods far below. Smoke from the fires added an acrid tang.

"Heavenly," Joan whispered and reached out her hand. She was quite unaware of the gesture, Lamont realized. He caught it and held it lightly in his.

"Like it?" he asked softly.

"Love it!" she answered fervently.

They watched the color in the west soften and the Big Dipper brighten and the Milky Way trail a gauzy bridal veil across the sky.

"I'm all made over. I feel as if my mind and heart had been cleansed of anger and distrust and had been hung out to dry in a golden glow from heaven."

Joan's voice had the magic quality of the twilight, warm, velvety, rhythmic. Lamont abruptly released her hand and threw a broken branch on the coals.

"Watch your signal fire, girl," he reminded gruffly.

When he had stirred up a blaze, to keep her thoughts from the possible discomfort of their situation, he suggested;

"Read me more choice bits from your sister's letter."

"I can't see unless you light your electric torch."

"Better not, we may need all the light there is in that later. Can't you remember what she wrote?"

Joan clasped her hands about her knees and frowned at the fire.

"I can remember the close of the letter. She begged me to join her, suggested that I drive across the country in my car this spring. She said I'd better come in June, before hot weather."

"Would you like to?"

"Why the life or death tension in the question? Like to! I'd love it, wouldn't you? Love to take the trip leisurely and put up at tourist camps — I've never stopped at one and I'm crazy to — and at hotels often enough to shake the wrinkles out of my evening gowns. Thrilling's the word for it. Think of the material I would collect for my work. No use considering it, though. Mother and father couldn't go in June and they would fight and die before they would allow me to go alone and I'm sufficiently old-fashioned to consider their wishes before my own."

A possibility, a breath-stopping possibility burgeoned full-grown in Lamont's mind and set his pulses quick-stepping. He lighted a cigarette to assure full control of his voice before he agreed;

"It would be a grand trip. Of course you couldn't go alone, but, we'll see what we can do about it."

"We —"

He re-circuited her thoughts by a touch on her arm. "We can see all points of the compass from here. Look! The East!"

The one-sided moon, low and luminous, was poking an eye above the horizon. The river shimmered. A transparent opaline mist clung halfway down the mountain and from the meadow far below rose the night-fluting of innumerable unseen living creatures, with a shrill obligato here and there to accent its slow monotony.

"Venus is co-starring Jupiter tonight. How they glow," Joan said softly.

She asked if he thought that sometime there would be interstellar communication? He said he did. That he couldn't believe that the earth was the only planet to harbor life in the great universe. And did he think that planes and radio and science were speeding up life so that during their lifetimes the world would be an incredibly different place in which to live?

And he asked her what she thought of the European situation. And she said that it would be presumptuous for her to express an opinion when behind the conflict there were centuries of history, of diplomacy, and a labyrinth of political causes of which she knew nothing.

And she asked if he believed in the communication from one mind to another and he laughed and said, "Sure, that it had not been difficult for Carl and him to get an impression from their mother's mind when they had been in mischief."

The deepening dusk around them, the purple infinity of the star-spangled canopy above, set their deeper thoughts free. They talked, revealing ideas and ideals they had never before expressed in words. With the devotion of Indians signalling with smoke spirals, or priests burning offerings to their gods on pagan altars, they fed the two fires while they talked of life and death and immortality; of what their generation might and should accomplish toward the peace of the world; of the practical working of the

Golden Rule which the Man of Galilee two thousand years ago had set echoing through the centuries.

He spoke tenderly of his brother, of what his loss had meant to him. He told of some of their pranks and chuckled at the memory. She told amusing incidents in which she and her sister had been front page family news. He told of his ambition to serve state and country and she confided her burning desire to be rated as a number one commercial artist.

"Janvers thinks you're that now," Lamont reminded as he threw wood on the fire.

Elbow on one knee, chin in her hand, Joan frowned at the two tiny columns of smoke that a rising wind was spreading.

"I like Mr. Janvers," she conceded thoughtfully. "He has the truculence of a man who has made slathers of money, who has built up a career from scratch. He is a bit pathetic to me with his perfectly tailored clothes, his carnation and his slip-shod speech."

"Janvers is all right. I admire the man. Success hasn't turned his head. He doesn't drink. He has learned what some of the rest of us have learned, that even moderate drinking fogs the mind and that in the fierce competition of modern business, a man can't afford the slightest haze of a hangover. Tony and I cut out drinking years ago. Competition is what puts the kick into business, but one's mind has to be one jump ahead of the other fellow to make good."

She nodded thoughtfully.

"It's surprising to see how the sentiment against drinking is growing. It is because it is founded on common sense, I suppose. Every little while I meet a super-sophisticated man or girl who has cut it out. Notice how the wind has come up? It is fresh enough to supply the required oxygen once every second to my thirty thousand million brain cells. I — I hope it won't blow out our fires be— before our signals are seen. Cold, isn't it?"

Her quickly controlled shiver, the break in her valiant voice, hurt Craig Lamont intolerably. It was evident that while she had been talking and laughing she had been throttling anxiety. Even in these convention-free days a girl didn't care to spend the night on a mountaintop with a man.

He threw more wood on the fires. Jumped to his feet and stretched.

"I'm stiff as a poker. I'll bet you are too. Let's walk."

"Ooch! I am stiff," Joan admitted as she rose. "I feel as I do after I've played my first six sets of tennis of the season. Where shall we walk? How suddenly it has grown dark. We can't see two feet away from this fire."

"I can. It will be lighter when the moon is overhead. Hang on." He drew her hand through his arm.

"You're cold! Your hand is icy."

"Yours doesn't suggest the tropics. Didn't you bring a topcoat?"

"I did — an extremely good-looking one — but our friend tooling merrily along in the roadster doubtless is snuggled cozily within it, while he emits demoniac chuckles of glee at our predicament."

Joan stumbled, clutched and clung to his arm.

"You and your trusty torch," she flouted. "Didn't you see that blueberry bush?"

"Sorry. Hold on tighter. We must exercise. Come on."

She drew back.

"Don't go near that cabin — please. I don't like it. I — I hate the way that door swings — it's — it's blood-chilling. There's something about it, something eerie that seems to follow us."

As she stared at the creaking door every nerve in her body came quiveringly alive and twanged unbearably. Icicles hung from her hands where fingers should have been.

Her heart was a stone lodged immovably in her throat. So this was fear, she told herself scornfully. She tried to swallow the lump, tried to laugh as she admitted;

"For the first time in my life, I'm afraid. Afraid of a door. Silly!"

She turned her face against his shoulder. He had to bend his head to hear the last choked word. His arm tightened about her. He resisted an urge to press his lips to her hair. Instead he pulled her soft hat forward on her head to shut away temptation and laughed. Would she sense the love and longing surging through him and revert to her detestation of him?

"Take it easy, little girl. You're not cracking up now, are you?"

Joan freed herself from his arm.

"Of course I'm not. I — I — just — well, there's something about that swinging door that gives me the jitters," she acknowledged with an attempt at lightness.

"That's easily stopped. Stand here. Don't move or I may lose you. I'll fasten the door. Must be a latch or key on it."

He heard her little gasp as he turned away. She was frightened. Why, why didn't someone at Silver Birches see those signal fires. She was cold. The air had an exhilarating sting born of frost. If only he had kept

290

his coat and the robes. Fortunately there was coffee in the hamper. He would reserve that until it was drastically needed.

"When I'm with you," he whistled softly as he approached the cabin. It looked comfortable and harmless enough outside. If it were fairly clean inside, Joan would better stay in it out of the cold. He could keep the signal fires going.

He pushed open the door and threw his light around the one room. Table. A jar of milk. A pile of canned goods. Bunks. Fireplace. Wood stacked beside it. That was a break. Joan needn't suffer from cold a moment longer. What was that on the floor?

Had his jumpy imagination fabricated the prone body? He averted his eyes. Stared up at a twinkling star.

He looked again. The figure was still there. Motionless.

XXII

For an instant indecision whirled Craig Lamont's mind like a windmill gone mad. If there were even a faint beat of the heart in that inert body he might save a life. If the man huddled on the floor were playing possum and attacked him Joan would be in danger. If he closed the door without knowing the truth he would suffer tortures of uncertainty as to what creeping horror might threaten her safety. He must go in and make sure.

He stepped into the cabin. Silence. Haunted silence. Outside a girl waiting. Inside the furtive creak of insects burrowing in the chinking between the logs. A small wind whispering in the chimney. A loose shingle flapping eerily. He flashed his light along the walls before he cautiously approached the huddled figure.

He bent over it. From it seeped the icy breath of death. Nothing to fear. A shot had ended the man's career. Had the person who had stolen the roadster disposed of an unwanted confederate first? Where had the two come from?

Memory sent icy chills coasting down his spine as it reminded; "The sedan! Up the mountain at three this morning. Down. Speeding by the gas station. Three in the car."

Had two of the passengers dumped this body or had the man been alive when they came? Must have been. One drove down the sedan, one made off with his roadster.

"Craig! Craig!"

Joan's voice brought the memory of the conversation she had overheard behind the spruces at the Club, of her recognition in the Library of the "Al" wanted for theft, crashing into his mind. It joined on to the mountain trip of the sedan with a jolt like two freight cars linking. Was this the man who had confessed that the police were after him, or was he the "sidekick?" Had a woman brought the men here to hide? What a break for one of them, what a tragedy for the other, that a fast roadster should have been conveniently parked in front of their hideout.

"Craig! Craig!"

There was a hint of terror in the call. Cruel to have left Joan in the dark so long. Long! It couldn't have been but a few minutes, though he felt as if he had lived through aeons. He stepped from the cabin.

"Coming!" he called and drew a deep breath of the fragrant, frosty air. He wound a handkerchief about his hand before he closed the door. There might be finger-prints on the handle that would furnish clues.

Joan caught his arm as he approached and declared breathlessly;

"You were in that cabin years! I thought that the roadster thief might have left a con-federate and — that you — Something did happen! You're white. I can see it even in this faint light!"

"Say, listen, Joan. You'll have me haywire if you keep this up."

His eyes were laughing at her. His hands were thrust hard in the pockets of his tweed coat to keep his arms from crushing her close. Mountaintops were heady, his mother had warned. She didn't know the half.

"Come back to the fires, Joan. They've died down. That won't do. We must keep the signals burning. It's getting colder every minute. If it's as frosty as this on our ridge across the valley, it will kill the young plants."

Why had he used that word "kill" he asked himself furiously. It gave him the creeps. He turned from throwing wood on the red embers, saw Joan shiver and her furtive look at him as she tried to control it. He came to a sudden conclusion.

He placed the two cushions close together on the side steps of the Inn veranda and said matter-of-factly;

"You're freezing. So am I. If we sit here we'll be out of the wind. I'll keep the fires going. Come here. Close beside me. We'll huddle and keep each other warm."

What would she say to that proposition? She didn't like him any too well. Would he lose the ground he felt he had gained with her today? Would she be insulted or would she —

She dropped to one of the cushions and looked up with an unsteady laugh.

"I've been wondering how long it would be before that brilliant idea would occur to you," she mocked gaily.

He looked down at her gravely.

"Joan, you're the most unpredictable girl in the world."

He seated himself beside her and drew her close within his arm. Her head fell against his shoulder as naturally as Peggy's might have done.

"This is better," she admitted unsteadily. "The world doesn't seem so frightfully big and lonely. I wish that door would stop banging."

She turned her head in the direction of the cabin. Hand on her cheek he pressed it back against his shoulder.

"Hey, none of that. Never mind the door. I like to hear it bang. Sort of friendly. The moon is giving us a break. It's lighting the mountain top. See that star skittering along the sky. I'll say it's in a hurry. Now it has blinked out. Let's talk."

She settled her head more comfortably against his shoulder.

"As if we hadn't already discussed and re-adjusted all the affairs of the universe, human and divine. Have you anything to suggest?"

"You haven't told me what New York shows you liked best last winter. I go over once or twice a month. I saw them all — perhaps you can tell me why the modern playwright has such a yen for the drab and sordid — or what music you prefer, or whether you're strong for modern art — can't see anything in it myself — or what books you read. I'm a Kipling addict — that dates me, doesn't it — I read him over and over."

She voted for Charles Dickens as a satisfying hardy perennial and declared that by some trick of manner, or striking oddity of feature, he made even the most unimportant characters unforgettable.

"Quick! Joan! The Aurora!"

They sprang to their feet. Lamont kept his arm about her as they looked toward the northern horizon from which shafts of eerie light shot up and sheets of white flame flashed and quivered like distant heat lightning.

"Reminds me of the fireworks at Monte Carlo," he whispered, as if the sound of his voice might break a magic spell.

Joan drew a long, unsteady breath.

"It's enchanting at the same time that it is weird and uncanny. The heavens are certainly putting on an all-star show tonight for us."

After minutes of thrilled silence, she said;

"Hope that brilliance doesn't dim the light from our signals. Let's pile on more wood."

"Don't be too lavish. One piece at a time. It makes a steadier fire that way."

He wasn't at all sure that it did, but it was unnecessary for her to know that the wood supply was almost gone, that they would have to wait for dawn until they could collect more.

"Wouldn't you think someone would miss us and look toward the mountain?" Joan demanded indignantly when they were again on the steps.

"Give them time," he glanced at the illuminated dial of his wrist watch. "It's only four hours since we lighted the fires. They wouldn't expect us home much before this. Perhaps they've just looked toward the mountain and seen the signal. At best they couldn't get here for two hours more."

"Two hours! That will be morning. Tomorrow is already today. This is the day we are to appear in Court. If we don't get there the judge will have us jailed for contempt. Wouldn't Señorita Nadja Donesca like to spread this adventure of ours — adventure is your word not mine — on the front pages! What will the girl you love say about that? I'm starting down the mountain now."

He drew her back.

"You are not. We'll start down as soon as it is light enough to see the road. Forget the girl I love. Put your head on my shoulder again and take a nap. With that storm on the loose last night, I'll bet you didn't sleep much."

"It wasn't the storm outside that kept my eyes open, it was my turmoil of mind. But that's behind us." She stifled a yawn. "I am sleepy which just shows the power of suggestion. You put the idea into my head."

He loved her voice, it was warm and clear

with a hint of gaiety. He slipped his arm about her.

"Comfortable?"

"It's perfect."

"Your head fits as if it were made for my shoulder, doesn't it?"

"Tell me about the girl you love. Where did you meet her?" she asked quickly, stiffly.

Apparently she intended to keep the girl to whom she thought him engaged between them. Just as well till they were off this mountain. He was neither wood nor stone.

"Where did I meet her?" he repeated reflectively. "In Boston."

"Is she a dyed-in-the-wool New Englander?"

A smile twitched at his lips as he remembered that she had said that of herself the first time they met. That question would be easy to answer.

"She is. It's rather curious about New Englanders, isn't it? Spot them anywhere. They are different from the rest of the world."

He went into the subject in detail and in a sing-song monotone. He smiled as her bronze lashes drooped and lifted, drooped and lifted until they rested motionless against her cheeks.

The Northern Lights went out. The stars brightened. Shrubs cast purple shadows in the moonlight. A frosty wind nipped by. He glanced at his watch. Surely by this time the Croftons would be anxious about Joan, would telephone Silver Birches and that would send his mother to the window. She would, she must see the signal fires. Why didn't Tony Crane see them? He would understand. Why hadn't Johnny Nolan noticed that his roadster had passed the gas station without stopping? Hadn't he told him he would report on the condition of the mountain road on the way down?

He'd better stop crabbing and think what he would do about that — that huddled body in the cabin. Why in thunder did the door keep up an everlasting creak?

Thank Heaven Joan was no longer disturbed by it. She must like him, she must trust him or she wouldn't sleep so quietly against his shoulder. When she had forgotten her anger at the announced engagement — which wasn't an engagement — he would tell her he loved her. Could he arrange his business to motor across the country to the Pacific Coast in June? What a honeymoon! The mere thought of it tripped up his breath. It would take some arranging but it could be done.

He fed the fires and planned until the horizon burned with color. Day slowly rolled up its curtain and dawn flushed and glorified the world. The broken moon paled. The purple sky turned to amethyst; white clouds to rose. The island was a green jewel set in a river of quicksilver that flowed under a bridge, unreal as a fairy's web. Gold roofed houses in white villages, their shapes suggested, not revealed, and stars winked out.

The serenity, the coolness, the isolation, the girl asleep within his arm, created a new universe for him. It was like being born again into a world of amazing beauty and spiritual exaltation he hadn't known existed.

He looked down at Joan. Should he waken her and tell her? Make her understand that he loved her, that the girl of whom his mother had spoken was herself?

He jerked up his head. He must have had a brain storm to think of it. He had told his mother that cool, calm friendliness was his role. Joan had given him no reason to change it.

The sound of birds twittering their morning salutation to the world rose above the rustle of the dewy fragrant woods below. The moment it was light enough, they would start down.

What was that sound? Not the twitter of birds. It was the hum of an engine! A car coming up the mountain! Two? Tony? The Senator? Better wake Joan —

The cabin door creaked. Closed with a bang. Suppose the car coming up the hill were coming for that — that grisly thing inside? Joan must not be seen here.

He spoke to her softly. Whispered as if the driver of the ascending car were already within hearing.

"Joan! Joan! Wake up, adorable."

She lifted heavy lids. Smiled vaguely and dropped them.

The purr of motors was louder. No doubt now that two cars were coming up the incline. She must not be seen until he was sure who was in them. He shook her gently.

"Joan! Cars coming! Wake up!"

The quality of his voice pierced her consciousness. Her lashes flew up. Radiance crowded out the haze of sleep. Her eyes met his.

"I — I love you!" she whispered fervently.

Something that flashed from his eyes to hers brought her wide awake. Even in the faint light he could see color dye her face as he demanded;

"What do you mean by that, Joan?"

She sprang to her feet. Acknowledged breathlessly;

"I was dreaming, really I was — for a minute — for one minute I thought you were someone else. Good cinema, wasn't it? Do I hear a car coming?"

"It's not only one car, but two." Her admission that she had thought him someone else when she had said, "I love you," had frozen his heart. It was as numb as the arm in which he had held her as she slept against his shoulder. Why was he wasting a moment thinking about himself? He must get her out of sight before the cars appeared. They might have come in answer to the signal fires, or for that gruesome cargo in the cabin.

"Come over into the black shadow of the Inn, Joan, until we are sure why those cars have come." He flexed his arm which prickled as if being probed by a million needles.

"Who could be in them but —" she looked up at him, then furtively at the cabin. She shivered.

"Something horrible is in there! I knew it," she whispered. "Each time I look at it, something grabs me by the throat."

"Forget the cabin! Come! Watch your step!" he warned and caught her as she stumbled over a low bush. He drew her close against the house which cast a black shadow over them.

"No matter what you hear or see, don't make a sound," he said close to her ear.

She nodded and gripped a corner of his coat.

He held his breath to listen. Except for the purr of engines, the twitter of birds, the world still slept in the rosy light of dawn. Most of the stars had blinked out. Light from the approaching cars was gilding tree tops. Lower now! A sedan took the last rise and stopped. The glow illumined every inch of the mountaintop except the black shadow in which he held Joan as in a vise.

A second car lurched into sight. The engines purred softly as men jumped out. Lamont couldn't see their faces, but he could hear a voice;

"Craig! Craig! Are you here?"

"It's Tony! Tony!" he exulted. "Come, Joan!"

He caught her hand to draw her forward but she shook him off and ran to the man standing beside the sedan. She sent her voice ahead of her.

"It's you, Jerry! Jerry, darling! I knew you'd find me!"

XXIII

Joan looked back as the green sedan in which she sat beside Jerry Slade, silently coasted into the mountain road. The scrub bushes were white with rime. Three men were walking toward the cabin. She had recognized two of them, Johnny Nolan of the gas station, and the sheriff who had served the summons on her. The figures of Craig Lamont and Tony Crane were motionless against the brightening sky as they stood side by side near the dying fires. There was light enough for her to see the whiteness, the tense lines in their faces. As she looked, Tony slipped his arm within Craig's. Something in the gesture brought a blinding rush of tears to her eyes. Why, why hadn't she refused to leave the mountaintop without Craig?

"Because you had been dreaming of him and when you woke and met his eyes, you knew you loved him and told him so, and then remembered that he was 'tenderly, deeply' in love with someone else," a voice within her answered her passionate question.

She turned and spoke to the silent man at the wheel.

"Who are the men who came in the second car, Jerry? And why did Tony and Craig refuse to come with us? There is plenty of room in this sedan for them."

"Don't talk to me, darling. I need to keep my eyes and thoughts on this road. It's fierce. The next time I visit a mountaintop I'll land in my plane. If we reach the level without a crack-up, I'll apply for a Humane Society medal for rescuing a lovely lady."

Joan regarded him from the corners of her eyes. He didn't intend to tell her why the three strange men were on the mountaintop, nor why Craig and Tony had refused to leave with her. The explanation was in that cabin. She knew it. She shivered uncontrollably.

"Cold, darling?"

"No, Jerry, and please, please don't call me darling."

"You called me that when you rushed at me back there on the mountain. Didn't you mean it?"

His husky voice hurt her but she said steadily;

"Not as you want me to mean it, Jerry. I — I had been watching and listening for hours for an answer to our signals and — and when I saw you — well, I would have called anyone — anyone darling — I was so relieved."

"Thanks for the compliment. Did Lamont get fresh that you were so glad to see me?"

"No, Jerry! No! How could you think it?"

"Don't be so horrified. You say you don't care a hang for me and yet you greet me when I appear as if I were the only man in your world, with your fiancé standing by, too."

Joan's head hit the top of the sedan with a resounding crack. Back in her seat she gasped breathlessly between laughter and pain;

"Ooch, what a bounce, Jerry. As I went up I saw you coming down. It — it was too — too funny."

"Stop laughing, Joan. You'll have hysterics, then what would I do with you? Lucky you didn't get a concussion from that crack. It sounded like a back-fire. Don't talk till we get off this fiendish road. If I hadn't been listening to you, I would have seen that hole."

Joan drew her coat collar high about her ears and slid down in the seat. She was glad not to talk. She couldn't tell Jerry that she had called him "darling" to counteract the fervent, "I — I love you!" she had whispered when her eyes had opened and looked up at Craig Lamont.

She pressed her hand against a hot cheek

as she remembered her passionate inner response to his deepening, darkening eyes. Her pulses had broken into double-quick. All the while they had stood in the shadow of the Inn waiting for the ascending automobiles, waiting an eternity it had seemed, she had turned over and over in her mind the best and surest way to erase those words from his memory. The instant she had seen Jerry she had known what to do. Apparently she had made a thorough job of it, for Craig had not spoken directly to her since. The memory hurt intolerably, but, she reminded herself, nothing hurts, nothing can hurt like this forever.

Her eyes were on the road ahead illumined by the lights of the car, but her thoughts were with the man on the mountain top whom she loved. She lived over every moment since they had left her home. She remembered his gaiety, his thought of her, his rich voice singing, the feel of his arm around her shoulder.

"Cold, dar— Joan?"

It was light enough for Jerry Slade to see the shake of her head in answer to his question. Lucky he couldn't see into her mind. Couldn't see it flash on and off like a neon sign "I love Craig! I love Craig!" Suppose she did? What could be done about it when he loved someone else?

"Asleep, Joan? I've spoken to you twice."

She sat erect.

"I wasn't asleep. I was thinking. Why, we are down the mountain!"

"That was the good news I was trying to get across to you. Thinking of your fiancé, I suppose. Well, take it from me, had I been in his place, I wouldn't have allowed the girl I love to go off without me."

"But, I'm not —" She stopped. Why pull down the story of the engagement it had proved so costly to her to build? She said instead;

"I wondered too why he and Tony remained behind. Something tells me there was a reason for it. Do you know, Jerry?"

"How would I know what was going on in the minds of those two? I had been crazy with anxiety about you after we heard you were marooned on top of that mountain."

"How did you hear?"

"I'll tell you after I've stopped at the gas station and phoned your house that you and Lamont are all right. The two families were about out of their minds when they heard that his roadster had speeded through town, and that kid, Peggy, and her dog and kitten were under everybody's feet."

Daylight had dimmed the string of colored light bulbs on the gas station when they pulled up before the door. Jerry Slade jumped from the sedan. It seemed years before he returned.

As the car slid smoothly homeward over the broad black road, Joan drew a long breath.

"Isn't the air exciting, Jerry? Fresh and clear and scented with the breeze from a thousand hills. Those clouds look like fluffs of pink down against the blue. Hear the birds! Watch the violet spiral of smoke rise from that black banded chimney. The roof below it is white with frost. When you see that can you believe this is the merry month of May? Someone's having an early breakfast. I sniff wheat cakes. Makes me ravenous. Hear the brook splash and tinkle? A cow-bell! I thought those went out when mechanical milkers came in. I'd forgotten that the early morning was so beautiful. Why did Nolan and the two other men come up the mountain with you, Jerry?"

She had trapped him as she had intended with her quick turn of the subject.

"To — to investigate. One of them is the sheriff —" the hesitation was but for an instant but Joan knew that he had derailed the sentence and substituted another when he said;

310

"I told you I'd tell you after we stopped to phone how we knew that you were stranded on top of that mountain. Remember when you left the gas station yesterday afternoon, that Lamont told Nolan he'd stop on his way back and report on the road?"

"I remember."

"Well, Nolan hung around his station till about eight o'clock. Then when Lamont hadn't appeared, he concluded that as it had been a fine evening, he was staying late to enjoy the moonlight. He didn't think it strange because he'd done the same thing many times himself. He left his helper in charge and drove to Carsfield to see his mother who is sick. He stopped at the town garage at midnight to swap stories with the boss. Just as he was leaving, the man said;

" 'A fella drove through town lickety-split a couple of hours ago. I ran out to see what fool driver was thumbing his nose at death and destruction, and who's car do you think it was? Craig Lamont's! He must have been takin' something. Couldn't believe my eyes. Those Lamont boys were just spillin' over with pep and high spirits but they was the most law-abiding citizens of this town.'

"That jolted Nolan's mind wide-open. He phoned Mrs. Shaw. She had gone to

311

bed. She phoned your mother and father who hadn't. They had begun to be frightfully anxious. Then Mrs. Shaw saw the signal fires on the mountain. They got hold of Crane, who got hold of me and well, we went haywire for fear that the man who had stolen the car had — had harmed you and Lamont. We picked up a state police who cleared the way for us to the mountain road where we picked up Nolan and the others. You know the rest."

"Do I? I'm still wondering why the sheriff was needed on top of that mountain. I am sure —"

After all, why tell Jerry that she was convinced that the cabin held a gruesome secret? Perhaps he didn't know. Perhaps Craig and Tony didn't want him to know. She finished her sentence.

"I'll be glad to get home," and for the present let the whole tangled experience go at that.

Every window in The Mansion was alight when Jerry Slade switched off the engine of the sedan in front of it.

Senator and Mrs. Shaw and Peggy, with the black and white dog, and the gray kitten squatting beside her, David and Patty Crofton were on the steps of the porch before Joan stepped from the car.

"Oh, honey! Oh, honey," her mother kept saying.

David Crofton's laugh was a praiseworthy attempt if not convincing.

"Let Joan get into the house, Patty. Come along, Slade. We have hot coffee and sandwiches ready for the return of the prodigals. You know your mother, Joan, her panacea for all trouble is food."

"Where's Uncle Craig?" Peggy pulled at Joan's skirt. "I heard them say he was missing and — and I went out on the balcony and knelt toward the mountain and prayed to the spirit of my father to keep him safe the way Uncle Craig told me the Indians did." Tears rolled down her cheeks.

Joan dropped to one knee and put her arms about her.

"He is quite safe, Peggy."

The child snuggled her head against Joan's neck. Whispered;

"I'm sorry I was an ol' meanie to you, Joan."

"Let's forget it, Peg."

"Okay, Toots."

"Suppose we get something to eat? I'm starving."

Joan felt as if she were moving in a daze as she entered the candle-lighted dining room. Was she really seeing the ivory paneled walls, the gold cornices with their blue damask hangings, the mahogany table with its exquisite lace doilies, plates and sandwiches and steaming silver urn or was she dreaming with her head against Craig Lamont's shoulder on the mountaintop under the stars?

She was awake. The aroma of coffee was real, Mrs. Shaw in her amethyst crêpe frock was real, so were her brilliantly blue eyes and her voice as she demanded brokenly;

"Where is Craig? Who stole his car? Why didn't he come with you?"

Her husband slipped his arm about her and bent his shaggy gray head over her white one.

"Steady, Sally, steady, my dear. You heard Joan tell Peggy that he is safe and unharmed."

"Craig is all right," Joan answered fervently. "I don't know why he stayed behind." She tried to inject lightness into her voice. "Perhaps he was fed-up with my company. Jerry knows why he didn't come with us. He won't tell me. Perhaps he'll tell you."

She saw Jerry Slade's eyes flash to the Senator who asked quickly;

"Where were you and Craig when the roadster was stolen?"

What message had been wirelessed that Senator Shaw should immediately switch the subject, Joan wondered, even as she explained;

"We were on the other side of the Inn from the roadster putting on a song and dance act for the benefit of the hills and valley, the river and incidentally ourselves. Craig opened the concert with the Battle Hymn. I wish you could have heard it, it was heart-twisting. Then we sang several verses of a one-time song hit. It must have been when we were lustily carolling the chorus that the thief seized the opportunity to make off with the roadster. It was a silent and simple stunt to coast it down the upper part of the steep road, and simpler still to start the engine as the key was in the ignition lock. When we discovered it was gone —"

"Why, why didn't you walk down?" Patty Crofton demanded.

"Craig said it was too dark, that the road was full of holes and that I might step into one and break a bone or two and where would we be then?"

"He had the right idea," Jerry Slade confirmed unexpectedly. "The road was tricky enough with powerful headlights. It would have been a crazy stunt to try to make it with only an electric torch."

"How did the thief get to the mountain-top? Had he walked?" Mrs. Shaw demanded.

"Nolan, who runs the gas station in the nearby village, saw a sedan start up the mountain road before daylight yesterday morning. Didn't think it strange then — but when he heard that Lamont's roadster had streaked through to this town without stopping at his place, he got busy, and as you know, telephoned to you," Slade explained.

"Did Nolan by any chance get the number of that sedan?" the Senator asked.

"He did. I could dally with another cup of coffee, Mrs. Crofton."

Why had Jerry so quickly switched from the subject of the mysterious sedan? Joan asked herself. What did he know? After she had stepped into the car for the journey down, he had stopped to talk with Craig and Tony.

"This night has seemed a hundred hours long," Patty Crofton admitted with a break in her soft voice as she filled Jerry Slade's cup.

"Make it a million and you'll know what it seemed to me," Joan attested fervently. "Craig was wonderful, he must have been tempted to laugh when I lost my nerve over a creaking door, but he didn't. It was an adventure but even so, I won't list a night on a mountaintop with a spooky cabin back-stage, as my favorite outdoor sport."

A surge of memory, memory of Craig's eyes looking deep into hers in the firelight was like a hand of steel gripping her heart. How like her after being unable to love men who loved her, to love a man who was mad — that had been his mother's word — over another girl. Her father had prophesied that when love came to her she would plunge in up to her neck. She'd plunged, all right, she wasn't able even to tread water. It was ter-rible to care like that.

Mrs. Shaw was looking at her. Was she reading her thoughts? She said quickly;

"Now that you know that Craig is safe and can see that I am, I'll say good-night — good-morning, rather — take a shower and change. I'm due at Philip Bard's office with some roughs at ten o'clock and then — good heavens, this is the day I am to appear in Court, isn't it, Senator?"

"It is, my dear. But don't worry about that. You won't be five minutes on the wit-ness stand."

"It isn't the time I mind, it is testifying for that poisonous woman, swearing — I have to swear that I'll tell the truth, don't I? — that I heard Peggy say that Mam'selle said that her mother was a schemer. I feel so disloyal to Mrs. Shaw and — and well, to Mrs. Shaw."

She had caught back Craig's name in time. For some inexplicable reason her voice showed a tendency to quiver when she said it.

Senator Shaw laid his kindly hand on her shoulder.

"What you testify won't hurt our case in the least, my dear. I wish I could keep you out of it, but I can't. Sally, now that we know that our boy is safe, let's go home — the sandman is getting busy with Peg's eyelashes — and give Joan a chance to snitch a bit of beauty sleep before she goes to town."

"Honey, after such an experience you can't go to town this morning," Patty Crofton protested.

Joan's laugh was genuine.

"Don't treat me as if I were the last word in invalids, Mother. Think of the nights I've danced till morning. That never kept me from my work, why should adventure. Except that I feel slightly swimmy above the eyes — I'd hate to tell you how many times my skull contacted the roof of the sedan on the way down the mountain road — I'm on top of the world."

She thought of her boast of light-heartedness as hours later she entered the office of the Art Director of the Bard Agency. She was no longer on top of the world, she was feverishly eager to submit the roughs and escape before Philip Bard should come in. That announced engagement would take some explaining. Engagement! It was the first time she had thought of it since she had left the mountain.

"I said these were bully, Miss Crofton."

Joan felt color warm her cheeks as her eyes met the quizzical green eyes of Scott Rand. For an instant she had forgotten that she was sitting beside his untidy desk. She twisted the good-luck bracelet Viv had sent her, gave an unnecessary pat to the white collar of her blue-sheer frock, and apologized;

"I'm sorry. A picture flashed into my mind. Ever have an idea for a rough come that way?"

Rand thrust thick-jointed fingers through tousled red hair.

"Not often and when they come that way, they're not much good. I've got a new account for you to try out. I — what's up now, boss?"

Philip Bard ignored Rand's question as he approached Joan. The fingers that brushed up the ends of his clipped dark mustache were unsteady, his voice was harsh as he demanded;

"When did you come in, Miss Crofton? I told them in the outer office to let me know the moment you arrived. Tried to get you on the phone yesterday, but all I could get out of that colored dumbbell at your house was that you'd 'done gone out.' Come into my office. I want to talk to you."

Joan shook her head.

"Can't. Mr. Rand is in the midst of some landing-the-consumer instruction. When he is through, I'll talk with you — if I have time. I have a very important date."

"Never mind Rand. I —"

"I want Philip Bard."

The voice came from the doorway. A policeman stood on the threshold.

Bard frowned at the interruption, apparently remembered that courtesy to the police made the road of the motorist easy and replied ingratiatingly;

"I'm Philip Bard, officer. What can I do for you?

The burly representative of the law consulted a slip of paper in his hand;

"Is the license number of your sedan XXX–70?"

"It is." Bard's voice was no longer genial.

A hint of anxiety had crept into his eyes. He snapped;

"What of it?"

"You're wanted at Headquarters."

"What headquarters?"

The officer's snort was half contempt, half derision.

"Police Headquarters."

"Police — look here, officer, is this a joke?"

"Joke! You said that XXX–70 was the license number of your car, didn't you?"

"I did."

"We'll, there's some parties that want to know what your car was doin' on the mountain road morning before last."

"Mountain road! Morning before —" Bard's voice caught in his throat. His face was livid. "But, officer —"

"Don't talk now! You'll have plenty of chance at Headquarters to tell all you know about that dead man in the cabin on top of the mountain."

XXIV

In a mirror in the ascending elevator at the Court House, Craig Lamont caught a glimpse of his tired, lean face and the little lines etched at the corners of his intent eyes — they hadn't been there yesterday — of his tense mouth, and tried to flex his lips.

No wonder he looked all in. Added to a morning packed with business appointments, had been questioning and requestioning as to his discovery of the body in the cabin, what he had been doing before he found it, what he had done every moment after. Not that it was thought that he was in any way connected with the shooting, he had been assured repeatedly — there was no doubt in anyone's mind that the men who had made the hasty early morning trip up and down the mountain in the sedan were responsible but he was the only person — he and Miss Crofton, who could, so far as was known at present, furnish any clues.

He had assured them that Joan had had no suspicion of what was huddled on the floor of the log cabin, had explained briefly that he had gone to close the swinging door to stop its confounded creak, had looked in to see if there were a fireplace in case the night grew too cold for her outside until someone came for them in answer to their signal fires — and then as he had flashed his light around he had seen — they didn't need to be told again what he had seen.

The District Attorney had solemnly nodded understanding. The sheriff's lips had twitched uncontrollably as he fitted together the fingers of his bony hands and inquired blandly;

"And after that, all the time you two were together on the mountain, you didn't let the girl know what you had seen? Didn't even let her suspect, Mr. Lamont?"

"I did not. Would you, had you been in my place?"

The sheriff had twisted in his seat, had twirled his thumbs before he had had the grace to acknowledge that he guessed he wouldn't have let the girl know.

As he stepped from the elevator and entered the corridor, crowded with men and women of a half dozen nationalities, cloudy with the haze from cigarettes which obscured the "NO SMOKING" signs, Craig Lamont's thoughts returned to the trip to Silver Birches in the speedy car the Senator had sent for him; to breakfast on the broad terrace and his mother's blue eyes which had brimmed with questions she would not allow to pass her lips. He had given a light touch to the adventure while all the time Joan's fervent;

"It's you, Jerry! Jerry, darling! I knew you'd find me!" had surged like a turbulent undercurrent through his mind.

Apparently it had taken a few hours only, marooned with a man she didn't like to make her realize how much she loved Slade.

Inextricably tangled with that conclusion had been the satisfying realization that Johnny Nolan had been quick enough to get the number of the mysterious sedan which had made the record-breaking early-morning mountain trip. The sheriff had been telephoning to the license department to find out to whom the car belonged when he, himself, had been dismissed with the cheering assurance that he would not be needed again for the present.

He'd better push last night's experience into the background of his mind. Nadja and her fight for Peg would need all his attention for the next few hours, he decided, as he faced a door on the ground-glass pane of which PROBATE COURT was printed in large black letters.

As he entered the room he had the curious

impression that he was looking at a picture on a screen. Senator Dan Shaw and a sleek-haired, thin-lipped man were conferring with the black-gowned judge on the bench, whose eyes were like slivers of bright blue glass beneath shaggy white eyebrows. Above him the glorious colors of the Stars and Stripes brightened the dull gray wall, below him the clerk of the court sorted papers, and the court stenographer arranged the pages of her note-book. Blue-coated officers slumped behind their desks. With a nice sense of theatric values the sun shot a shaft of light through an open window straight at the face of Señorita Nadja Donesca. It revealed haggard creases about her vividly rouged mouth, tiny lines about her brilliant green eyes, emphasized the tailored perfection of her gray suit and toque, struck glints of gold in her red hair and glittered sparks from the circlet of diamonds on one of the fingers with which she drummed nervously on counsel's table within the bar.

She's playing up her wedding ring for all it is worth, Lamont thought. What has wrought havoc with her usually unlined, hard-shell face? It can't be anxiety over this fight for her child, she admitted she didn't really want her. She had brazenly dared admit that, because she knew I wouldn't testify to the alternative she proposed. How, how could Carl have loved the woman? he asked himself as he had asked himself hundreds of times.

As if in telepathic response to his thought she turned and looked at him. There was no hint of recognition in her eyes but there was hatred and a trace of fright.

He crossed the room to his mother who in a thin black frock, and black turban, with a double string of lustrous pearls at her throat was sitting rigidly upright on a settee.

"Relax, Sally Shaw," he whispered. "You look as tense as if you were about to be shot from a cannon."

She smiled and leaned back.

"My looks do not belie my feelings. I am glad that Nadja has turned her back on us. I would hate to have her realize that I am nervous. Here comes Mam'selle whom I discharged. Nadja must have summoned her as a witness."

An over rouged, heavily mascaraed woman in a bright blue print frock settled herself on a bench across the room with an air of importance and much fluttering of skirts and jingling of chains and bracelets.

"What line will her evidence take?" Mrs. Shaw wondered softly. "Why, why did

Nadja do this? She doesn't want Peggy. It is cruel, unforgivable, to drag family quarrels into the spot-light."

Lamont laid his hand lightly on his mother's.

"Steady, Sally Shaw. Unless I miss my guess the spot-light won't get the chance to show up much of this family quarrel. The Senator's expression reminds me of the cat who swallowed a canary. Where's Joan? I thought she might drive in with you —"

"She had a morning business appointment." Mrs. Shaw glanced at the wall clock. "She still has five minutes leeway. Here she is."

Lamont rose. His mother caught his sleeve.

"Sit down, Craig. Nadja's lawyer won't let Joan sit with us. She is his witness."

The thin-lipped, sleek-haired counsel for the plaintiff quick-stepped toward Joan. He said something in a low tone to her and waved her to a seat beside the French woman.

Lamont followed her with his eyes. She was even lovelier in that sheer navy frock with the small white hat pulled low over one eye, than she had been in the blue tweed yesterday. Had soft color stolen to her hair when her eyes had met his, or had imagination tricked him? Now that the excitement of last night's adventure had given place to cold reason — if he could exercise cold reason where Joan was concerned — there was something unconvincing in her impassioned greeting of Jerry Slade when he had stepped out of the sedan on the mountaintop. Twenty-four hours before, to stop his persistent love-making, she had told Slade that she was engaged. Was it possible that in the short time which had intervened her sentiment toward him would have changed sufficiently to warrant that fervent;

"It's you, Jerry! Jerry darling! I knew you'd find me!"?

It didn't make sense. Not nearly so much sense as the radiance in her eyes when they met his own and she had whispered;

"I love you!"

Her quick explanation that she had been dreaming, that when she opened her eyes, she had thought he was someone else, had been breathless, panicky. Had she told the truth? Why should he think she hadn't? Since the moment she and he had met their acquaintance had been strewn as thick with misunderstandings as the mountain road with holes. In between there had been moments when she had been heart-warmingly friendly. Even when he had backed up his mother's story that he was madly in love with a girl —

Could that touch of diplomacy be the reason Joan had thrust Slade between them? When she had wakened with her head against his shoulder, his arm about her, had her heart wakened to a realization that she loved him? Had his love for her penetrated her dreams?

Was it possible that she cared for him? He would tell her at once that she was the girl —

"Craig! Where are you going?"

He looked at his mother's hand clutching his coat, at plaintiff's counsel unctuously addressing the white-haired judge. He chuckled and resumed his seat.

"Sorry," he whispered. "Forgot where I was. Suddenly thought of something I must tell Joan."

"The Croftons are dining with us tonight. If we win our case, we will want to celebrate, if we lose, we'll need cheerful company. Keep what you have to tell her until then," Sally Shaw answered in a low voice. She colored with the sensitiveness of a young girl reproved as the Senator turned and looked at her.

He'd better not let his thoughts wander to Joan again or he might follow them and be ejected from the hearing, Craig Lamont warned himself. The Clerk of the Court was administering the oath to the witnesses. Followed the lawyer's presentation of Nadja's case. The man used his voice like an organ, pulled out tremolo keys when he referred to mother-love, rolled out bass notes when he denounced the guardians of the little girl appointed by the father; craftily insinuated that the grandmother and uncle would gain much if — er — in case of the child's death.

"Strike that last remark from the records!" the judge ordered sharply. "Counsel for the plaintiff will keep to facts and avoid fiction. State his case, not argue it at present. Proceed!"

Counsel for the plaintiff suavely apologized and suavely proceeded. He called his first witness.

"Miss Joan Crofton."

As the girl went forward to the witness stand, two men entered the room, Janvers and Philip Bard.

Arms crossed, knees crossed, Craig Lamont frowningly regarded Bard as he seated himself on a bench near the preening Mam'selle. She rolled dark eyes toward him, shrugged a Frenchified shrug. Her whispered greeting elicited a sharp glance of reproof from the presiding justice.

Just where did Philip Bard fit into this case, Lamont wondered. Apparently Nadja had expected him. She had nodded to him. He had been in her stag line the last year of her husband's life, but there had been others. Had fear of what the Senator's cross-examination might bring out turned his olive skin pasty, made his fingers unsteady as he pulled at one end of his clipped dark mustache?

As Janvers sat down heavily beside Mrs. Shaw, she touched her son's arm. Her lips formed a word.

"Look!"

Lamont's eyes followed hers. Drucilla Dodd was huddled in a back corner of the room as if hoping to escape notice. She must have been behind the two men when they entered. He glanced at Senator Shaw who was listening to the questions being put to Joan. Did he know that "The Pest" was among those present? Why spend a moment's thought on her when Joan was being questioned?

Counsel for the plaintiff turned to counsel for defense. Conceded urbanely.

"Your witness, Brother Shaw."

The Senator rose. He smiled at Joan.

"No questions."

Joan returned to her seat. He remained standing.

"May it please the Court to listen to me for five minutes?" he asked. "I know that remarks from the defense are out of order, but I can produce a witness who will save your Honor's time and throw this case out of Court."

Counsel for plaintiff was on his feet.

"I protest this irregularity, your Honor!"

The judge fitted almost transparent fingers together. His shaggy white brows lowered like ragged canopies over his keen, blue eyes.

"In the interest of a docket crowded with important cases and on the statement of Counsel for the defense, the objection of Counsel for the plaintiff is overruled. Counsel for the defense may call his witness."

"Augustus Janvers!"

Craig Lamont looked quickly at Nadja Donesca as the name boomed through the court room. She started from her seat. Her eyes were enormous, incredulous. Her counsel caught her arm and pulled her back.

Janvers stepped to the witness stand. The fingers of his left hand stroked the red carnation in the lapel of his gray coat as he took the oath.

Counsel for the defense threw back his

shaggy gray head as if preparing for battle. Every question he asked, every statement he made cut with the hiss of a keen-edged scimitar in the hands of a savage avenger.

"Mr. Janvers, look at the plaintiff in this case. Have you seen her before?"

The expression of the witness was a cross between a smile and a sneer.

"I have."

"Where?"

"In a small city in Pennsylvania."

"When?"

"Twenty-odd years ago."

"It's a lie! I've never seen the man!"

The plaintiff's sharp denial stripped of foreign accent, brought a curt order from the judge.

"Quiet! The counsel for defense will proceed."

"Mr. Janvers, tell the Court as briefly as possible of your acquaintance with the plaintiff."

"Acquaintance!" the word stung. "I first saw the woman who now calls herself Señorita Nadja Donesca, twenty years ago. I hear she claims to be the daughter of a high-class Mexican, that her home was a *hacienda* called La Torranca. That must have been in another life because for ten years we lived in the same tenement house, it would be called an apartment house now. Her mother did my mother's washing. Her name then was Maggie Dawn. She married me when she was seventeen with the full consent of her parents. Then — then we just naturally drifted apart."

"And you've not seen her since?" the counsel for the defense queried smoothly.

"Not until I saw her come out of the Lamont Agency a short time ago."

"And during that time you made no effort to locate her?"

"Why should I? She left me. Said she intended to rise in the world. Said I never would." The witness stroked the red carnation. His laugh was a gruff bark. "She had me wrong. I'm Janvers of the Straight As A Crow Flies Bus Line."

The man bulged with pride. The judge covered suddenly twitching lips with transparent fingers. Counsel for the defense asked smoothly;

"You and the woman, Maggie Dawn, were not divorced?"

"Not that I know of."

"It's a lie! I've never seen this man before! I've never —" the plaintiff's voice rose and cracked.

Counsel for defense interrupted sternly.

"If you are not Maggie Dawn, why did

you drive a man whose name is Al Dawn to the top of a mountain two nights ago and leave him dead in the cabin?"

Tense silence in the court room. The tick-tock! tick-tock! tick-tock! of the wall clock accentuated the uncanny stillness, stillness as haunted as if a gray-faced, glassy-eyed man lay in its midst.

The woman pulled off her hat as if she couldn't bear the pressure. Her eyes were enormous as she stared at the judge —

"Al! Dead! I — I—" she stammered. "I —"

Her counsel caught her as she swayed.

XXV

Craig Lamont's eyes were on the woman whose face was buried in her arms outflung on counsel's table, his thoughts were of his brother as voices of judge and counsel rose and fell. Nadja never had been Carl's wife legally. Incredible. How had the woman dared? Tough medicine for little Peggy. Why need she know? This had been a private hearing. Nadja, herself, wouldn't be likely to broadcast the truth. It might jeopardize the income Carl had willed her. She —

"Craig! Quick! Stop Drucilla! Don't let her —"

His mother's strained whisper broke. He glimpsed her colorless face, her eyes brilliant with pain before he started for the door.

Drucilla and her nose for news, he said to himself as he sprinted after the thick-set woman who was flat-footing along the corridor with the speed and grace of a racing turtle. He caught her shoulder.

"Just a minute, Drucilla!"

Her small eyes were mere pinpoints of excitement, all the color in her face had concentrated in her nose which was as red as a Stop signal. She tried to shake off his hand. His grip tightened along with the line of his jaw.

"Don't detain me, Craig! I have a date to have tea with —"

"Never mind the date. Come in here!"

He propelled her into an empty court room and closed the door. He backed against it and with his arms crossed, faced her. She was too angry to do more than splutter protest.

"Listen to me, Drucilla. I was sent after you to inform you that if one word of what went on in that hearing you sneaked into gets on the air through you, the income the Senator gives you will stop. Get that? Stop! There won't be a cent more for you, ever."

He hadn't been so instructed but it looked as if his threat would work, he told himself as he saw dull color suffuse her face. She tried to laugh but the sound was a gasp. Her voice was a shaken ooze.

"How can you accuse me of such un-friendliness to your dear mother and my cousin the Senator as to mention the fact of —"

"That's enough, Drucilla. Am I to go back and tell the Senator that you've for-gotten everything you heard in that room, or shall I tell him you prefer a fee for gossip to a steady income?"

She looked at him as if considering in which segment of his face to set her vicious yellow teeth. He glanced at his wrist watch.

"Well?" he reminded. "Better forget it. A steady income is not to be sneezed at these days."

She looked at him as if weighing the pros and cons of his proposition, humped her thick shoulders.

"I'll take the income. I promise not to mention the — the late unfortunate revelations."

He ignored the venom in her voice.

"All right, I'll report to the Senator and — don't think you can undermine that promise with innuendo, Drucilla. I'll make it my business to see that you don't."

"It would be like you. Pity that Carl didn't have some of that liquid granite that runs in your veins in his, then he wouldn't have been fooled by that cheap actress. The Lord help the woman who marries you!"

Drucilla Dodd's waspish prophecy echoed in Craig Lamont's mind as after dinner he looked at Joan sitting on the step of the terrace at Silver Birches. Her head was tipped back against the parapet. Moonlight did magic things to her eyes and to her white satin frock which glowed and shimmered as she moved. Did she think that the girl who married him would need Divine help to make life bearable?

Her eyes flashed to his. Had his mind drawn hers? Color stained her face. She said hurriedly;

"When I look at you three men in your white clothes, I can't believe that this balmy evening is only twenty-four hours removed from the frost of last night. New England weather is as temperamental as a cinema headliner."

She held out a silver and porcelain coffee cup to the hovering butler.

"Just a bit more, Saxon."

"You won't sleep, honey, if you drink too much coffee," warned Patty Crofton, who was sitting on a low stool at her husband's feet, her white chiffon skirt with red poppies scattered over it spread like a fan about her.

"Not having slept for forty-eight hours plus — that is, not much — a high-pressure swing band serenading under my window couldn't keep me awake tonight, Mother."

She had colored brilliantly when she had interpolated "Not much," Lamont reflected. Had she suddenly remembered that last night she had slept with her head against his shoulder?

He looked across the valley. Looked beyond the river, pure silver now, beyond the foothills to the mountain. It was an indigo shadow against a night sky of dark majesty so thick with stars that it resembled a purple velvet canopy spattered with gold.

Had only twenty-four hours passed since he had flashed his torch around the walls of the cabin, since he and Joan had tended the signal fires, since she had looked up at him with drowsy, radiant eyes, had whispered, "I love you"?

"That will be all, Saxon."

His mother's voice recalled him to the present. The unsteadiness of it reminded him that she had requested that no mention be made of the events of the last twenty-four hours during dinner. "After coffee," she had said to her husband and to him, "I want you to tell the Croftons and me everything that happened after Joan and I left the Court-room."

"Craig, I wish you and Joan would come and sit near us. Voices carry," his mother suggested.

He felt her tenseness. The revelation of the afternoon had been a cruel blow for her, but he had never seen her lovelier than she was tonight in a dress of sheer pale mauve with bunches of purple and white Parma

340

violets printed on it. He liked the bouffant skirts women were wearing, he thought as he drew forward a fan-back chair for Joan and seated himself beside her.

"By the way, where is Peggy?" he asked. "She hasn't made her usual after-dinner appearance."

To his relief his mother smiled.

"She fell asleep over her supper and didn't register even a faint protest when Miss Hopkins suggested bed. I didn't know until Joan returned at dawn that she had spent most of the night praying to the spirit of her father for your safe return, Craig."

Her husband patted the white fingers resting on the arm of his chair. He said tenderly;

"That's all behind us, Sally. All behind us. We have Craig and we have Peggy." He smiled at David Crofton and his wife. "And our neighbors. Blink those tears out of your eyes, my dear."

Craig Lamont glanced from his mother's face to Patty Crofton's. Life had disciplined them both but also it had endowed their spirits with a lovely light which shone through their eyes and touched their lips with tenderness and beauty. A woman need not dread advancing years when she has met heart-twisting experiences with faith and valor and gay courage.

Senator Dan Shaw tamped out his cigar and dropped it on the stand beside him. He laid his hand over his wife's fingers.

"I'll have to go back several weeks to make my story hang together," he began slowly as if marshalling the facts, "to a diamond theft in Hollywood."

"Viv's bandit?" Joan exclaimed incredulously.

"Have the ripples from that amazing episode reached across the continent?"

Her father held up a protesting hand.

"I'm sorry," she whispered. Lamont laid his hand on the arm of her chair. The Senator went on;

"Your sister is tied up in this, Joan. The man who returned her handkerchief — you see, I know all the details of the story — was a man named Al Dawn. He had aliases but his real name is the one that concerns us. He and his pal overheard Vivian tell Mrs. Bankton about her family and ours. He knew that his sister Nadja was in Carsfield and conceived the brilliant plan of mailing the jewels to her."

"Nadja, Carl's wife, the accomplice of a thief!" Mrs. Shaw interrupted passionately.

"She is not the accomplice of a thief!"

The denial was flung from the long open

window. The three men rose as Señorit Nadja Donesca swept forward and stopped in the middle of the terrace. Trust her to make a theatrical entrance, Craig thought. Her face was livid, her green eyes glittered like glass, the tremor of her body set the sequins on her revealingly thin black frock a-shimmer. She denied again fiercely, "I am not the accomplice of a thief! My — my brother sent the diamonds his — his sidekick stole to me — yes — but days ago I mailed them to a jeweler in Hollywood."

"But I saw a mass of diamond bracelets taken from the pocket of the man you call the sidekick when he was brought into Police Headquarters today," Senator Shaw protested.

"You deed?" The Señorita had gone high-class Mexican again. She shrugged one shoulder. Her glance flicked scornfully from face to face and returned to the Senator.

"You deed see them? Deed you examine them? They were rhinestones of the first water. I put them in the box in which the stolen jewels had come and gave them to my brother when I left him and his treacherous friend in the cabin on the mountain." Her mouth twisted convulsively. "He never knew that the real jewels had gone back to their owners."

She whirled and faced Sally Shaw.

"Well, thees settles who shall have Peggy. I am no fool. Weel the judge give the child to me now? No. I don't want her — thees you shall know — when after seven years I could not trace Gus Janvers, I divorced him. I was legally your son's wife. *Adios!*"

Her exit was as theatric as her entrance had been.

"Nadja! Wait!" the Senator called and followed her.

After what seemed hours of tense silence Craig Lamont leaned over his mother. Hands on her shoulders he said tenderly;

"Pull yourself together, Sally Shaw. Remember your philosophy. Things will straighten out. Things have a marvelous, unbelievable way of straightening out. Here comes the Senator. Did you find out anything more, sir?"

Senator Shaw lighted a fresh cigar.

"Yes. After I had assured Nadja that because she was Peggy's mother I would see her through the Grand Jury investigation of the murder, she poured out her story so fast that I followed with difficulty. She said that when she went to the Coast to fulfil a picture contract, she took her brother with her hoping he would go straight in a new environment. He stayed in California when she came east. She said she was stunned — I believe her — when a few weeks ago she opened a package which came through the mail and discovered therein six diamond bracelets. Then came a letter from 'Al' in Hollywood, explaining that the 'merchandise' he had sent her, was not a present, that he would be along soon to claim it, that she was to keep 'mum' about it, if she didn't he would be in the hoosegow for years.

"She knew what that meant. He had boarded at state expense several times before. She packed the bracelets in another box and mailed it from a branch post-office in Boston, as 'merchandise,' to the jewelers in Hollywood from whom she suspected the diamonds had been stolen. She used an assumed name and town for the return address. They would get to the owners even if she had mistaken the firm, she reasoned. Two weeks later her brother telephoned her that he must see her. She agreed to meet him at the Public Library in Boston. On that very morning she saw his picture posted in the office here in Carsfield and knew that his part in the diamond theft had been discovered. He did not meet her at the Library. That evening he trailed her to the Country Club here."

Joan looked at Craig Lamont. There was

question in her eyes. He shook his head. She nodded and smiled.

Her friendliness sent his thoughts off at a tangent. She must like him. There had been something in her eyes just now —

"As I was saying, Craig."

The Senator's quizzical reminder brought him sharp up against the present.

"As you were saying, sir? I'm all attention."

"The brother and sister met secretly at the Country Club. He told her that detectives were hot on his heels, that she must hide him and his pal until they lost the trail. She refused. He threatened to drag her into the mess as a receiver of stolen goods if he were caught. With her fight for Peggy coming up at once she didn't dare defy him. She borrowed Philip Bard's sedan, drove the two men to the top of the mountain and left them with the understanding that as soon as she felt it safe she would come for them and drive them to some distant town from which they could make their get-away to South America."

"Phil Bard mixed up in this! He would be. How like him," Mrs. Shaw interrupted passionately.

"Steady, Sally, steady," her husband soothed. "Granted that Bard is a double-crosser and a false friend, I'm sorry for hi. His political career in this town is com. pletely washed up. The taint of last night's events will cling to him though his only connection was loaning Nadja his car with no suspicion of her reason for wanting it."

"Go on, Dan," Mrs. Shaw prodded tensely. "Go on!"

"Nadja left her brother and his pal in the cabin on the mountain with provisions for two days, and the package they thought contained the diamonds. The temptation to escape with the jewels was too much for the person known in our story as the sidekick or pal. He expertly disposed of Al Dawn and made his get-away in Craig's roadster with the unopened box he thought contained the stolen jewels."

"How did they find out that Nadja was mixed up in the deal?" Craig Lamont asked.

"Johnny Nolan took the number of the sedan that went up and down the mountain in the early morning. He suspected something was wrong. It was but a moment's work to trace the owner. Bard was invited to Headquarters. Explained at once that his car had been loaned and with but an instant's hesitation, to whom."

Mrs. Shaw's face was the tint of transparent alabaster as she admitted fervently;

'I am glad, glad that my boy Carl is spared this humiliation. What put you on the trail of the woman's former marriage, Dan?"

"Tell your mother, Craig. Let's get this all cleared up now."

Craig Lamont told of Janvers' recognition of Nadja at the Country Club, of his sneering repetition of her stage name. He had asked the Senator to question him with the thought that he might tell of something in the woman's past which would help in the fight to retain guardianship of Peggy. He had been stunned at the revelation of the truth.

The Senator made him think of a great lion stretching as he rose and shook back his shaggy hair. He put his arm about his wife.

"Nadja knows that if she wants my help I'll see her through the mess. The lawyers for the prosecution will try to implicate her — after that she will leave the country and never return — she says. I believe she means it. Now, Sally, we'll close that book on the past forever, will we, my dear?"

The expression in his mother's eyes as she looked up at her husband, brought the sting of tears to Craig Lamont's.

"The book is closed, Dan. Thank you for everything." She cleared her voice and smiled at David Crofton and his wife.

"Shall we go in and have a little game c contract?"

"I can think of nothing more soothing to our jangled nerves," David Crofton agreed lightly. He looked at his daughter. "Coming, Joan?"

"She is not," Craig Lamont answered for her. "This seems to be clearing-up night. There are one or two questions she can answer for me. Come on, Joan."

He held out his hand. In the instant she hesitated, he felt his mother's tense regard, knew that the eyes of David and Patty Crofton were on their daughter.

"The Dictator speaks. I go!" Joan declaimed melodramatically and ran down the terrace steps.

Craig followed her along the flower-bordered graveled path till she stopped in an enchanted patch of moonlight and looked up.

"I've always wanted to study astronomy." There was a hint of emotion in her voice. "There's Scorpion rising from the South-east. See that bright star? It is Antares which marks the Scorpion's heart. You're not looking!"

Lamont agreed.

"I'm not. I'm not interested in the Scoron's heart. I have my own and yours on my mind. As has been said before, there are one or two little matters to be cleared up between you and me. I love you, Joan."

Her eyes flashed to his.

"But, but your mother said —"

"That I was mad about a girl. It was a bit of Sally Shaw diplomacy. She's right, I am. You're the girl. I had told her that." He cleared his voice of huskiness. "Why did you call Slade 'darling' up there on the mountain?"

She looked down at his hands which had caught hers.

"I was glad to see him."

"Why? Because you had told me you loved me?"

She looked up with gay defiance.

"You've missed your vocation. As a prosecuting attorney you would make your mark, Mister Lamont."

"Was that the reason?"

Laughter left her eyes. Their radiance set his heart pounding.

"It was," she admitted in a voice so low that he had to catch her close in his arms to hear.

A throbbing interlude, before, with her head tipped back against his shoulder, she looked up and suggested unsteadily;

"Having settled those one or two littq questions — that's a quotation — in cas. you care — perhaps we'd better join the families."

His arm tightened. He laid his cheek against her soft hair.

"Just a minute. There's a little matter of a cross-country motor trip to the Coast in June I'd like to discuss with you — adorable."

XXVI

June! June at last!

The beat of Joan's heart broke into double time. Her wedding day! She looked about her room strewn with tissue paper and white boxes containing presents which had arrived too late to be unpacked. Open on a chair was a dark blue alligator dressing case with extravagant silver fittings. Her tulle veil with its Juliet cap of point lace was spread on the bed. Near it lay a spray of pure white azaleas and white orchids.

The filmy chiffon of her frock drifted and floated about her as she crossed to the window. What a day! Fields emerald and gold. River platinum. Amethyst hills deepening to purple, as they loomed to touch a turquoise sky. Below in the garden glossy rhododendrons, colonies of pink, lavender and white lupin, siberian irises, roses, patches of velvety green lawn. Girls gowned in flower tints and wide brimmed hats, men in white clothes everywhere except in a place roped off with garlands where she and Craig were to stand — and the clergyman, almost she had forgotten him. From somewhere drifted the exquisite music of harps.

"Time to put on your veil, honey," Patty Crofton's voice caught on the familiar word. "That chiffon frock is perfect for a garden wedding, satin would have been such a mistake," she added with what briskness her soft voice would permit and blinked long lashes.

Joan's lips trembled in a smile.

"You are rather ravishing yourself, mother, in that silvery gray frock. Choosing the American beauty hat and bag and sandals as a contrast was a positive inspiration. Gorgeous day, isn't it?"

"Gorgeous, honey. Stand still while I place the cap on your head and arrange the veil. I couldn't let anyone else do it. Your father is coming to go down with you and Peggy is already in the drawing room. She is fairly trembling with pride that she is to be your maid of honor. That must be your father. Come in!" She answered a knock on the door.

David Crofton dressed in white entered.

"Long distance call for you, Jo. Take it in your workroom."

"I will! I will! It's Viv! I know it's Viv!"

Her mother caught up the flowing end of her veil and followed as she ran into the adjoining room. She pleaded;

"Be careful of your gown, honey. Try not to be so excited. You're shaking."

"Me! Excited! I'm calm as a summer sea," Joan declared and wrinkled her nose at her father. She spoke into the phone.

"Yes. Yes. Ready — Viv! Viv, darling. No. No. You haven't made me cry. Hearing your voice makes everything perfect. I can't believe you're thousands of miles away. Love the traveling case you sent — Of course I'm taking it. It's packed except for the clip I'm wearing with my wedding gown — Craig gave it to me. Star sapphire set in gorgeous diamonds — have to wear something blue, you know — Old? Mother's wedding handkerchief as a cap for my veil. Borrowed a dime from Seraphina to put in my slipper, and with everything else new, I have all the good-luck talismans. Not that I need them when Craig loves me — Yes, gorgeous day, we can have the ceremony in our garden for intimate friends and the families. Reception at Silver Birches. Mrs. Shaw begged to have it. In about five minutes — Think of me, darling! — Don't cry, Viv. You'll see me in two weeks and after we leave, Mother and Father are coming out to you. They are turning this house over to the newly-weds for the summer. Isn't it like them? Craig and I are to plane home. We'll leave the roadster for Patty and

Davy to motor back in. Isn't it exciting? —
is lunch time there? He is! — Mother has pu
her hand on my shoulder to remind me that I
— I — have a date. It's a gorgeous day here
— Mother's a dream — Viv —"

Joan looked at her father. Her lips trembled.

"She said 'Cut the film,' and rang off
before I could say good-bye. I — I think I
heard her sob," she added unsteadily.

"She would," David Crofton agreed, "but
I'll bet my last year's Fedora that already
she is faring forth to celebrate."

Joan blinked wet lashes and laughed.

"Davy Crofton, you are positively psy-
chic. Jerry Slade is taking her to lunch."

"Jerry!" her mother and father exclaimed
in unison.

"Jerry," Joan repeated. "The fact that he
has flown out to her makes everything perfect. I can see the finish of her cinema
career. Gorgeous day, isn't it, Mother?"

"It is, honey," Patty Crofton agreed for
approximately the tenth time, "Take your
flowers. Exquisite, aren't they? I'll go down
now. Seraphina will be at the terrace door to
arrange your veil. I — I —"

She left the room without finishing the
sentence. Joan looked at her father and said
unsteadily;

"I'm starting out on that 'high adventure,' Davy."

"Keep your marriage a 'high adventure,' Jo, darling. You can do it." He kissed her tenderly. "There's our signal. Let's go," he said gruffly.

As she went down the stairs, Joan felt as if she were progressing like a girl in a slow-motion picture with her veil and chiffon skirt floating and drifting behind her. She heard the musical drip of the harps strengthen into the wedding march. She knew when Peggy in an enchanting rose color frock and a big leghorn hat tied with rose and blue ribbon, slipped into place to precede her, knew when pink gowned, grinning Seraphina, arranged her veil and whispered loudly;

"You sure done look grand, Miss Jo-an!"

From the terrace she looked across a sea of color and faces to where Craig stood waiting with Tony Crane beside him. His eyes shining, unguarded, possessive, met hers, lifted her heart and steadied it. She stopped floating and walked toward him.

Portions of the service rang through the emotional confusion of her mind like trumpet calls.

"Dearly beloved we are gathered together —" "To have and to hold from this day forward —" "To love and to cherish till death

do us part —" Craig's fervent, "I do." H[...]
own response. The clergyman saying; "I[...]
this new united life you now begin together."

After that, a flood of impressions, registering, passing, the pattern changing with
the quickness and color of a kinetoscope.
Guests coming. Some of them kissing her.
Guests going. Voices shrilling above the
throb of music. Rainbows of color. Hearing
the same good wishes over and over.
Making the same response over and over.
Awareness of Craig beside her. A sharp
close-up of Janvers wishing them luck and
hoping she liked the diamond bracelet he
had sent her. The gaiety and beauty on the
terrace at Silver Birches; cutting the cake;
Craig's mother, in an amethyst net frock
and orchids, clasping a string of pearls
about her neck; running back to The Mansion along the brown stone path; changing
to the thin wool beige frock; another clear
close-up of Babs Shelton and Tony
standing together, Babs catching her bridal
bouquet; Craig waiting at the foot of the
stairs; their dash under showers of confetti
for his roadster miraculously free of white
ribbons; looking back to wave to her father
and mother, to Sally Shaw and the Senator
and wet-lashed Peggy with the black and

nite dog beside her looking as if he were about to burst into tears; out of the drive into the highway faring forth on that new united life they now began together.

It seemed to Joan that they drove for miles in silence. Beyond the village, along a road bordered by brilliant green shrubs, through another village, and on into the country. She must shake off the feeling that she was in a dream. She moved her left hand. That was real. The square-cut diamond of her engagement ring was real, so was the gem-set platinum wedding ring. She looked up quickly. So was Craig beside her. His eyes met and held hers.

"You act as if you were afraid of me, Mrs. Lamont," he teased.

His laughing voice quieted the pulses his look had set throbbing. She responded with unsteady gaiety;

"Believe it or not, all this time I have been scrambling round in my mind for something to say to you, something sparkling, debonair, as if — as if being married happened every day, but it wouldn't come."

"Just to start the conversation, you might say, 'I love you, I'll always love you.' "

"As long as I live, Craig," she said fervently.

She saw the color surge to his hair. Saw

his eyes deepen and darken. Saw him glance over his shoulder before the roadster slid to a stop under the spreading branches of a benign old oak.

"That promise can't be properly acknowledged with one hand on the wheel," he declared huskily.